FILL THE GAPS

A NOVEL

ANDREW JOHNSTON

This book is dedicated to me, for thinking I could never do this.

A mystery, and, I thought, not of a favourable complexion, appeared to hang over his conduct; but to ascertain if my suspicions were just, it was necessary to throw him off his guard. We cut for the deal, and were soon earnestly engaged in our play ...

— *Rob Roy*, by Sir Walter Scott

CHAPTER ONE

Winter, 2010. Edinburgh.

Isaac raised his eyes from his phone. He had been writing yet another lengthy text to the woman he had broken up with earlier that day. He had not been paying attention to his surroundings and now he scanned the scene in front of him: small circles of people drinking and talking. But the sounds of the party had sunk to a low murmur.

Something in the room had made him look up. But there was nothing obvious he could see that should have caused him to do that, no physical thing caught in his eyeline. It was all very ordinary. Just people standing around in groups, sipping drinks and making conversation. No one had said anything to him. He remained quite still for a second, a wild animal caught in the eyeline of an ethereal predator. Stared at, examined from a distance. Something unseen waited to see what he would do next.

That second passed. There was nothing in the air to suggest he was in any danger. Isaac finished his text and sent it, then looked around at the people closest to him.

He was in a circle with Will, Mary and Mark. Will was his flatmate and old university friend. Mary and Mark were old friends of Will, and they were hosting the party. Will was talking about a new online course he was doing which would improve his job prospects by getting him away from working in a call centre.

Isaac spoke with a sneer and at a volume only he could hear. “What’s so good about that?” Isaac wasn’t in the habit of speaking to himself like this. He paused, waited. Will was still telling Mary and Mark about the details of the course. He’d been talking like this for ten minutes. Isaac looked at the three of them as they continued to talk to each other. They did not look over at Isaac or ask him what he meant by his unheard comment. Isaac shook his head. He had not been paying attention to what was going on around him.

He breathed out slowly. Ambient music started playing at a low volume from a set of speakers in the corner, the music playing underneath the conversation around them. The main hall light was off, the room lit up by lamps in the corner and fairy lights on the walls. Other partygoers stood close together, talking at each other, straining forward to listen and forcing each other to concentrate on every word.

Mary was asking about the course, what Will needed to do and how much he had already done. Will paused, trying to remember. Mary and Mark looked at each other. Mark said something quietly, and Mary nodded before he finished talking. Will glanced at them for a second, mumbling out a response that was too quiet to make out. Mary and Mark nodded along anyway, not looking away from Will.

Isaac forced a groan, keeping his mouth shut as he did so. Will was smiling now, enthusiastically going on about his course and how he was optimistic about learning accounting, getting his life back on track.

Isaac looked at Mary and Mark, then put his phone away. He spoke up, his voice louder than Will’s. “I need a drink.”

Will stumbled over his words. Isaac continued, talking

over him. “You know, it’s amazing that he’s trying all these things to get him out of that call centre gig, but he needs to start at home a bit more. I tried telling him to put stuff away instead of doing all that ‘business skills’ stuff. It’s a bit daft.”

Will’s shoulders fell. Isaac opened his mouth to continue, but Mary spoke up again. “I mean, you shouldn’t give … What else are you planning to work on, Will? You mentioned you were drawing again.”

Will answered, his voice suddenly at a higher pitch and almost too loud. “Doesn’t matter. The stuff I’d done in the past wasn’t that great anyway – all derivative of stuff I was working on years ago. Isaac is right, I should probably have tidied up first before doing anything.”

Isaac laughed. “Beer bottles everywhere! An entire collage of stuff – that’s real art! Just wish you’d put it away.”

Mary and Mark managed to raise their glasses to their mouths at the same time. They didn’t look at each other. Will continued, quieter. No one leaned in to listen. “Our flat has always had an issue with mess, to be fair, but it’s getting out of hand. I’d help more but the job I do is draining. It’s hard speaking on the phone all day.”

Mary piped up, speaking to Isaac. Will stopped talking immediately. “How’s your job going? Will said you’ve been doing it for a while now.”

Isaac looked around before he talked. There were no women near him, but he talked loudly anyway. “Yeah, corporate IT security. It’s a private firm and you won’t have heard of it. Lots of checking corporate networks. It’s quite intensive and I have to be there most of the time. Worked hard to get it. Pretty intensive stuff.”

Mark replied, “Wow, that’s … And you dropped out of university as well.”

Isaac kept going. “Yeah, but I’ve always had the graft, you know? The real world only cares about how hard you work. It's not all about qualifications. We'd be better off if the world was more egalitarian, more … you know what I mean. Are there more folk coming tonight? It's a bit quiet, but it's early days. I mean, Will said there were more folk coming."

Will kept quiet, taking a long drink. Isaac looked over at Mary, who turned and said something to Mark. The couple reached out across the short distance between each other and joined hands.

Isaac continued, "Will said there was tons of folk coming, but, I mean, Will's always lying. Would you honestly trust a guy like him?"

"Thanks, man," Will said to himself.

Mary and Mark said nothing, moving a little closer to each other. Will didn't look at them. Isaac changed the topic back to his job, talking about the nuances of his work, before changing the topic back to Will again. "Do you honestly trust that face? He works on commission, so it's all just salesmanship. Just as well they can't see his face!"

Will spoke to himself again. "I am a great liar, to be fair."

Isaac laughed again, louder than before. "Will's a smart guy, you know. Four years of art college well spent, mate."

Will didn't look at anyone. "Yeah."

Isaac didn't look at him. "Should have dropped out, pal."

Will looked at Isaac.

Isaac put his hand on Will's shoulder, looked at the can of beer in Will's hand. He turned his head to observe the door of the flat. It remained closed.

Mark spoke up. "I mean, we're happier that it's more … well, quality not quantity. We haven't seen anyone for a while, so it's good to see folk here."

Mary joined in. "I mean, we're quite happy to have any friends round. The usual guys from our work are all here.

They've never missed one of our parties. I think it's just a bad week for it …"

Isaac exhaled, still watching the door. Then he turned to Will, whose shoulders were tense. "Have you seen Lyle anywhere, Will?"

Will looked away for a second before managing a murmur. "I think he's in the kitchen." Will paused, then found his voice again. "Was everything good today, Isaac? With … I know it's … difficult to talk about … " Will trailed off as Isaac looked away.

Mary glanced at Isaac, opening her mouth as he turned his head. "What happened today, Isaac, with her? I heard that she was in tears …"

Isaac walked away from her question.

Mary and Mark whispered to each other. Will looked around the room, fiddling with the rim of his beer can with his thumb. In years previous the hallway would have been packed full of people staying into the early hours. It was quieter tonight. Some people were leaving already. Will was gritting his teeth.

There was one picture in the far corner, hung up on the wall, away from everything. An art print that Will had made for Mark as a moving-in gift, back when they had just graduated. A white background with a black square, straight red streaks alongside it. The print had been damaged at some point: the black square had cracks in it, the paper ripped slightly. Will looked at it for some time, not looking at Mark and Mary, before returning his attention to the empty space where Isaac had stood.

As he had moved away, Isaac had looked at Mary, his eyes scanning down her long skirt, which fell to just above her ankles. It shifted from left to right as she made subtle movements with her hips. Isaac turned to face the music coming from a nearby bedroom, which was punctuated by the sound of loud female laughter.

Again Isaac spoke under his breath. "Well, fuck."

He moved towards the kitchen with some urgency, blocked by a crowd of five men standing outside the kitchen door, laughing and shouting. They were Mark's friends. They had been the first ones at the party. Isaac hadn't talked to any of them. They were taller than Isaac; some by about an inch, some by a few more. Isaac tried to move past them, turning his body sideways. One of them turned his head as Isaac passed behind his back. They were talking about video games. One wore a suit jacket which was two sizes too big for him.

It was a cold, late-winter night; the darkness long since set in the sky came through the kitchen window. There was a lingering smell of cigarette smoke. Isaac immediately moved to shut the window, closing it with a cracking noise. Wood against wood. The smell of smoke remained, along with gasps of cold air. He tutted and rolled his sleeves down, shivering.

He turned back towards the kitchen doorway. No one had followed him in. He went to the large standing fridge and opened it, locating a pack of beers which resembled the can in Will's hand, a six-pack with four left. Isaac took one of them and looked around at the other things in the fridge. There was a shelf full of hummus, labelled as homemade, small round tubs piled up on each other. Isaac put the beer to one side, looking back towards the kitchen door. He lifted out one of the tubs of hummus. The noise of the party was far away, blocked out by the occasional raised voice of the men outside the kitchen. One of them was describing a video game and his friend was laughing about it. Isaac breathed out through his nose. Still holding the hummus with his right hand, still in the cold of the fridge, he opened the tub with his other hand. He sniffed it. He dipped a finger into it, taking a small amount from the top and putting it into his mouth. He let it rest on his tongue before swallowing it. A few seconds later, he stuck three fingers in, taking out a larger dollop of it and putting it in his mouth. Isaac frowned. He looked at the items in the fridge again, moved the hummus around in his mouth with his tongue. He pressed the lid back onto the tub, placed it at the back of the shelf. He closed the fridge, picked up the beer and went back to the party.

Isaac sneezed as he left the kitchen, causing the group of men to look round. Isaac muttered out loud, not looking at any of them. "It's cold in there. You guys should have closed the window, at least."

Isaac looked back down the corridor. Will and Mark were not there. Mary was standing by herself, staring at her phone. Isaac looked at her behind, slightly straining against the back of her long skirt. He looked at her for a couple of seconds, turning away as she turned her head towards him. He walked towards the bedroom where the female laughter had been earlier.

Lyle, Isaac's other flatmate, was in the bedroom. He was silent, his back against the radiator by the window, his legs extended outward on the floor. Three women were sitting on the bed across from him. They sat close to each other. Isaac didn't recognise them. He looked back at Lyle, whose legs were framed by some empty cans of beer. Isaac moved closer to him. Lyle shuffled away from Isaac as he walked over, shifting his back, leaving the beer cans behind. Isaac went to sit next to him but stopped, hanging in mid-air for a second before standing up again. Lyle hadn't left him enough room but didn't budge any further. The women were talking over each other, their responses to each other immediate.

"The castle was so nice!"

"So nice!"

"Edinburgh is so pretty!"

"It's amazing how old everything is!"

Lyle didn't join in with them.

One of the women, a redhead with long curls, watched Isaac sit down. He held his beer can out in the general direction of Lyle, tilting it to begin a toast. Lyle didn't look at him. Isaac opened his mouth, then closed it. He took his can back. He looked away from Lyle and asked a question. "You want anything from the kitchen?"

Lyle replied, "No, I've had enough."

"Suit yourself."

Lyle did not respond. He was looking at the far corner of the bedroom ceiling, his eyes resting on a fixed point. He straightened his back, taking another drink, not looking away from the far corner. He did not try to insert himself into the conversation.

Isaac looked at the open doorway, out into the corridor. He began to talk. "Not that many people here. Not as many as there were in August – obviously, but August is a different world. Couldn't get into this room at all last time. Those dancers came along. Mind, Dylan brought them here. Some guy, Dylan. He's not mentioned turning up but I'd assumed that he'd be here, and he always brings folk. Some sort of strange drama always following him around."

Isaac glanced up at the women on the bed. Lyle, taking another drink, muttered something under his breath. Isaac talked over him. "We saw some good stuff at the festival this year, didn't we? Do you still hear from that big Greek bloke? That stand-up show – that guy we saw? Lyle? We went for a few drinks with him after. You stayed in touch with him, yeah?"

Lyle kept the drink in his mouth. He did not look at Isaac when he spoke a few seconds later. "I haven't thought about that boy in a long while."

Isaac snapped back immediately, "Thought you liked that kind of guy? Like, your type?"

Lyle looked at Isaac for a second. "I've never said that to you."

Isaac looked over at the women, then back to Lyle. He lowered his voice. "Yeah, but – *you know what I mean*. Big hairy chest, all that stuff." Isaac looked away, back at the women.

Lyle did not say a thing for a few seconds, taking another drink before opening his mouth. "Please stop talking, Isaac. Absolutely fuc … Horrible, as always. It's not right to do any of that—"

Isaac tutted, interrupting. "You're really stroppy recently. It's happening too much just now."

Lyle closed his eyes, breathing in. He pressed his fore-finger and thumb together on his free hand, hard enough that the tips of them turned white.

Isaac looked down at his beer. "What's wrong now, Lyle?"

Lyle breathed out a response. "You know what it is. You're always making those sorts of comments, then you spin it into being about my job."

Isaac nodded. "Been telling you to chuck that waiting job for years."

"I know, but what help have you been? You've said your place won't hire people like me, whatever that means."

Isaac shook his head. He snapped back angrily, "Didn't mean it like that, don't be so sensitive. It's just they need more than – whatever it was you did. Modern languages? Really helped out with that holiday you went on for a year."

Lyle finally turned to Isaac. "You know fine well it's what you did today that's pissed me off. How could you?" He took a drink, splashing beer from his own can into his face.

Isaac flinched and got up, moving towards the bed the

women were on. There was enough space for him to sit a little away from the trio, but he chose to sit close to them. They shifted up the bed away from him. The women looked at him, not saying anything.

Isaac made a small wave with his hand. He spoke up. "I'm Isaac. How long you guys in Edinburgh for?"

They talked rapidly to each other, not towards Isaac.

"I think we're here for another few days."

"Lyle's been such a gentleman."

"Lyle! Come up here!"

One of them turned to Isaac. "Lyle said that you were having a bit of a dramatic day, something about a break-up?"

Isaac turned his head back towards Lyle. "Wait, sorry, you told them?"

Lyle had his head pointed at the ceiling, saying nothing.

The women hesitated. One of them spoke. "I think Lyle was talking about … We got chatting to him at an art exhibition today, a pop-up thing near the university. I'm thinking of applying there for a postgrad."

Isaac was still glaring at Lyle when he said, "Lyle doesn't really invite me to that sort of thing."

The same woman spoke up again. "What about – was it Will, Lyle? Was that his name? – I think he's coming. I think there's more stuff on tomorrow."

Isaac said, "Will's our other flatmate. It's not really my thing, art stuff."

The women did not respond.

Isaac waited. After a second, he held his hands up. "It's not really my thing."

One of them spoke quietly. "They had a free bar."

Isaac laughed. "See, that sort of thing I can get behind. Lyle doesn't really advertise these things, but I can endorse getting shit-faced on a budget. I thought that was the whole point? Anyway …" Isaac raised his beer can to the women, who were drinking wine. There was evidence of some spillage: the white wall nearest them was smeared with a crimson colour. The stain extended to the bed, the smell of red wine sinking into the fabric of the covers.

Lyle continued to drink by himself. He kept taking a swig, then putting the beer can between his forefinger and thumb, tapping it, letting it swing. He did this a few times and it always swung the same way.

Isaac studied the three women. One of them, the redhead, was drinking from a bottle of wine. Isaac took a drink himself. She wiped her mouth. "The gallery was amazing, some really nice paintings—"

Isaac spoke quickly, interrupting her. "You guys must be doing well if you're getting to flat parties on your travels!"

She nodded. "Oh, it's great, this is the best place we've been to – Edinburgh's just magical, you know what I mean? There's a real buzz around the place. It's just so pretty, just nowhere else like it. Have you been travelling? Don't know if you've had the same feelings, you know. Being elsewhere."

Isaac nodded, biting the inside of his lip. He waited a few seconds after she finished before responding. "What are your names?"

Lyle spoke up. "Isaac, what happened to her today? She's been texting me, she's upset."

Isaac kept looking at the redhead and spoke quietly. "It's not really any of your business." He shifted position to look at Lyle.

Lyle kept going. "You never said you were unhappy with her—"

Isaac interrupted him. "Don't start, we can talk about it later. It's a bit dishonest that you're—"

Lyle cut in. "Is that one of Will's beers?"

"We bought the same stuff," Isaac snapped back.

Lyle responded quickly. "I don't think you did."

"Calm down, Lyle. You're a bit out of order."

Isaac drank as he turned back to the group on the bed. One of the women was whispering. The redhead was staring at her friend, concentrating on her. Isaac looked at her green sequined top, her freckles scattered down her bare arms, glancing at the section of the bed near her, the whispering words, anything she was doing.

He closed his eyes. He groaned quietly, tilting the side of his head and rubbing the palm of his hand under his chin. He made himself as comfortable as possible, leaning backwards and looking up, glaring at the lampshade, the patterns indented on the ceiling. The bed was soft and his legs began to sink into it as he slouched.

Lyle continued. "Isaac. Be serious – you're never this chipper. It's odd that you've done this to someone we've spent years with. She was meant to be coming tonight."

Isaac raised his voice. "It's weird that I don't want to talk about it? I don't talk about that stuff anyway. Didn't need your permission to—"

Lyle interrupted him. "It's odd, that's all."

Isaac, grinning, snapped back. "This is a bit dull."

The women sitting on the bed exchanged looks with each other, then stared at Isaac. He straightened his back, pushing out his chest.

Lyle did not let off. "You're going to talk about her at some point."

Isaac looked back towards the ceiling, tilting his head to the left a little. The redhead was leaning over to listen to her friend. He turned back to her, looking away from Lyle. "What was your exhibition about?" he asked.

Lyle spoke back, quieter now. "I thought you didn't want to go. You've never shown an interest."

Isaac, his voice a little strained, kept going. "How was it?"

Lyle went to mouth something, but one of the women spoke up. "It was quite busy. Lots of locals were there. It was quite homely."

The redhead began to speak. "There was some great stuff. I loved that painting of the boat; it had really deep colours."

Lyle cleared his throat. The women looked back at him. "I liked it as well," he said. "Think it got bought by some local business owner who has a coffee shop somewhere. Decent guy. He's got a place on Nicolson Street. It's nice."

Isaac took a drink as the women replied to Lyle. Then he interrupted their conversation. "You all liked a picture of a boat?"

The women looked back at him. "It was a great painting," one said.

Isaac sneered. "Was it a big boat? Boats, man."

One of them mumbled, "You mentioned you didn't like art."

Isaac was smiling now, harder than before. "Boats are rubbish. People use planes to get anywhere. What's the point of getting on a boat nowadays? Good chance you'll die, all alone, no one to give a fuck about you."

The redhead made a shrill laughing sound.

Lyle spoke up. "Isaac's from the Borders," he explained.

"From where?"

"Countryside, south of here. He hasn't seen much of hereabouts. Not near the sea. He's not used to boats."

"Oh, that sounds lovely, we should—"

Isaac breathed out through his mouth before interrupting. "Can we go back to this amazing painting of a fucking boat for a second?"

The redhead tried to speak, a little flustered, and Isaac asked again before she could say anything, "What makes your boat painting so good?"

She tried to speak again. Some small words came out. "I don't know."

"You like it, but you don't know why? I don't get what's so exciting about a boat."

The redhead waited. She was looking at the expression on her friend's face. The friend had her back to Isaac, and he couldn't see what she was doing.

"I just liked it, I guess," the redhead said. "It just sort of worked for me, you know? It was a Scottish artist, I guess? It just looked really … I just liked it. Sorry."

Isaac nodded. "Just liked it. Cool." He looked away and pressed his hands into the bed to push himself up. He checked his phone. No new notifications. He pressed the phone into his hand with his thumb.

No one was speaking.

Isaac sank his shoulders down again. He spoke in frustration. "Where the hell is everyone?"

The redhead spoke again. "It was a fishing boat."

Isaac screwed up his face before responding. "A wee fishing boat? Not even a battleship or anything?"

Lyle interrupted him. "Isaac, no one's here because you … It's you they're avoiding."

Isaac turned his body to face Lyle. "I want to hear about the wee fishing boat that was so good you couldn't even—"

The redhead interrupted Isaac. Quieter to begin with, but she found her voice as she talked. "It was a fishing boat approaching a storm. It looked quite terrifying, actually. Like it was going to be lost at sea but then … then there's this glimpse of something on the horizon, something out there, out of reach, a glimmer of light. We don't know if it'll make it there, but at least it is trying. It has to go forward, further into the dark."

Everyone in the room was silent. Isaac breathed through his nose before responding, raising his voice. "Sounds brilliant. Don't get me wrong. I'm not saying that it's rubbish or anything like that, but where is the painting put? Where does it go? Nothing happens to it, it doesn't do anything. Some rich Yank buys it, sticks it somewhere next to a plant or something. It doesn't mean anything. By the sounds of it, the boat's pretty fucked. Who gives a fuck about a boat? Why does it need to go into the dark? Why does it need to do anything? Stupid boat driver, who gives a fuck about him?"

Lyle was looking directly at Isaac but moving further away from him. Isaac looked back at him but did not say anything. The redhead was whispering something to her friends. Isaac curled his toes and relaxed them. He straightened his back, the bones clicking at the top of his spine. He smiled and muttered, "This beer is absolute shite."

Lyle spoke up again. He had not moved from the radiator. The women were turning their heads as the two men spoke, caught in the middle. "Isaac, you *always* do this when you get annoyed – start fixating on what other people have been doing, start needling and chipping away. Stop trying to change the subject, for fuck's sake. I've heard from her, Isaac. She told me what happened, how you did it—"

Isaac was shaking his head. "Doesn't matter, it's my choice," he spluttered.

"She told me about how you did it," Lyle snapped back, repeating himself.

Isaac shook his head. "That's … She's lying. She's a liar."

Lyle opened his mouth, but Isaac kept going, raising his voice. "You weren't with us all the time, Lyle. You don't get to decide what happened. You don't get to decide what happened with me, only I do. You don't get to decide anything, Lyle, that's your issue. Always has been. You pick up strange friends all the time and act weird when they walk away from you."

The redhead looked at her friends. One of them made a move to get up but the other held onto her leg.

"How is this about me all of a sudden?" Lyle said.

Isaac shrugged. "You're just happy that you get to have a real conversation for once, instead of just being a tour guide again!"

"You had her round last week and you were talking about taking her abroad. She started asking about your jo—"

"You know what this is? It's boring. This is boring. People break up all the time. There's no reason to get upset about it."

Lyle focused, concentrated on his words. "I'm not upset about it. It raises questions. Lots of questions."

Isaac laughed again, his laugh the same as his previous in length, in volume, in high-pitched tone. He smiled, showing his teeth. He did not say anything back.

Lyle flashed a look towards the women.

Isaac laughed the same laugh again, right down to the smile with his mouth open.

The music reached a lull. Mark could be heard from outside the corridor.

Isaac spoke. "Lyle."

Lyle waited a second before responding. "It raises questions, Isaac, that's what I'm saying."

Isaac sneered at him. "You're a pal."

"I'm allowed to *ask*."

"You don't know what you're talking about."

"That's what I mean."

"You don't know what she was like with me. You've got no way of knowing anything about what we … about what I was going to do. She'd tell you anything to make you feel like I was the bad guy all along."

Lyle closed his eyes. "I'm not saying you're a bad guy, Isaac. No one is. You've been weird ab—"

Isaac interrupted him to speak to the women on the bed, his voice still raised and aggressive. "What was so good about the boat?" He took a swig from the empty can. He tried to shake it.

"Isaac, look at me," Lyle pleaded. "She asked about the—"

Isaac ignored him. "What was the thing with the stupid boat about?"

Lyle tried to stop him. "Isaac!"

Isaac kept going. "What was the boat … Where was it going? What made it so good? Sounds like it's done for. Can't imagine getting excited for a boat which is doomed."

The redhead muttered out a response. "You don't know that."

"Excuse me?" Isaac snapped back.

The redhead spoke up again. Her friends were silent, looking at their phones. "You don't know that. You don't know what's going to happen. It could capsize, but it could make it. There's a chance it could make it. But now, no one knows. But it has to head towards the storm. It has to keep trying."

Isaac replied, "It's literally just made-up colours. Shapes and stuff." He scratched his nose again.

The redhead spoke again but didn't look at Isaac. "I found it quite moving."

"So you're just saying anything, talking about nothing. You guys should try living in the real world." He looked away.

Lyle sighed. "What is it, Isaac?" he asked.

A new song had kicked in with a low bassline that looped, again and again. "Will's always playing that hip-hop shit. I've told him, it's just people talking quickly, I'm always telling him …" Isaac got up without looking at anyone. "Where is everyone? It's like you've all gone into hiding. Come on, fuck sake."

The hallway was empty. Isaac whined. "Come on, man." He went back into the kitchen. Will was looking inside the fridge. Isaac watched him, placing his empty can on the kitchen counter behind a pair of half-full wine bottles. "What are you … Where have you been, Will?"

Will's shoulders sank. He breathed out. "Yeah, I'm alright," he replied, not answering the question.

"I'm out. Do you have any spare?" Isaac asked.

Will sighed a response. "Some of mine are gone. I think … I don't know who would have taken it."

"One or two?"

Will hesitated before replying. "A few. Don't know who could have–"

Isaac interrupted him, talking quickly. "Yeah, Will, it's happened to me too in the past, at other parties. You just have to keep going. That's what life is all about."

Will closed the fridge, two beers held tentatively in one hand. He shrugged apologetically and muttered, "You can have one of mine. Sorry they're a bit shit."

Isaac reached out his hand quickly. "That's fine."

Will continued muttering. "Couldn't really manage anything decent, but they were on offer."

Isaac opened the can within a second of it being in his hands. "It'll have to do, I guess."

Will muttered some more. "Feels crap having to cut back on it. We haven't been out in a while and I'm only buying this cheap stuff."

"Don't mention it. By the way, he wasn't here. Lyle. You said he was here in the kitchen, and he wasn't. He's been in that other bedroom. You were wrong, Will. Wrong again."

There was still a chill in the kitchen. The window had been left open again.

Will gritted his teeth a little, looking away as he asked, “He wasn’t?”

“I came in here and he wasn’t here. He’s been acting weird next door.”

Will stammered out a response, breathing through his mouth. “Sorry, I thought he was—”

Isaac cut him off. “Sure.”

Will looked out the open window at the endless dark; at the shapes of the buildings outside lost to the night, the windows all dark, curtains firmly closed. He tried talking again. “I’d seen him earlier, but I thought he was leaving soon.”

“Well, he’s here, being shit again.”

“Sorry, I thought I said it. Sorry.”

“He’s off on one. He’s always like that after a bad day of work, then he pretends that he’s the one who’s hard done by. It’s his own fault, really.”

“Sorry,” Will muttered.

Isaac tutted. “You need to stop apologising. It’s boring.”

Will muttered to himself again, at a volume only he could hear. “Sorry, I—”

“You remember the day we met? You apologised for buying me the wrong drink.”

“Whisky and soda, that’s what you wanted, I remember. Haven’t forgotten that.”

Isaac sneered at him. “Don’t know how you ever got that wrong,” he said, then laughed.

Will sighed. “Yeah. Long time ago,” he said.

Isaac took a drink, staring into space as he rolled his tongue around in his mouth. He turned back to Will. “What’s up with Lyle? He’s acting weird.”

Will took a drink, then asked his own question. “You dumped her today, Isaac?”

“What’s it to you?” Isaac snapped back.

Will did not say anything. He kept watching the window.

Isaac kept going. "What's it to you, Will? Nothing to say? Good stuff."

There was a brief pause, broken by the sound of the front door slamming shut.

Isaac tutted. He took another drink.

Will spoke up. "Are you feeling okay? You seem tense."

Isaac responded immediately. "I'm not. Is Dylan coming?"

Will paused a second before replying, holding his breath immediately after he spoke. "No, he's not."

Isaac shook his head and looked out the window. "Why isn't Dylan coming? It's not like him to miss these things."

Will opened and closed his mouth before speaking. "Mind how we all … how we'd been saying things about him? Last time we were out, we were all trading stories."

Isaac interrupted him. "I mean, we did. It's just … Never mind."

"We've had enough of him now."

"I know he said that stuff to her, but it's not like … Oh come on, he's good for some things. You know what I mean."

"I think he was always a bit weird. He just brought a lot of, erm, you know …"

"Women, drama?" Isaac piped up. "A solid mix of the two?"

"We've stopped talking to him," Will said. "Probably best that you do as well."

Isaac stammered, biting his tongue for a second before responding. "I mean … whatever." Isaac moved the can up to his face with some force. He began to speak again, this time at a slower, concentrated pace. "Yeah. It's probably for the best. You can't have that kind of person around for long. It's good that everyone talked about it, at least. I guess no one's ever said it out loud before."

Will spoke slowly. “He was mean to you a lot of the time.”

“He was rude to me a lot of the time. I’ve always hated spending time with him. He always talked over me when other people were present.”

Will started to smile as he spoke. “He’s no big loss. I mean, it’s a lesson. He’s a lesson. He’s not learnt from—”

“You can’t always learn things from people, Will,” Isaac interrupted. “You need to be a bit more responsible. That’s all.” Isaac looked back towards the kitchen doorway. He could hear more female voices, saying goodbye. His shoulders sagged.

Will continued to talk. “Mind when he bought a round of drinks for those girls, spilt it in front of them and tried to get them to pay for it?”

Isaac nodded and laughed. “That was one of his better moments.”

Will watched Isaac for a few seconds before continuing. “He used to be quite pally with you. You surely remember a few of his worst—”

“This party is really dead, Will,” Isaac interrupted again. “Why is it like this?”

The front door shut again. Isaac pressed into the top of his can with his fingers. His body swayed towards the countertop.

Will shrugged. “This happens sometimes. They can’t all be big raves.”

Isaac shook his head. “They should be, though. They should all be big. Otherwise, what’s the point?”

“You know what I mean,” Will replied.

Isaac took another drink then put his hand on the kitchen counter, picking up a thick line of dust on the outside of his palm as he moved it across the surface. He tutted and waved his hand in the air as he spoke. “We used to get really good folk at these parties. But yeah, they're all working now. It's crap. You'd think folk would be up for going out, be more into getting into … you know what I mean. It's daft, people are being daft. Sitting around talking about paintings – those girls that Lyle brought are the most *boring* people. Nothing interesting to say. Not even worth it." He bit the underside of his lip.

"I think Lyle bumped into them," Will piped up. "They all seemed pretty chatty."

"I mean, can you blame them?" Isaac asked. "They're white American women. They're always a little weird around black people, right Will? Probably scared shitless of you. Must have thought you were going to sell them drugs or something. But you know what I mean, right? God, I'm fucking starving."

Will bit hard into the side of his mouth and shook his head. "That's awful, Isaac – Jesus."

Isaac tutted before replying. "I'm joking, asshole, what are you getting upset about? Christ, you're always making this weird. The hell is with you now? You're always in a bad mood, always being snappy with people. What is it now, Will? What is it now?"

Will looked away for a few seconds before answering. "I mean, it's difficult with … You're quite lucky with your job; it's impressive what you've done. I've always struggled to talk about what I do for a living. It's been difficult." He turned to open the cupboard behind him. It was full of plates and cups. In the corridor, the women were saying their good-byes. The front door closed shut and the flat fell silent.

Isaac shook his head and said, "Fucking Lyle, man. Set me up in there. Absolutely walked into that. You know, I've always felt like he's been capable of doing that, doing that just out of spite, just because it's …" Isaac looked back towards the door. He leaned over, poking his head out into the hallway. On a beat, he came back into the kitchen. “What is it with him? It’s not like we’re *competing* for the same type of people or anything. You know – you know what I mean, right? It’s just daft.”

“Isaac, come on, that’s just crass—”

Isaac continued to talk, speaking over Will. “He’s just doing that out of spite. He’s a bad guy, Will. He just acts like he’s better than everyone, but really, what’s he done? Fucks around for a bit at university, fucks off travelling, works in the same place for a few years, gets nowhere and hates everyone else for it. He’s directionless, fucking around, going out all the time. At least you understand about work.”

Will took a drink, unwilling to engage in the conversation. Isaac continued anyway.

“We need to be careful around him.”

Will raised his eyebrows and turned to face the door. “Should we go find everyone?” he asked.

Isaac paused a second before nodding. “Let’s go find everyone. Come on.” They went out into the empty hallway. Isaac said, “You’d think they would have said goodbye or something.”

Will looked at Isaac. “Who?”

Isaac ignored the question and snapped, “Where’s Lyle, that fucker? Hate him so much.” He went back into the bedroom where he’d spoken to the American women. Will didn’t follow him in.

No one was in there.

Isaac sat back on the bed. Impressions from where the women had sat were indented into the soft duvet. It smelled of rose perfume and it filled up his nostrils. He scratched his nose. Glancing back at the wine stain on the wall, he took another drink. He muttered to himself, “No, no, no.” He lay back on the bed. He was silent.

He stayed like that for a few minutes.

He went back into the corridor, turning his head left and right, swaying a little bit. He went back into the kitchen. He opened the fridge again. He stared back at the stacks of hummus in their tubs. He slammed the door shut. The kitchen was silent. Someone had opened the window again and the cold wind blew in.

He went back into the hallway. The music had been turned off.

He tutted.

He went into the living room. Lyle was lying on an armchair, resting with his back on the side, legs wrapped over one armrest, looking at his phone. Will was also fiddling with his phone, perched on another armchair, his knees up to his chest. A sofa across from them was occupied by Mark and Mary, who were occupied with each other.

Isaac stood in the doorway, arms folded. No one said anything. Isaac spoke again. "This is awful."

Lyle responded without looking up from his phone. "What's awful, Isaac?"

Isaac tutted. He addressed the room. "Mind we were playing ring of fire a few months ago, when we had forty people in this room and everyone was focused on it? That never-ending game of spin the bottle? Mind when Will threw up on that girl?"

Lyle smiled. "That was pretty funny, to be fair."

They were silent for a moment. Will yawned. Lyle looked up from his phone at Isaac. "Everyone's just busy tonight. We should probably get home, anyway."

Isaac's shoulders fell. He muttered, "Awful, man, awful."

Lyle got up from the seat. "Come on, let's go."

Isaac flapped his arms for a moment, looking around him. "Where's my jacket? I left it here. Where's it gone?"

Mary and Mark left the room, muttering goodbyes to the three.

The others looked around the flat for the jacket. Isaac went quickly from room to room, Will following him. Lyle got up after they left and checked the backs of the sofas. He found the jacket behind the armchair; it had fallen near where Isaac had left his beer cans in the corner. Lyle picked up Isaac's cans in both hands and, carrying them to the kitchen, walked past Isaac and Will. After placing them in the bin Lyle went back to the living room and picked up the jacket.

"It's here." He gave it to Isaac, who put it on without saying anything.

Isaac didn't follow them down the stairs straight away. He looked into the empty hallway one last time as the door slammed shut with the barest momentum from his finger, a small amount of effort. The click of the lock was loud. They made their way downstairs, Isaac stuffing his hands in his pockets, watching his feet as he went down, step by step.

It was cold outside. They were in an area removed from the central parts of Edinburgh, the Old and New Towns, separated from it by the flat parkland of the Meadows. Home was a relatively short walk away, closer to the outer suburbs. Isaac glanced across the darkened pathways across the Meadows, lit by a thin line of lamps, away towards the nightlife of town. Away from where they were going.

Isaac kept looking towards the sights as the other two began to walk away. He spoke up. "I'm pretty drunk, guys. Could go for a few more—"

Will interrupted him. "We're all a bit drunk, man. It's going to work out fine. Things will work out the way they should."

"Are the girls in Iona's flat still up?" Isaac asked. "We could go see them?"

"No, Isaac. Let's just go," said Lyle.

Isaac clenched his fist. "They're always up, or they normally are."

Lyle responded, half talking to himself. “Just leave it, just leave it.”

Isaac sighed and started to walk behind them.

They walked up the street and turned the corner. The dark night sky cut across the tops of the buildings, the endless rows of clean tenements and polite shop fronts. The silence was broken by a howling wind which cut down the street, pulling dead leaves and dust with it. The three of them held on to their jackets as the wind hit them.

Isaac kept his fists curled in his pockets. They crossed a junction which turned off into more rows of flats. Isaac turned his head up towards the top-floor flats on the left-hand side of the road. There was no light in any of the windows. No movement, nothing happening. Street lights lit the way.

Isaac spoke to himself. Louder than he had before. “Please. Come on, please.”

Isaac paused in the middle of the road as they crossed over, his eyes looking down the street where Iona lived. The other two stopped a short distance away, both looking back at Isaac. His eyes scanned the window of Iona’s flat; the curtains were closed. There was no movement.

Where they were was not a classic postcard view, by any means, but one that was fine enough. More tenements, parked cars. At the end, all the way at the end, were more roads, more houses, the hill curling downward, the north of the city beyond it.

The history embedded into the Castle rock, the Victorian and Georgian streets in the distance – its history is already done. It does not continue. New homes are built around them, spreading out from the centre. Life happens out here, in small rooms and quiet streets. Young people meeting others in galleries, clubs and pubs. Families raising kids, old couples watching them go. Old friends drinking crap beer in dirty flats. Angry young men standing in the street, staring tearfully at windows, hoping that a light will turn on. The light will not turn on. There is no worthwhile history recorded around here, only minor happenings and quiet personal lessons.

Isaac glanced towards this vast emptiness ahead of him, looked around himself for a few moments, spinning slowly. Lyle and Will were moving on. Isaac walked up the street, hands in his pockets. Lyle and Will let him catch up with them before they walked on together. Isaac spoke out loud. "Bloody freezing."

No one answered him. He kept looking down at the way back, keeping his distance from the other two, hands stuffed in his pockets. A taxi passed them on the way into town, full of people. Isaac looked away from it.

Their flat was on a street to the left, in a tenement that looked murkier than the rest even in the pale street lights. Mumbling a series of nothings as they came in, Isaac went into his room, the first one on the left. He sat down on the bed. He could hear the other two moving around the flat, heading for their rooms. Then, silence. He was left alone, sitting in the dark, listening to the creaks and cracks, the wind howling against the window outside, sputters of cold coming through the pane of the glass.

He spoke to himself, louder this time. "I deserve better. I deserve more than you all."

His phone answered his cry.

It was a text. He looked at the number. It was one that he didn't recognise. He tutted, not looking at the message. He fell asleep, fully clothed.

CHAPTER TWO

When Isaac woke up the next day, it was mid-morning. He grabbed the top of his duvet and threw it forward. It landed on his open laptop, which was sitting on the desk near the end of the bed. The laptop's mouse fell to the floor. He moved quickly from the bed over to it, grasping at the duvet and pulling it off.

The laptop was fine. He lay back on his bed without covering himself up, the duvet lost to what little space there was left on the floor.

The curtains did a poor job of keeping out the light. He had slept through an earlier alarm.

He moved to the bottom of the bed, planting his feet on a pile of unwashed clothes, trousers and jumpers he had worn last week, some the week before. He picked up items one after the other, smelling them, then put on a jumper which did not smell strange.

He sat himself on the chair, the backrest making a loud clicking noise. His fingers reached for the dusty exterior of his laptop and turned it on. It was propped up at a slight angle, the keyboard tilted forward to allow some comfort for his wrists. The arrangement was a makeshift one composed of old textbooks he had bought when he studied computing. Isaac tapped the keys to check they were all working. A few were worn with age. He hammered the on button and the laptop's fans roared into life.

When he had bought the laptop, it took about a minute to load. It would take another five, maybe seven, sometimes eight minutes now. His eyes remained blank as he watched the loading screen. A plain blue background, the computer whirring away. He did not move from the chair.

When it finished loading up, he opened an internet tab to show his emails, but he didn't look at them. He kept opening up more tabs. He looked at a lot of news articles on the internet, reading through comments. He gritted his teeth, foul air rolling across the tips of his teeth. He read articles on foreign affairs and social equality. He read a lot about local issues relevant to Edinburgh, about the building of the trams, issues about the influx of tourists. People argued over everything.

Isaac did not have an account and had never created one. He kept reading articles, flicking through the comments, reading through every argument.

He checked his emails. He had one new message. He had a meeting today with the job centre about his search for gainful employment. If he failed to attend, he would lose his benefits and have to re-apply. The email had been sent yesterday. The meeting was in thirty minutes.

"Aww, *fuck*."

Isaac ran to the bathroom to get himself ready. He came back to the room, swirling mouthwash around in his mouth and spitting it onto an empty part of his bedroom floor. He stuck his feet into his shoes, fingers grasping at the frayed laces. He dragged his jacket up from the floor, tapped all the pockets and made his way outside, down the stone steps and out of the building.

. . .

He moved quickly out from the shadows and into the faint sunlight. A brief section of blue sky lit up between the patches of assorted shades of grey. It was cold but manageably so, the kind of weather that would frighten tourists into wrapping up too much. It was only made worse by the state of the trees. The few large ones on Isaac's street were barren, their leaves already gone from the ground. It was the sight of the trees that made it feel colder, more than anything.

Isaac moved quickly but his pace slowed as he came to the main road into town, closer to where people could see him. The main road was busy. There was a queue of cars stuck at a set of traffic lights near the flat. The cars were large, angular and clean. Isaac glanced at the drivers, some older, some young professionals dressed smartly, from the limited view he had of them.

He walked on and approached Tollcross, an area of town leading elsewhere. Small shops and smaller cafés, people avoiding both. The traffic forked around the clock in the centre of the road in shifts, straight down to the city centre one way, the other way leading towards the hospital, through to the Old Town. A tall grey and glass construction, belonging to a major bank, stood on the corner. Behind it was a building with mustard gas brickwork and bright blue painted along the windows. Isaac made his way towards it.

In other cities and towns there are job centres near to where people live. The main Edinburgh job centre, which Isaac was walking towards, was close to the centre of the historic Old Town, far away from anyone who actually lives in Edinburgh. It was a walk away from the Grassmarket, Princes Street and Edinburgh Castle.

Tourists coming to the city for the first time might wander about these ancient places, might wonder what it must be like to live here. They are unable to sample all the sights and sounds around them, to take in the vast expanse and expense of it all in the short time they stay here.

When they leave, a strange guilt starts to set in.

It takes root and never goes away – a sinking feeling, the shudder of a life lived half-full because they have never really been here, never grew up here, around the greenery, the ancient rock, pubs and shops, the Edinburgh that exists in their heads. Even then, if they were to then move here, they would only ever live here on the surface, living in their impressions of it, always dipping in and out, only ever able to sample it.

Edinburgh is a place that is never the same in anyone's imagination, never quite as good as anyone wants it to be. It's a city of desk jobs and jobseekers in a city with a castle.

A security guard greeted Isaac as he entered the building. Isaac did not try to make eye contact but mumbled his name. He looked at the man's gut, pressing out of the front of the white shirt and striped tie curving round it. Isaac tensed his own stomach muscles. He was told to go upstairs and he did, turning to go without saying anything. His foot missed the fifth step up, making a slamming sound on the tiles. He stopped for a few seconds, breathing through his mouth. He continued to walk up to the first floor without looking back.

A second security guard, on the first floor, pointed Isaac to a waiting area in the middle of a large open-plan office. The seats were arranged in a circle, armless cushioned seats. The circle was surrounded by an arrangement of desks and chairs, men and women in smart clothes working away. Some had claimants sitting across from them; others were sitting by themselves.

There was a murmur of conversation in the room, punctuated by a loud exchange between a stressed claimant in the corner talking to an impassive employee. The members of the circle would turn their heads on occasion, but the workers paid no attention to it. Isaac joined in, looking over at where the noise was coming from, turning to look at the others in the circle when they were not looking at him.

To his left was an older couple sitting together, still in winter jackets. The older woman had a perm and not a hair out of place. The man was balding, the hairs at the side of his head fading as they approached the top. His feet barely touched the ground and he kept rubbing his knees in discomfort.

To their left was a bald man who chewed the inside of his mouth, the motion of his jaw moving up and down, up and down. He was moving his hands together. His mouth was also moving as he spoke to himself, his eyes not looking at anyone.

There was also a young woman with a pram.

Isaac moved towards the right, then the left, before falling into the seat between the couple and the man moving his hands. Isaac looked around, the waiting people taking no interest in him. He slouched down. He looked to his left again and adjusted himself, squaring his shoulders and straightening his back.

He looked over at the woman with the pram. The pram had a large metal frame with thick wheels to match. Isaac glanced at the woman's pale neck, at her blonde hair tied into a ponytail.

He looked back at the man who was moving his hands constantly. The man held his hands together, palms against each other, fingers wrapped around each other. His lips were trembling. Isaac watched him for a while, then glanced towards the woman with a pram for a second before never looking at her again. He took out his phone with one hand, rubbing his eyes with the other, raising his eyebrows and yawning. He did not cover his mouth.

The text on his phone from the unknown number had remained unread.

His thumb tapped on the button to open it and to read it. He stopped. He put it away, muttering to himself. "Fucking … scam shit."

His finger hovered over the button to open the message.

Isaac's name was called by a voice from the back of the room. A man near the end was standing there with a sheet of paper in his hand.

The employee sat back down at his desk. Isaac sat on the opposite side of it. The employee stared at his computer screen without talking, his fingers tapping away on the keyboard.

Isaac's innards made a noise. He took a long breath out. There were leaflets on the desk for working in the health service. Isaac picked up one and looked through it. They were desperately looking for social workers, nurses and others. The woman on the leaflets had bright blonde hair, her slim figure in a nurse's uniform. Isaac pocketed the leaflet. The man kept typing.

"So, you've not found anything. I know it's tough out there now, but you have been unemployed for a few months, so I need to be a bit more thorough, you understand? I've been passed your details by my colleague … you worked in a supermarket for a bit, that large one out of town. That must have been quite a commute."

Isaac kept his arms folded. The man continued.

"I just need to check. Why were you let go from the supermarket?"

"I was looking for other work."

The man pursed his lips. "Sure thing."

"It wasn't what I wanted to do."

The man opened his mouth to ask a question, but he stopped. He muttered, "Sure thing." The man ignored Isaac for a few seconds after this, alternating between scribbling notes on a piece of paper and typing on the keyboard. He kept his eyes open without blinking. Then, he spoke up. "So, you've been claiming for a few months, by the looks of things. Are you aware of what else you could claim for?"

Isaac sat up, leaning forward and running his forefinger along the bottom of his nose, hooking his thumb under his chin. "Yes. I'm fine."

The man sighed and continued. "Okay, Isaac. I'll need to check how active you've been. By the looks of it, you've not been active. Let's see here …"

Isaac bit the inside of his cheek.

"You've put something twice in here. See here? You've applied for the same job twice, it says. I'm sorry, you won't be eligible – I'll have to stop your payments."

The argument happening in the far corner had died down a while ago.

The man kept going. "It'll be a couple of weeks before you can claim again. You'll need …"

Isaac watched the man's hands, currently resting on the keyboard. There was a wedding ring on his hand. It looked worn with time, with little dots of chipped paint. It looked small compared to his fat fingers. His fingernails looked short, uneven. The skin around his hands was wrinkled. There were flakes of dead skin on the back of his hand.

Isaac looked back up with a smile. "I'll get that all sent over."

"I'm really sorry, Isaac – by the looks of things, you've been doing a lot to look for work, but it's odd that you've not had any success for this amount of time. Do you need CV advice? Can we put you on a placement somewhere?"

Isaac waited before responding. He spoke firmly. "I'll sort myself out, thank you."

The older man didn't react.

Isaac muttered, "*Thank* you."

Isaac turned around to look at the circle of people. They were all gone, speaking to people across the room, replaced with new people.

He started making his way back home. There were men and women in thick, warm-looking jackets leaving their offices. Isaac kept his hands in his jacket pockets. He blew air slowly out of his mouth, his arms shaking, curling his toes in his shoes. The wind had picked up and he walked faster.

Isaac heard the click-clack of heels next to him. He turned his head and made eye contact with a woman a head shorter than him, black hair in a bun, wearing a green coat. She looked away from him as she passed. Isaac watched her move, looking back towards the job centre before crossing the road.

After walking for a few minutes, he came to a cash machine. Reaching for the wallet in his trouser pocket, Isaac looked from his left to his right and back up the road. He squeezed the wallet and it folded in his hand with ease. Isaac hesitated, the cash machine flashing up an advert with a smiling couple in an expensive-looking kitchen. Bold text described the rates for a loan. Slowly but surely, Isaac took out his debit card. He typed in his PIN and requested his balance on screen. It appeared a moment later.

A very small number appeared.

Isaac held his breath.

Two passing parents with prams moved to avoid him as he backed away from the machine, the sound of their children crying drowned out by the noise of a nearby bus reaching its stop. Isaac stood in the middle of the pavement and put his card in his wallet, then his wallet into his jacket pocket. He looked back towards the way he had come, back towards the job centre.

He had nothing. He had argued enough with his parents about his lack of employment. They had cut him off financially. He would not have any money in for the next month. He could not afford rent. There was nothing he could do.

He muttered, "Absolute bastards, bastards."

He kept walking, passing by an old pub he had been to a few months ago. He saw someone inside turn their head to him and he moved away.

The wind blew downhill as he walked back towards Bruntsfield. There was a new upmarket coffee shop with small furniture and white walls. It was empty. According to the sign outside, it opened at ten each day. There was a sign advertising a job. He glanced inside at a young woman behind the till, who was looking at her phone. He looked at the sign again. His phone buzzed again. He turned away quickly when the woman looked up.

These were sights he had seen many times before on the way back home. He walked past the edge of the Meadows, the trees bare and empty across the green parkland. In the light of day, Arthur's Seat was clear in the distance, the ancient rock a still fixture above the houses in the distance. Isaac did not look over at it, staring at the ground ahead of him the whole way back, not looking at the young students making their way towards their lectures across the Meadows.

He breathed through his mouth again. His breath was warm and stank of booze; his teeth were still sore.

When he was back in the flat, he went straight into the living room. The kitchenette was on the immediate left of the room, a sliver of vinyl flooring cutting across a small part of the room at an angle. The two sofas were wedged into the far opposite corner, a television on a cabinet opposite one of them. Lyle and Will had been drinking before they had left last night. They had left beer bottles everywhere.

Isaac pulled one of the wooden drawers in the kitchenette open with some force, the base of it dragging on the handle of a pan in the drawer below. He turned on the electric hob, fiddling with the plug in the wall to make sure it was still turning on. He boiled the kettle on the counter and reached for a mug from one of the cupboards, hands moving slowly over a vast collection of novelty glassware.

There was a large pile of dirty plates next to and in the sink. There were no clean mugs left. He looked at the pile without touching it; crockery piled up unevenly. The kettle finished boiling. He made a cup of tea and cooked some soup out of a tin, leaving the pan with the rest in the sink.

He went back into his room and lay on his bed for a few hours, keeping his eyes half-open for most of the time, not falling asleep. He gave up on drifting off and stared at the ceiling; covered in shadow, faint cracks in the corner which had always been there.

After a while he raised his head, looking at the desk across the room. He rolled over to his side. Lyle and Will were talking to each other somewhere in the flat, laughing loudly. Isaac grabbed the thin pillow to his left and stuck it over his head. The conversation ended, replaced by the washing machine thudding into existence in the kitchen, the foundations of Isaac's bed shaking.

Isaac called out, "Christ, you wee fucks."

There was a knock on the door. Isaac didn't move. The door was pushed open. Lyle popped his head round. "Isaac, how are you feeling today? Were you meant to be at work?"

Isaac did not respond at first but then said, "I didn't feel like it today, took it off."

The washing machine dipped into a lull, the wheel spinning slowly. Lyle nodded. "That's quite good that you can do that."

"Happens when you have a proper job."

Lyle sighed and said, "Isaac, I feel like last night you were … out of order. I don't think the way you speak to me or Will is nice enough."

Isaac blew air out of his mouth when Lyle started talking. "So, you can't take a bit of light ribbing now? Jesus wept."

Lyle waited for a few seconds before replying. "You're also behind on your rent. Is that job not paying you enough?"

Isaac raised his voice. "Don't start on my job – why are you interrogating me?" Isaac glared at him.

Lyle spoke softly and slowly. "Can you just please set up a standing order? I've asked a few times already. Really need it by end of this week."

"You're always begging for stuff. It's grim, Lyle, really grim. Honestly, I'm tired of you. Don't you have tables to clean or something?"

Lyle sighed.

Isaac kept going. "I can't understand what's gotten into you recently. Why are you acting so tetchy? Why?"

Lyle moved away.

Isaac called after him. "Why?" He went over to the door and called after him. "Why, Lyle? Why do you always run away, Lyle? Why can't you stick it out, Lyle?" Isaac turned back into his room and closed the door, forcing it shut over the last short distance, just as the washing machine started up again, the sound of it muffling the slam of the door.

Lyle went back into his room. The curtains were drawn. He sat on the end of his bed. After a few moments he put his head in his hands. He stared up at the photos on the wall, a collage of the past few years. There were a few photos of Isaac on the wall from when he was a student, when he had more hair. His smile seemed to light up in the dark. Lyle got up and slammed the door shut.

He opened up his laptop. It woke up from its snooze mode with the sight of Lyle's CV still being worked on. He minimised it, opening up his emails. The majority of the staff he worked with were students, men and women younger than him. They took fewer shifts, turned up hungover, their shifts working around their studies. Lyle worked most of the time, taking shifts whenever possible. He hadn't had a day off in a few weeks.

His other emails were mostly marketing-related, from airlines and foreign hotels. He hadn't left the country for some time now. He had some unread emails from his grandmother. There was an email from some friends he had made abroad from a week ago. Lyle opened it up again. The email was lengthy, filled with descriptions of foreign hotels, upmarket bars and shining seas. The sender managed to mix up 'their' and 'there' every single time. Lyle had looked at this email a few times over the last few days.

He put his head in his hands.

He glanced over at his phone. There were some missed calls from his parents. He had not spoken to them for a while. He pressed his feet forward under the desk. His travelling rucksack remained under it as a footrest.

Lyle pressed his feet into it, re-reading the email from his old friends.

He began to type out a reply to the email.

Will had gotten out of bed to check what had caused the noise. He did not make it to his bedroom door. He stepped on some scattered pieces of paper that he had left on the floor, things unfinished, things torn into pieces. Will had been crying all day and continued to do so.

His phone was ringing. He was receiving calls from work, from his boss. Will had missed work again.

He had spent the day attempting to draw. He drew some shapes, representations of the things in front of him, squares and rectangles. Every time he found himself drawing he stopped himself, muttering noises under his breath, screwing the sheets of paper up and slamming them onto the ground behind the desk. They made no noise when they hit the ground.

He had given up after an hour of this and spent more time on the internet, looking up symptoms of mental illnesses and the price of therapy. In the dark, the room around him was blank, the walls bare, frames of his older work piled up on one side of the room. He kept his eyes open, gasps of cold air wrapping around his strands of hair.

The phone rang again.

He didn't get up.

Back in his room, Isaac could feel phlegm creeping down the back of his throat. He curled his hands together, rubbing his face with them. He yawned and went back to his laptop, going straight to the internet, looking at various content aggregation sites. He watched a few film trailers for some upcoming films and a few that he had already seen in the cinema.

He opened a new tab for the jobseekers website. He entered his username and password into the relevant boxes. It took a while to load so he went back to reading the forums.

About thirty minutes later, he clicked back to the jobseekers page. Wrong password. He typed it in again.

He looked at a few advertised jobs on the website. There were roles for senior cooks, managers, supervisors. There were minimum-wage jobs, sales jobs, restaurant jobs. He closed his eyes. "Come on, come on, come on – I deserve better than this, this … Arseholes, all of you."

He moved back to the bed and lay down facing the white wall. Isaac did not close his eyes.

He did not have a screensaver, so the screen with the job offers stayed on, a bright pale background with black lines and words.

His phone buzzed again.

Isaac fell asleep.

He woke an hour later. Isaac went back to his laptop, not touching his phone.

The phone buzzed again. He checked where the messages had been coming from – all from the same unknown number. He put his phone down on the desk and spun it round, watching it do several spins before losing momentum. It was a black phone with very little in the way of expensive features, a small screen with black text on a faded green background. It was light enough to keep going when it was spun hard enough, weighted well enough to not spin out of control.

Isaac clicked through some of the management positions on offer, scanning their details. The jobs all required degrees.

His flatmates were back in the kitchen again, cooking something; he heard the hiss of a hot frying pan. Isaac kept looking through the pages – not bothering to click the job descriptions, continuing to scroll, a little faster but more methodical.

His phone started to ring. Isaac watched it ring away, dancing across the table, the vibrations shaking the desk. The same unknown number flashed on the screen. Isaac stared at the phone. It rang out.

He went back to the internet. He re-opened the internet forums.

It was getting darker outside.

He opened up the phone message. It was from Cullen.

Cullen was a name from the distant past. He was someone that Isaac knew from university. He was the first person Isaac became friendly with when he had first arrived at halls. They had been close friends until Cullen suddenly dropped out. Isaac had lost touch with him. Cullen was someone who, for all intents and purposes, had vanished from Isaac's life. Now he was in Edinburgh. He wanted to meet Isaac at an address on the outskirts of the city.

He wanted to meet tonight.

CHAPTER THREE

Isaac stared down the length of the bus to the very front, his eyes resting on the only other passenger on the top deck, a man with large spots on his bald patch – red splotches of strained skin. The man stared forward into the dark. Isaac looked away, taking the phone out of his jacket pocket.

He had texted Cullen earlier, confirming that he wanted to meet. Cullen had sent him a location to go to later that day. Isaac did not respond. Cullen had not texted back to check if Isaac was on his way.

Isaac tapped the phone with his fingers. According to Cullen's texts, his house was around here.

The bus had long since pulled away from the centre of town, picking up speed as it encountered fewer traffic lights and crossing pedestrians. It had driven past endless street lights and lines of houses and parked cars. Isaac reached for the button to request the bus to stop and started to make his way off the bus.

It had pulled up to a bus stop on a street far off the main road. There were rows of low houses on one side and an overgrown patch of grass on the other, which was not lit up by anything. A street lamp shone over the bus stop, lighting up the lines of dirt on the wall of the nearest house, its curtains pulled shut. There were only a few parked cars around. Isaac made his way outside.

He watched the bus move away, glancing at a trio of women sitting and talking by the back window, lit up by the bright light inside. They did not look back at Isaac. He moved towards the closest street lamp, standing directly under the light.

As the bus departed, the sound of its whirring engine was replaced by a muted stream of concrete breath from far out to the west. The sound of traffic from the bypass, the motorway that ran around the city, an eternal white noise audible even late at night. Isaac had never been out this far from the city. He sniffed the air. There was a faint smell of diesel but it faded away. He looked across the still space around him.

He was somewhere in a housing estate. There was no one outside. Towards the east, high-rises rose up over the surrounding houses. The street lights made them glow, a virulent maroon swirling around their bases, the colour turning darker as the light blended into the night sky.

Isaac walked down the street, looking behind him every couple of steps he took.

Under his thick jacket he was wearing a warm jumper with sleeves that were too long for him, a cheap buy from his student days. He kept his arms down by his sides so that they would rub against the side of his body, compressing his armpit sweat against him. The sweat felt like a warm, solid object. He hadn't washed in a few days.

He turned a corner, close to the address Cullen had given him. From where he was on the pavement, it was difficult to make out the numbers on the front doors of the houses around him. With a nervous gait, Isaac kept walking and looking around, occasionally pausing at a house, squinting at it, checking his phone. They all looked quite similar, their curtains closed, some with lights on behind, some entirely dark. He looked around him, spinning in a circle.

Isaac walked for a few more minutes, taking his time. The ground was cold, damp in places. Ice had formed, lit up by the amber street lamps.

Near the end of the road was the entrance towards something he could not see, the front fence overwhelmed by a thick hedgerow. The roof of a small house was poking above it. Isaac checked his phone again. He went to the front gate and opened it.

This was definitely the address Cullen had given him. It was less a house, more an extension of the house connected to it. There was not much of a front garden; the grass was thin around the edges of the lawn, which was circled by a muddy path leading directly towards the house. This house was smaller and the roof lower than its immediate neighbour. It was difficult to see all this with the nearest street lamp just poking over the height of the hedge.

Crossing over the grass, Isaac went up to the door and looked at the number and letter scrawled on it in black ink, something that looked like it was from a permanent marker. He had left the gate open.

Isaac knocked on the door, which swung open on the second knock. The only source of light came from upstairs.

"Hello?" he called.

There was no reply.

He called out again but still no answer. He went inside and closed the door behind him. He called out again. "Hello?"

Nothing happened. Isaac waited with his hands in his pockets. He stood, his right hand curled into a fist, his thumb pressed against the top of his forefinger.

"Who the hell do you think you are, Cullen?" he muttered to himself.

Isaac moved steadily upstairs. His hand gripped the handrail. He made it all the way up but stopped at the penultimate step and muttered, "Vanishes out of the blue, now wants … fuck knows."

He hesitated for a moment. The light came from a room to his left. The walls of the illuminated room looked faded from where Isaac could see into it, with parts of the wallpaper peeling off. The colour of the carpet became visible: it was a dark charcoal, and sections of it were ripped close to the skirting boards.

Isaac stepped into the room.

He immediately covered his eyes; there was an intense warm light from a low-hanging bulb just above Isaac's head. The room was small and bare and the light from the bulb cast shadows on the small objects at the far end of the room.

Cullen was in the far corner. He said nothing when Isaac entered, making eye contact with him for a few moments before going back to the bag in front of him. His shadow in the room stuck to the far wall, a second layer to him, gripping the pale paint. Isaac stared at the shadow before he looked at Cullen.

On the floor were three small piles of books unevenly stacked. A mat was rolled out in front of them with a small pillow at the top. At the very foot of the mat was a small hiking rucksack, and Cullen was pushing something into its side pocket.

After a moment Cullen said, "Hey, you're a bit late. I was going to get into things here, but we should probably head off in a bit."

Cullen wore black combats with large pockets. His hair was cut short, quite different to the longer hair he had in university. Isaac waited for him to continue talking. When he said nothing more, Isaac said softly, "Christ, Cullen, you look different."

Cullen did not look up, still packing. He spoke again with a sense of urgency in his voice. "It's been a couple of years. Really want to get going, come on."

He got up and Isaac stepped back. Cullen was a head taller than him. Isaac stammered a little before he started talking again. "Yeah, but … where are we going?"

Cullen shrugged and replied, "I mean, we're going there anyway. I'd figured you'd just sit there and blast out tons of questions, but I can just show you when we're there, no sense dragging things out. Best way to learn things. Better than you normally did, anyway. I never forgot, man. I remember you so well, Isaac. You've not … You look exactly the same. Christ, man. A little bit older, sure. But you're the same." He had put the bag on his back, looking at his hands to wrap straps around his waist.

"What did you say?" Isaac asked.

Cullen laughed. "I mean, you were always one for asking questions, like, over and over. Didn't really get anything out of it, not sure what you were after. But I think I worked it out."

Isaac shook his head, trying to process what Cullen had said. "Worked out what? Don't speak to me like that. You just turn up and then … What, we're leaving now? We aren't even going to talk?"

Cullen opened his mouth a little, looking to his left, towards a map. His eyes snapped back to Isaac. "You look like you're ready to move already. You used to always make me late for things, mind? Don't think your classes took attendance that often. Not even sure you ever went to yours."

Isaac's mouth was open. His response was muted. "You've lost your accent."

"It comes on every now and again," Cullen said. "I

haven't been home to Ireland yet. Don't think I will, if I'm honest. Feel like I can do more here. You know, have to move on with things, all that university stuff was years ago."

"Cullen?" Isaac began, but Cullen was already starting to talk again.

"This is going to be more of a thing where I do things and you follow me. It'll make sense if you just keep going along with it for a bit and then figure it out." As Cullen spoke, he moved towards the door.

Isaac wobbled backwards and held his arms up, a look of *Excuse me?* on his face.

Cullen shook his head, impatient. "Come on, this is the pace I'm going to go, and you need to go with it."

Isaac stammered out a response. "What happened? You vanished, dropped out after a few weeks. You lived in the dorm right next to me, walked to class with me. You just dropped out – where have you been?"

But Cullen was already making his way downstairs. His placid expression didn't alter. The fingers in his right hand began to curl and uncurl. He paused to pick up a pair of hiking boots with scratches around the front. He stood at the bottom of the stairs, looking back at Isaac, who had moved onto the landing. "I went travelling. I learnt some things. Grew up a bit. Did some jobs along the way. Met some interesting people."

Cullen turned, putting on his jacket as he did so. Isaac glanced at Cullen's biceps before taking his own hands out of their pockets and folding his arms.

Cullen kept talking. "It's always interesting, actually. Folk are really relaxed when they're abroad and you tend to get more out of them, like they're not really that open about themselves back home. Like there's something holding them back. Only when they're abroad do they start being more – I don't know, man, unhindered? Not sure how much they bring back of them when they go."

Isaac screwed up his face. "What?"

Cullen paused. Isaac couldn't see his face in the dark. When Cullen spoke, it was quietly. "I do wonder, I do wonder a lot."

"Cullen, what the hell, man!"

"Not about everything, just trying to get a sense of perspective."

"We're heading out already? You're only just back in town?"

"I've been here for a few weeks."

"A few weeks? In this shithole?"

Cullen shrugged. "Shouldn't be this bit for much longer, mind," he said. "I've been looking at places."

Isaac paused at this. He lowered his shoulders, speaking slowly. "Do you want to just hang out a bit?"

"You've just watched me put my boots on – you think we're staying here? What is there to do here?" Cullen screwed his eyes up a little and turned away. "We're going for a walk."

"We aren't going to a pub?" Isaac asked.

Cullen turned back. "I gave up drinking a long time ago."

"What? You gave up drinking?"

"I gave up drinking after uni," Cullen snapped, talking in a low growl. "Mind that night in that big club – what was it called again? Don't think I told anyone, but then I wasn't out that much afterwards, I remember. Nah, haven't been drinking for years."

Isaac nodded, acknowledging the memory. "The one in the union …"

Cullen nodded. "That one, mind that? One pound drinks on a Tuesday, DJ with the ponytail. Mind him? Used to remix the bassline from that Simon and Garfunkel song over and over?"

Isaac nodded again. He muttered, "Christ."

"A few years ago, wasn't it? But it's fine though. Been out in a few other places around the world, but nah, I don't drink anymore. Can't go back to those days, can't go back now. Don't need to go back, it's all forward."

Isaac smiled a little. "Do you mind that first night we'd all gone out?" he asked. "The bar in town that the old guy had dragged us to – mind how he was repeating a year, didn't have anyone to talk to? Think we ditched him somewhere."

Cullen nodded. "He was a nice bloke, I remember," he said.

"You always rambled on a lot, remember? Couldn't get a word in edgeways – you always talked over me a lot. I think the only time you stopped was when I told you to stop, remember? We were in that big circle and no one was talking, just you, and I had to tell you that no one could understand a word you were saying. Remember?"

Cullen didn't say anything in response.

Isaac made his way downstairs, continuing to talk. "Those were good days. Then a few weeks later you up and vanish. Completely out of the blue, you just go, you aren't there anymore."

"Yeah, that's right."

Isaac looked directly at him and asked, "What happened?"

"I moved forward." Cullen paused. "Let's head out, we're wasting time here …" He moved away quickly.

Isaac watched him leave and began to follow him. Isaac muttered under his breath, "Come on, man."

Cullen held the door open for him, hooking a small length of string at the base of the door to a hook on the side. Cullen pulled onto the side of the door as he left, the door fitting into the door frame quietly. Isaac looked at him.

"What are you doing that for?" Isaac asked.

Cullen didn't respond, his fingers resting on the door. He held his hands against the door. Isaac opened his mouth to ask another question, but Cullen had already turned his head and moved away. Isaac watched Cullen follow the path around the front lawn before he stepped back onto the grass to follow him out.

Cullen turned right out of the gate, walking in the very middle of the pavement. Isaac tried to walk next to him but ended up hitting the wing mirror of a car. Cullen whispered to him, "Careful, Isaac."

"Where are we going, Cullen?"

Cullen stopped, and Isaac flinched. Cullen turned and said, "Look, I'm going to keep walking, you're going to follow, we're just going to be quiet on our walk. No need to draw attention to ourselves. It'll be better if you just come along, right? Great, man. Let's go."

Isaac raised his voice in reply. "So, I can't ask questions? Not a fan of fr—"

Cullen turned back quickly, hissing at a much lower volume. "It's not a freedom-of-speech thing. It's a basic matter of comprehension. You're better seeing it for yourself, in a manner of speaking."

But Isaac did not lower his voice. "Why can't you just tell me what it is?"

Cullen grinned. He hissed, his tone a little lighter. "I mean, I'm not going to tell you now, am I?"

"Because you can't answer it properly?" Isaac snapped back.

Cullen looked into the night sky. "No, because I know you're just going to keep asking forever and ever until I get annoyed, then get a sense of superiority knowing that you know I don't know what it is. If I just keep going there, you'll follow behind anyway. Man, I've sort of missed this."

Isaac finally lowered his voice. "I don't know what you're talking about."

Cullen walked on. Isaac watched him go. When he got to a few metres away without stopping or turning around, Isaac started after him, periodically turning his head to look behind at the empty, still streets. Cullen kept going, walking a route parallel to the main road and heading east. They came to an empty patch of land beside the housing estate they were on and saw more houses out in the far distance. Cullen stuck to the footpath; Isaac started to cut across the grass. The grass was wet and the dampness sank through the light material of Isaac's trainers. Cullen kept walking and only stopped when he reached a four-way junction leading out of the council estate. He waited.

"How far are we walking?" Isaac asked as he caught up.

Cullen crossed the road diagonally, looking left and right. Isaac reached for the button to activate one part of the crossing, but Cullen walked on, unimpeded.

"Oh, fuck off, Cullen," Isaac muttered.

They were walking along a long main road that ran under a railway bridge, piles of old brickwork with a high archway. Isaac's footsteps started to echo. He stopped for a second, falling behind Cullen again, who made no sound when he walked under the bridge.

They walked past a large, fenced-off park that was vast and empty, and then came to a row of bungalows planted on a hill. For the most part the curtains were closed. Cullen slowed his pace, his head turning left and right, left and right, as he walked past driveways and roads turning off. He took a left turn down a side street, one not immediately visible from a distance. Isaac picked up his pace as Cullen vanished around the corner.

Isaac coughed. Cullen's head snapped around. He stopped. They both stopped.

Isaac was out of breath but he managed to speak. "Cullen, what's going on?" he asked.

"No names," Cullen hissed before setting off in the same manner as before. And on they went. Isaac walked with his head down, spitting phlegm onto the pavement at intervals.

They came onto roads with wider pavements, trees casting cracked shadows onto the tinted amber concrete. The wind cut across the trees, the sound of branches scratching the night sky in peaks and troughs. Because the houses were so short in stature the night sky became larger, framed by the barren trees hanging over them. There were no visible stars in the sky, and the ground was lit well enough by street lamps for them to see only in front of them but nothing of the world around them.

Cullen took another sudden left turn down a narrow pathway. When he vanished again, Isaac spat on the ground, with the full weight of his spit landing on his trainer. Disgusted, he tried to wipe it off with the foot of his other trainer, but to no avail.

He caught up with Cullen, who was already in front of a house. They were in a cul-de-sac, the road out of it lined by barren trees. None of the lights in the houses around them were on. One house looked different to the others, after first glance. It seemed to have sunk into the earth, branches sticking out of the front hedge at odd angles, the front lawn overgrown in random blotches. No car was in the driveway. There was something stuck in the letterbox, an errant letter which had not fallen inside.

Cullen walked towards the garage door, taking a pair of leather gloves out of his pocket and putting them on. When he got right up to the door he turned around, staring at Isaac. Isaac looked to his left, back down the cul-de-sac. He stepped back to look down the path they had walked down. No one was there. When he turned back, Cullen was still looking at him with his arms raised by his sides.

Cullen hissed at Isaac with a firm tone in his voice. “This is the place. Come on.”

Isaac hissed back. “I don't know what you want me to do.”

Cullen looked dead into Isaac’s eyes. “I want you to come over here so I can push you up onto the roof of the garage. Then you can pull me up.”

“What the *hell* do you want me to do?”

Cullen replied with a tone of exasperation in his voice. “Get over here.”

But Isaac did not move.

Cullen cupped his hands together and lowered them to his waist, planting his legs a little wider. “Come on.”

“Cull—”

“No names,” Cullen snapped.

Isaac closed his mouth. His hands were shaking. There were shadows on Cullen’s face, the curve of his nose, his straight, serious mouth. His eyes were focused on Isaac.

Isaac walked slowly towards Cullen. He stretched his leg upward a little. Cullen kept his hands by his waist, not lowering them to catch Isaac's foot. Isaac struggled, raising his leg higher, planting his foot in Cullen's hands. Cullen pushed his leg up immediately. For a moment, Isaac was in the air with nothing to hang onto, his entire weight in Cullen's hands. Isaac was leaning backwards, his weight carrying him, his hands reaching forward, gripping at the night air. His fingers found the edge of the garage roof, the hard concrete scraping the tops of his nails. He flattened his palms and pushed his leg forward into Cullen, forcing him into the garage door with a sharp movement. Isaac paddled his legs, lamely attempting to press something to hoist him upwards.

Cullen growled, “Push with your hands, get on the roof. Have you seriously never done this before?”

Isaac exerted as much force onto the garage roof as he could muster, his fingers curling, his shoulders burning as he moved upwards, the front of his stomach scraping against the lip of the garage roof, banging his left knee against the edge of the roof. There was a small puddle near the edge, near where he had put his hands. He managed to accidentally clamber into it, water spreading around his waist. It felt dirty, cold, staining his crotch.

“Now get me up,” Cullen said. “Quickly now, don’t want to be hanging around.”

Isaac did not respond. He looked around. He was more exposed to the elements, high enough to look out of the cul-de-sac and into the back gardens of the houses surrounding them, back towards where they had come and in every other direction. The thin wind buffeted his back as he turned around, leaning forward, finding his balance. He could see lines of houses, aerials stuck into the night air. He could see the high-rises in the distance.

Cullen was waiting by the bottom of the garage door, his eyebrows raised. He did not move when Isaac shuffled towards him. Isaac got onto one knee, muttering as he managed to land it right in the puddle again. He put his other knee slightly in front. He reached forward, his arm extended downwards.

Cullen shook his head. “No. Bend your arm, open your hand.”

Isaac sighed, turning his arm a little. Cullen jumped to grab it, getting a few feet off the ground. Isaac grunted.

“Cullen–”

“*Shut*—”

Isaac, unable to balance himself, did not pull his arm up. A shot of pain snapped through his back, just left of his spine.

He reacted by lowering his arm, trying to drop Cullen, who managed to reach with his other hand and grip the edge roof. This action pulled Isaac forward so that he was inches away from losing his balance and falling face first onto the ground.

Cullen planted his hand on the roof, letting go of Isaac with his other hand. Isaac wobbled forward and fell onto his stomach, the top half of his body hanging over the edge.

"Christ!" he gasped, then sneezed. The phlegm and saliva that had built up in his mouth hit the ground with a well-defined splat that reverberated around the cul-de-sac. He could feel the roof vibrate as Cullen stepped around it. He pulled himself backwards, tenderly lifting his arms. He moved up slowly, coming onto his knees. He put his hands on his hips, bending his elbows. Isaac turned his head to look for Cullen, who had walked to the back of the garage roof. As Isaac rose off his knees, Cullen was planting his foot on the sloped, tiled roof, moving towards a skylight.

Isaac moved across the roof, past Cullen, to look into the back garden. The grass was overgrown, bare bushes reaching into the dirt, a tree leaning against the tall back hedge, its roots on display, poking into the lawn.

Cullen was close to the skylight, leaning his body on the roof. He unzipped the side of the bag on his back without looking. He whispered, "Keep down and keep your eye out. I'll be out in—"

"Cullen, what the *fuck*!" Isaac hissed.

Cullen was shaking his head, never looking up from what he was doing. "The security system is broken. Garage is new and they've not moved or shut off the window. Shut up and keep your head down."

Isaac's mouth was open, staring at Cullen. He stammered out, "I have no idea what's going on."

Cullen was moving and talking quickly. "You don't actually have to do anything, so the fact you don't understand at this particular point in time is immaterial, if I'm honest with you. Stop going on about it, it's boring to listen to. Keep low. Won't be anyone around at this time, but if anyone does come, text me."

Cullen put his hand into the bag and removed something from it in one smooth motion. It was a multi-tool, which he pressed underneath the top of the skylight. He waited for the wind to blow and then he opened it with one sudden movement, the sound of something metal tearing, the noise muted by the gust of wind. Isaac watched him, squatting down, his knees bent. Cullen opened the window and let himself in. He pressed a finger against the pane of glass, letting the weight of the window close before he stopped it, shutting it without making a noise.

Isaac was alone.

There was no noise from the trees. There was not a hum from the electricity running through the lights. The house was far away from the rumble of traffic.

He curled his hands into fists, then stretched them out again.

He crouched and turned back to look at the cul-de-sac. The pathway they had entered from was practically invisible from the roof. Isaac looked right, left, right again. The wind began to howl again.

The wet patches around his waist were not drying. He coughed again, phlegm forming in the roof of his mouth and throat. He rubbed his hands against his sides. He looked at the palms of his hands. Lines of black dirt filled the lines of his hands; his fingers were sore from being pushed against the roof. There was a cut on his right forefinger, a line of blood seeping out of it.

Isaac stayed still as he looked at his hands. He brushed the cut with his thumb. He had cut his hand somewhere. His blood could be anywhere along the edge of the roof.

He whimpered to himself, "Wanna get off. Wanna get off …"

He got on his hands and knees and studied the edge of the roof, looking for signs of dirt, signs showing he'd gripped onto it, signs of anything. He looked down at the gathering of snot and saliva which he had coughed up at the foot of the garage. Muttering under his breath, he frantically moved his hands over the edge, then took them away sharply, placing his hands on the top of his head, running his hands through his hair.

His eyes diverted to the sight, real or imagined, of any minor movement from his vantage point. Shadows on the ground moved as nearby tree branches moved in the wind. The branches reached out to the road, the tips of them clawing against the ground towards him. Isaac could feel the air whip around the tip of his nose.

Isaac bit the inside of his bottom lip and looked again at his bloody finger. He pushed it into the puddle, despite being reluctant to expose his cut to the dirty water. He looked at the water. He couldn't see his reflection, save for a sliver of his shadowy face. He put his other hand in and, after a few seconds, he lifted it and wrapped it around the edge of the garage roof, soaking the part where he had clambered up. He did this a few times for good measure, so that most of the edge had been washed in the dirty water.

He breathed out. "No fingerprints."

Isaac, down on his knees, rested his cold, soaking hands on his wet thighs. He sat there for a minute, watching the empty space of the cul-de-sac, the closed windows, the lack of life anywhere. He turned his head after a few moments.

Cullen was behind him, his knees bent, watching Isaac. His black bag was resting on his shoulder.

Isaac stood up slowly, grunting as he bent his legs.

Cullen whispered, "Why are you giving yourself an infection? Why do you feel the need to stand up suddenly? Keep down."

Isaac squatted down quickly.

Cullen continued, "We need to get off the roof. Are you planning on standing up and jumping off? You need to stay low, don't move around so much."

Isaac didn't say anything. He got back onto his knees, reaching for the edge of the garage roof.

"Use a bit of common sense," Cullen said.

Isaac dropped down. He did not look down when he landed, nor did he look up at Cullen's face. He did not set his feet when he fell down, landing with his left leg straight. He cried out in pain. He balanced himself by reaching out for the garage door, the noise of the impact making a sharp noise against the metal sheet.

Cullen whispered from above, "Isaac – you're panicking, for fuck's sake. Plant your fucking feet properly. Eyes up: catch!"

Cullen gripped the strap of the bag and swung it over his shoulder, dropping the bag down, missing Isaac by a matter of inches. The bag landed with a solid, heavy sound. Cullen bent down, gripping the edge of the garage with one hand, swinging his body round in a fluid movement to catch the edge with his other hand so that his front was facing the garage door. He took his time, adjusting himself for a few seconds, bending his knees before dropping down.

Isaac stared at the bag. It was zipped up, an arm's length away from him. His arms stayed at his side. He did not look up from the bag when Cullen dropped down. He did not look at him as he spoke. "Cullen, what's in the bag?"

Cullen whispered, leaning forward to Isaac, "It's full of air from inside the house. Gonna trade it somewhere for some magic beans."

Cullen sniggered. Isaac whimpered.

"Cullen—"

"You need to stop saying my name."

Isaac managed to say, "We walked together to class when we were students, and now you're robbing houses. Christ, man."

Cullen was walking up the driveway, back into the cul-de-sac. Cullen did not look back at Isaac or at the bag. He said, "You want to know what's *in* the bag, but you aren't willing to carry it to find out. Good stuff."

Cullen stopped, turning around to face Isaac, his hands shoved into his pockets.

Isaac muttered, "I have no idea what's going on."

Cullen grinned. "I know you well enough – you're acting confused to get out of carrying the bag. God, even after all these years …"

The howl of the wind interrupted them.

Isaac finally said, "No."

They paused. Cullen didn't move. Isaac shook his head.

Finally, Cullen began to walk away.

Isaac didn't do anything. Cullen was walking away without looking back. Isaac snatched at the bag and began to follow him. The weight of it strained against his back as he lifted it. Something metal ground against metal. He slung it over his shoulder, the force of the strap cutting into his body. Isaac followed Cullen, just as he had before.

Cullen looked back with a grin.

The bag pulled at Isaac's shoulders. When he walked, he twisted his body a little to the left to accommodate the weight, the bag hanging down to just above his waist. Isaac moved his hand up to grip the strap just as Cullen had done on the roof.

When Cullen was at the entrance of the pathway, he stopped, looked right and turned left, away from where they had come.

Isaac struggled with the weight of the bag. Cullen would look back occasionally to see Isaac slowing down to breathe and steady himself, or mutter to himself, or rub his eyes from tiredness. Cullen kept going.

There was no traffic on the roads. No one else was walking around this late at night in the cold weather.

They headed further into the suburbs, away from where they had started. Then Cullen took a left, so they were heading west. Further along, he took another turn left, so they were heading south, downhill, back towards the direction of the high-rises.

Isaac was sweating now. The cold settled into his feet and hands. He shifted the bag across his back, but he just felt the pain more keenly. Something clicked in the lower part of his back. But he could not stop and would not lose sight of Cullen.

They made it back to Cullen's after walking for another thirty minutes. They had not encountered anyone on the way back. Cullen opened the gate without looking behind. Isaac walked through it, came to a halt, turned back to the gate and pushed it shut. Cullen was already inside.

Upstairs, Isaac found Cullen sitting cross-legged against the wall of his room. The light was still on from when they had left and he had taken his coat off. In one movement Isaac lifted the bag and attempted to hurl it at Cullen. But it stopped a short distance in front of Cullen – far enough so he had to change his stance and reach for the bag strap to pull it towards him.

Cullen did not react to this potential attack. Isaac curled his fist into a ball and put it to his mouth to blow air onto it, trying to warm it up. Cullen unzipped the bag. He checked the contents, then looked up at Isaac.

"Cullen, I didn't take anything out of it."

Cullen pursed his lips. He held the bag up by the straps, lifting it just above the ground to get a feel for the weight.

"Fuck sake," Isaac sighed.

Cullen put the bag down.

"Cullen, are you in trouble?" Isaac asked.

"Isaac, are you asking if you're in trouble by association?"

Isaac groaned. "Jesus, man, I—"

"If I was, I wouldn't be here," Cullen interrupted, "I just … picked up some things when I was abroad, that's all. It's amazing what you can learn when you travel."

Cullen started smiling and took off his gloves. He reached into the bag and pulled out a wad of cash. He ran a thumb over the edge of one set of notes, the noise of the crisp currency vibrating in the air, filling the silence in the room between them.

Isaac's jaw dropped open. "Is that cash? Did they … They had rolls of cash in there?"

Cullen nodded. "Yeah, in a safe. Few other things too."

Isaac remained slack-jawed. "You found … How did you get into it?"

Cullen shrugged and continued unpacking the bag.

"I mean, I learnt some stuff abroad. I scout out people, places, follow them home. Harmless stuff. It was easy abroad, I just looked like another drunk foreigner."

Isaac looked away for a second, muttering again. "Just … Crying out loud …"

Cullen looked up at him. "Isaac, you're shaking. Are you upset?"

Isaac slumped back onto the floor, his back against the opposite wall.

Cullen went back to unpacking.

Isaac said, "Fuck, man. Mind the last time I saw you?"

Cullen tapped some of the notes, not looking up. He muttered, "No."

"Christ, man. I do – that club in town, the one with like six, seven floors, remember? Everything was open, that perfect balance of, like, fullness? Right amount of women. It was really good. You vanished that night, man, you don't remember? Someone thought you died or something."

Cullen looked at the notes, his hands firm as he reached for a roll, never looking at Isaac, who was watching for Cullen's reaction. Cullen smiled but not too much.

Isaac continued, "You got lost or something, whatever. Then you vanished. That's all we knew about you. We all stopped talking about you, to be quite honest. Like you were never there."

Cullen held out a roll of money towards Isaac. Isaac reached out for a second, as if going to shake Cullen's hand, but he snapped his hand back.

Cullen grinned. "You tell your friends you've got a new job," he said.

Isaac spoke carefully and slowly. "I've got a job."

Cullen, still grinning, shook his head. "Your job is fake. I've looked it up. Low-end website, no content, poorly coded. Definitely your handiwork. You'd probably be better off working in a supermarket."

"You've been stalking me?" Isaac snapped.

Cullen shrugged. "I've checked up every now and then. I'm surprised you've kept it up for this long, you could just get a real job—"

"You don't know me."

"You wouldn't have agreed to come all the way out here to meet me like this if you hadn't got nothing else on. You would have wanted to meet up in town, try to get fired into some eighteen-year-olds. So, I know, Isaac, I know."

Isaac said nothing. There was a buzzing sound coming

from the light above, audible in the silence between them. Cullen tossed the money at Isaac. It landed in front of his lap.

Cullen spoke firmly. “Don't put the money in your bank account in one go; keep it under your bed or something like your sock drawer. Be smart – I know that’s a difficult concept for you, but please try your best.”

Isaac still didn't look at the money. His hands were fumbling with his pockets, and he was muttering to himself. “I don't understand why you're doing this.”

Cullen looked at Isaac and said, “But you do understand that you now have money in your hand, probably more than you’ve ever made in a month. You’re a lazy fuck, always were.”

“I'm not doing this again, Cullen,” Isaac snapped. “I’m going to get a job and sort out my rent, and I'm going … going to be fine. Right? Right. Don’t need this.” He grunted, snatching the cash in front of him and pocketing it.

Cullen did not look up as Isaac left the room, but he called out after him, “I’ll text you in a few days.”

Isaac shouted back, “You always were an odd one, Cullen.”

Cullen said nothing. He looked through some of the other items he’d taken – a watch, some jewellery. He slapped them down to the ground as soon as Isaac left.

Isaac made his way downstairs and slowed as he reached the bottom step, turning back for a second. No sound came from upstairs. It was as if the room was empty and tonight had never happened.

He stepped out into the street, where the wind was stronger and icier than before. He kept his hands in his pockets as he made his way back onto the street and back to the bus stop. There was not a timetable attached to it. He waited for ten minutes before becoming agitated, swearing and spitting as he walked on.

He walked east, finding himself on a main road into the city centre. A bus sped past him but Isaac did not look at it. His hands fumbled with the cash inside his pocket, and he kept looking over his shoulder.

The money he had in his pocket would last him a few months. All he was being asked to do was carry a bag, be present, on time, keep his mouth shut. That was all he had to do.

CHAPTER FOUR

Isaac did another job with Cullen a few days later, and then another a few days after that. They were all done much the same way, in similar houses but different locations. They travelled on foot at all times. There were no witnesses to their crimes.

Isaac woke up in the afternoon after the last job to the sound of rain stroking the window in waves. He was still tired. His legs ached.

An hour later he was back on his laptop, sipping a cup of coffee as he browsed through job sites. He had applied for couple of low-level technical jobs which did not require a qualification but did ask for some coding knowledge. He went searching for coding tutorials, opening the first few links he found. He started working his way through them. He opened his notebook to take notes. His writing was erratic and littered with small errors or errant letters sinking through the lines on the page.

He sneezed onto his keyboard, phlegm littering his broken trackpad. He didn't clear it off. He was watching a video on the basics of coding, going over things he had learnt during the first weeks of university.

He switched to a different tab. He found some text documents with coding exercises online. He downloaded a few at once, creating a folder on his laptop.

Another tab led to a website which did lectures on programming for free. He signed up for them, opening the video with the first set of lectures. He sat through the introductory video, which introduced the course prospectus. He kept the sound off and watched the subtitles.

He watched the second lecture in the series. The online lecture began to run over the basics of coding, using plain language to express some simple points. Isaac twirled the pen in his hand as the man spoke, clicking the top of the pen occasionally, mumbling to himself. "I know, I know, I know ..." He stopped after about ten minutes, opening a new tab to look at some internet forums.

Isaac reached for his duvet, which was hanging on the edge of the bed. As he dragged it towards him, something else hit the ground. It was the cash which Cullen had given him, money raised from the stolen things. Isaac reached for it and threw it under the bed. He glanced at the door after the money hit the floor. He squeezed the hand he had held the money in tightly, squeezing it hard enough to make his nails dig into the skin, his fingers gripping the invisible space where the money had been.

He turned his attention back to his laptop, muttering, "Cullen, you arsehole ..." He stopped himself. He had been muttering to himself more over the last week – muttering when he woke up with a sore throat, muttering when he left things untidy in his room and muttering when he could not sleep in the evenings.

He checked his emails. There was one new email from an address he did not recognise – it was a response from one of the emails he had sent out a few hours before. He read the email a few times.

They were asking him to come in for an interview the next day. The email was short. The manager's name was Ben, and he had ended his email with a smiley emoticon.

Isaac hastily sent a reply, writing down the address of the company, his hands shaking as he typed.

He went back to the tabs with the lectures he had been looking at, screwing up his face as the lessons continued, skipping past parts, skipping back to go over parts he had missed. He glanced at the scribbles on the notebook, grinding his teeth.

His phone buzzed inside his jacket, and he scrambled for it in frustration. A new text from Cullen, who wanted him back out again tonight.

Isaac swore out loud. "Fuck off, actually fuck off." He threw his phone across the room. It hit the pillows on his bed.

He got up and walked into the corridor. There was a hissing noise coming from the kitchen, the sound of something being fried. Isaac made his way towards the sound.

Lyle was in the kitchen wearing a heavy, hooded jumper. Isaac glanced at this food before saying anything. "Hey, Lyle, are you working today?"

Lyle did not answer. He threw some vegetables from a chopping board into the frying pan with a forceful flick of his wrist, the noise of oil crackling and spitting, drowning out the last part of Isaac's question.

The kitchen worktop looked like it had been wiped down, the clutter cleared up and put away. Isaac repeated himself, a sweet tone in his voice. "Lyle, I thought you were working today?"

Lyle answered without turning around. "I'm working later."

"Any gossip from that night out? I heard you come in late. Did you throw up? You look worse than normal."

Lyle looked around for a knife. He was shaking his head

and his voice was low. "Well, back when I was travelling a few years ago, I met these two women in Greece who said their dad owned a place. Turns out it was an island they owned. Met some friend through them, bumped into them at work last night. Rich people."

"So – what? You milked those girls for all they were worth, right? Are you …?"

Lyle didn't look up, concentrating on his food. He spoke up but the low growl was still there. "No, they were awful people, actually. Like, I'd thought they were down to earth but … they were weird, a strange pair."

Isaac shrugged again and spoke a little more forcefully. "You didn't take advantage of them? You said you didn't like them, so what would it have mattered? With all that money, connections, all that."

Lyle shook his head, turning to Isaac to show his disdain. "No, Isaac, that's *gross*, you can't use people like that. Some of their friends were okay. I didn't try to ask too much from them, you know? I've never had that kind of life, and it's awkward when you're standing around them, wanting more for yourself. Or … Never mind." Lyle went back to what he was doing, moving his food around.

Isaac spoke up again, a little quieter this time. "Fair enough. Anyway, I got you the rent and everything. I've tidied up my stuff and we're all good. I've had a lot on my mind in the last few weeks, the break-up and all that stuff. "

Lyle did not look up when Isaac spoke to him, keeping the knife in his hand. He pressed it down hard on a tomato, slicing it cleanly before replying, "Sure thing."

"I'm doing late shift work now," Isaac said over the sound of the hissing pan. "Emergency work. Bosses fucked up, so I'm stepping up." Isaac waited for Lyle to say something, but he didn't, so Isaac kept going. "Can't really talk about it too much, lots of emergency work …" He trailed off as Lyle remained uninterested. “Okay, then,” he said. “You're not really being that chatty.”

Lyle put down his knife. He paused, turning to look at Isaac, one hand on his hip. He glared at Isaac.

“Mind when we used to bounce around the Cowgate till the wee hours?” Isaac asked. “Skulk around nightclubs and down all sorts, remember? I can remember you used to blag your way into big parties.”

Lyle nodded. “Yeah, of course I do.”

Isaac nodded, pointing at him. “Exactly – now you aren’t doing that anymore. You’re just picking up random Americans and, I don’t know, what? Showing them around? Those girls from a while back weren't even talking to you. You were just a story to them. They’ll go back home and talk about how they love the experience of it all, but they’ll never remember your name.”

Lyle went back to his knife, back to his food. “You were well out of order that night, you know you—”

“No, you’re talking nonsense again,” Isaac interrupted, his hands held up. “Don’t need to say that stuff any more. We’ve been over that. But what about you, Lyle – you weren’t just in a huff about me. It’s not just that. I know it’s not. You’re not doing enough – not like me. You and Will …”

“Will’s going through some stuff – he needs help, Isaac.”

“We should get him out then. What was that club we used to get into? The one with the pillars and the staircase and the carpet on the floor. It was a massive place, never had to queue for the bar …”

“Well, yeah, that was a while ago.”

Isaac kept going, speaking faster, louder. “That place was good. The music was good. Can you remember that? I can remember the music being good, like soul or whatever. I mean, I didn’t get it but, man, it got a really good crowd, like a *good* crowd, attractive and all, everyone was quite chatty …"

"I think we went there twice, Isaac."

"So why didn't we go again?" Isaac snapped back, exasperated. "Why didn't we go back? You were always able to get us in."

Lyle's hand twitched. It was somewhere close to the knife, the sound of vegetables buzzing away. He turned back to Isaac and spoke.

"You started dating her, remember? *You* stopped going out so much, you were struggling with work and you said you weren't going to go out that much any more. Then, well, you stopped seeing us all. You used to be round her place all the time. It happens. You found other things to do. That's all there is to it. We got a bit older – not ancient or anything – but we're all just working away. I mean, I know it's different for all of us – you got your awesome job, that sort of thing …"

Isaac had looked away when his ex was mentioned. He didn't try to cut in and did not look away. He was grinding his teeth. When Lyle trailed off, he started talking again. "Oh, so it's a jealousy thing, right."

Lyle snapped round to Isaac. "No, it's just that I'm working all the time now; we're all working all the time now. We can't go out to clubs all the time any more." He turned back to the worktop, distracted, shaking his head. "My work's changed up," he said. "I'm doing more now, doing more shifts, and there's this new guy managing the place and he's … he's harsh. He's got this new girl in who's new to it all and gets one or two things wrong, but she's … quick. Or maybe I'm slow. I'm not slow, but I'm slower, I'm not as quick as I was. Not by a huge amount, I'm not useless. There was something there before with what I did – I don't get it, Isaac. You know? What happened? Where did …? I don't remember arguing this much at all. But then, I wouldn't do anything differently. I can't do anything differently."

Isaac did not respond. He was focused on the food Lyle was cooking, fumbling with the phone in his pocket.

Lyle continued to talk. "It's annoying. Sorry."

Isaac grinned. "At least you had a good time, though! Still, you've got to grow up some day. But whatever, you'll be fine. Is that—"

Will came into the kitchen, squeezing past Isaac to get in.

Isaac looked away from Lyle. "Sold much today, Will?" Isaac asked.

Will didn't answer, not making eye contact with Isaac or Lyle. He grabbed a hummus pot and some celery in the fridge before heading back to his room.

Isaac looked to the ceiling as Will passed him by. Lyle opened his mouth to say something, closing it. Isaac whispered to Lyle, "He needs to get his head examined."

Lyle turned off the heat on the stove. He breathed out before talking. "You need to try talking to him."

Isaac shrugged. "I *do* talk to him. See how he just ignored me? He gets selfish sometimes."

Lyle looked back at Isaac. His response was flatter in tone, more concentrated. "I mean, you need to talk to him about his problems, is what I'm saying. It's … I don't know, I feel like it's trickier now to get a hold of things."

"Lyle, you always let folk walk all over you. You always do this. It's not about standing up to people and making a big scene – no, that was rubbish last time. It's ab … You make such a big deal about your big travels, then you … Life is about taking charge, realising that some people in life aren't going to be in it forever, that people use you, then you use them. If you're so worried about this boss of yours, why don't you get one over him, or something?"

When he finished speaking, Isaac turned quickly, went back to his room and closed the door behind him.

Lyle was left to go back to his cooking. He stared at what he had made. He spent more time cooking than before. At work he had spent his breaks watching the way the chefs in the restaurant had made their meals, the way they used knives, fried things. He didn't ask too many questions.

He looked back at the empty place where Isaac had been.

When he had finished cooking he brought his meal back into his room. He opened up his laptop, looked through his email. He'd received another email from his grandmother, still unread. His friends from abroad had sent through a reply to his earlier email.

He took out his phone and started texting his boss.

Back in his room, Isaac went to his laptop, opening the web browser. He went into the lecture series again. He watched the second lecture, speeding up the video to run at double speed, the lecturer sounding cartoonishly high-pitched as he started going through some of the lecture slides. He cupped his head in his hands from the bottom of his chin. He didn't open his notebook to take any notes, and he watched the lecture in one sitting. He glanced at the questions attached to the lecture that he was meant to complete as part of the course. He did not write them down or answer them, instead going to click on the third lecture in the series.

He rose to turn on the light in his room, letting the lecture run on. The world outside had turned dark again.

The lecture referred a lot to things discussed in the previous lecture. He watched it at double speed. He stopped it and closed it after five minutes. He put his head in his hands, digging his fingers into his face.

Isaac went back to bed, lying down on his side. He turned over his pillow. From where he lay on his bed, he could see the space between the curtain and the wall, out the window – a sliver of the amber glow of the street lamp outside.

It was dark already. He would leave for Cullen's in a few hours.

Someone in the flat put on loud music. A solo piano tune, long drawn-out notes in a minor key. "Fuck – *Will.*"

He rose to seek out the source of the noise and found Will sitting in the living room. A low drumbeat moved out of time with the song, the speakers next to the television shaking with noise. Will was looking through his phone, his bare feet up on the couch.

"Will …" Isaac mumbled.

Will took a few seconds to look up from his phone.

"Just – turn it off. Can you do something this year? You're fucking about and it's worse than Lyle, you're just – an absolute fuck-around …"

Will turned down the music and said, "Sorry, won't do it again."

Isaac shook his head. "I need to rest before work, can you keep it down?"

"Sure."

Isaac shrugged. "Or maybe turn it off. Do you ever get anything done with that music on?"

Will paused, looking at his reflection in the dark television screen. "I'm not trying to get anything done."

Isaac nodded. "Yeah, I got that. Music off, please, some of us are doing things with our lives. Fuck sake."

He turned and left. The music continued but at a lower volume. When Isaac left to see Cullen later that night, the music was still playing. Isaac did not check up on Will before he left.

Will had long since put the phone down. He had a sketch pad on his lap, his hands shading in a set of geometric shapes, some incomplete, broken in places. It was similar to what he had been working on when he studied art. Objects with set forms, representations of things. They looked out of sorts, and there were wet patches spread across the page.

He picked up the piece he'd been working and screwed it into a ball. He wiped away another tear that was dripping down his chin.

He began to draw on a new page. He glanced back at the reflection of his face in the dark screen, the curve of his head, his shoulders tensed. He kept drawing, his pencil moving slowly. He hadn't drawn portraits since his teenage years.

He paused.

He looked back towards the doorway, back out into the corridor, back where Isaac had been standing.

He sketched the doorway, the outline of a man staring down at him. The man was taller than the doorway, the fingers of his hands sharp and claw-like.

Will continued to sketch for a few hours, all the way into the small hours of the night.

CHAPTER FIVE

Isaac picked up his pace.

He was twenty minutes late for his interview.

He turned to examine the numbers on the buildings around him. He had walked past the office where the interview was due to take place.

He slowed his frantic pace as he approached and walked into the building. From the outside it looked the same as any of the other tenement buildings around. Bronze plaques hung by the entrance and the front windows.

He found himself in a small reception area. There was a woman behind the desk ahead of him. She did not get up. Her hands rested on each other on her desk. She looked up at him. "Can I help you?"

"I'm here for the interview," Isaac muttered back.

"I'm sorry?"

Isaac tried again. "I … I'm here for an interview."

"There are a few offices in this building. Do you know—"

"Are they all having interviews for applicants today?" Isaac snapped. "Was that information not passed down?"

She did not look away from him. He looked down at her

desk, then back towards the door behind him. The silence was filled by music from a radio in the corner.

She piped up again, keeping her tone consistent. "Do you know who you're having an interview with?"

Isaac did not answer.

She spoke again. "So, you don't know who your interview is with?"

Isaac looked out the window.

"I see. What's your name?"

"Isaac. You don't have any idea … Never mind."

"If you can just take a seat by the window, I'll see who you have your interview with."

Isaac stood looking at her for a few seconds before moving to the nearby sofa, which was a lighter shade of grey than the carpet. He spoke up from where he sat down. "It's an IT company. They're hiring me. They …" He trailed off.

The receptionist responded in the same tone as before. "Okay then."

Isaac looked away from her, taking his phone out of his pocket, turning it to silent mode. He had been texting constantly over Cullen the last few days, ignoring the other messages he'd been getting. Cullen tended to text around this time about work. He still had not taken off his jacket, so he removed it after he had put his phone away in one of the pockets, letting it rest on his lap. He tried picking up and folding it several times.

A police siren started blaring from far away, but as it became louder and louder, Isaac turned his head and twisted his body to look out the window.

The receptionist spoke up. "What time was your interview for?"

Isaac did not turn around to look at her. The siren grew louder still.

She repeated herself without raising her voice. "Sir. What

time was your interview for?"

Isaac turned around and spoke. "Sorry, I didn't get that."

"Isaac, what time was your interview for?" she replied, still not raising her voice.

Isaac hesitated for a second before talking. "For just now, I think. This morning. There wasn't a name on the email. They would have told you ..." He stopped talking when the receptionist looked back to her computer and tapped a few keys on the keyboard. The siren faded away, and Isaac breathed out.

The phone on the receptionist's desk rang and she picked it up. She started talking, a little quietly but with the same tone and inflections that she had when she spoke to Isaac. She looked up again, holding the phone away from her mouth for a second. "Okay, if you go upstairs and ask for Ben, he'll sort you out."

"Ben. Yes, Ben emailed me. That's right." Isaac got up and gathered his jacket, unfolding it and holding it in his left hand. "How ... how do I get upstairs?"

"Just go through the door, up the stairs." She nodded her head towards a door to the side of the desk.

Isaac looked back at her. She was already tapping keys on her keyboard, focusing on her work. He closed the door behind him. The staircase rose up sharply, the walls on either side close together. He muttered, "Fat bitch, not helpful."

As Isaac reached the top of the staircase, a door opened and a face appeared in the doorway. It was a man a head shorter than Isaac.

"Isaac? I'm Ben, it's good to meet you!"

Isaac took a second to look over the man's head before looking down. Thin lines of hair stuck up from the back of his bald head, his scalp flaky in places.

Ben stepped back to let Isaac into office. He walked with an uneven gait, flapping his arms downward, almost waving his hands. He led Isaac past a row of desks which extended to the walls. The room was packed with computers and wires and people with looks of firm concentration on their faces.

Ben turned to speak to Isaac as he walked. "Did you have any trouble getting here today?" he asked.

Isaac, still staring at the back of Ben's fraying hair, said, "No, I was really organised about it, actually." His response was drowned out by the noise of ringing phones, men chatting together at small desks, working behind computer screens, rows of them. There were no windows. The room was lit by lights overhead, almost duller than outside. There was a strong smell of sweat.

Ben pointed to his office, a section in the far corner with walls of clear glass and a small desk.

Isaac's eyes did not follow Ben's finger. At the end of the office on the left-hand side was a pale redhead sitting at a desk, answering a phone. She was nodding as she talked. She did not look up from her desk, even as Isaac's eyes never left her. Isaac had not been around women in a while, only ever working with Cullen and returning home. Isaac continued to stare at her.

He nearly walked into a glass door held open by Ben.

Isaac fumbled with his jacket as Ben went to his desk chair, the headrest a full head above his body. Inside the room, the office noise dropped significantly, the faint insulation of the glass walls reducing the chatter to a whisper. Isaac glanced past Ben, not looking him in the eyes. Behind Ben's plain wooden desk was an assortment of pictures of racing motorbikes on the wall, next to small, framed certificates with writing too small to make out from a distance.

Ben spoke up. "Can you close the door behind you, Isaac?"

Isaac was about to sit down, his legs bending. He moved

back up in one movement, going back to the door. He misjudged the force that he needed to close it. It slammed shut, making the noise reverberate around the room. A few people in the office looked up, including the woman with the red hair. Isaac looked at her then down to the ground. Everyone went back to work.

Ben did not seem to react to what had happened. His eyes were already on his computer screen.

Isaac perked up. "Thank you for inviting me to interview for the—" he began, but Ben interrupted.

"That's fine, Isaac. We're a little behind schedule, so let's get into it. Why don't you tell me about yourself?"

Isaac made his way back to the chair, sitting on the edge of it, his hands on his knees. He spoke quickly. "Well, my name is Isaac. I'm twenty-four. I grew up in the Borders, the Scottish Borders and, um, I moved here for university. I currently do … I've done some work at an IT agency …" Isaac trailed off a little.

Ben said, "Yes, I saw that."

"And now I'm here," Isaac continued, "and I'm interested in the role. I'm a capable guy and, um, I think I'd be good here, a good fit here, yes." Isaac slammed his mouth shut, hard enough that his teeth felt the impact. His shoulders tensed.

Ben nodded with a smile, glancing over a piece of paper in front of him on the desk – Isaac's CV. There were neat red marks stencilled all over it. Ben concentrated on it while he talked. "I mean, it's an impressive-looking CV. What kind of clients were you dealing with? I've checked the website of the company you work for and there's not a lot of information on there."

"Well, we look after client security, database structuring, that sort of thing. Yeah, I can't really … It's hard to …detail that sort of thing. It's all very confidential. You understand."

Ben nodded as Isaac spoke, still smiling. "Oh, oh, I see. I understand what you mean, confidentiality and all that *jazz*." He raised his hands up, showing his flat palms, putting them back again with a small giggle. "I suppose if I contacted them for a reference, they'd be okay with that? Would be good to get an idea of what you're used to working with."

Isaac shivered a little. "They're generally … Sorry …"

"Pardon, Isaac?"

Isaac opened and closed his mouth. He tried again. "They're pretty … We're quite, um, it's just … It's all confidential, you understand."

Ben paused, the smile on his face faltering for a second, before giving Isaac a nod. "Sure. I understand," he said.

Isaac rubbed his nose.

Ben looked back down, pointing a finger at a large red circle he had put around a line on Isaac's CV. He smiled at Isaac as he spoke. "I have to say, it sounds like you're doing quite well there, from what I've read."

Isaac nodded. "Thank you."

Ben's finger left the page, his hands now resting on his desk, a little further forward. "Why would you want to come here? It feels like, if I may say so, a bit of a step down."

"I want a new challenge."

"Pardon?"

"A new challenge. I enjoy working in a large team and I'm a very quick learner."

Again, Ben paused, his smile fading, then the smile came back, the nods again. "That's good. That's good ..." He trailed off, his finger hovering at the top of the CV and moving down the page. He stopped at another part, looking back up. "I'm impressed with your qualifications, you—"

"I … Sorry?" Isaac interrupted.

Ben held his hands up, still nodding, still smiling. "No, I mean … I believe the great thing with computing is that sometimes a degree isn't always the way forward. University isn't for everyone."

Isaac's shoulders relaxed a bit. He began to nod back as he spoke. "Yes, thank you. I think it's a waste of time for some people, like they're just wasting time and money."

"Do you mind if I ask why you dropped out, Isaac? No wrong answers, no judgement here."

Isaac moved back into the chair, one hand gripping an armrest. He looked out the glass again. The view hadn't changed. "I dropped out due to personal reasons. University isn't for everyone."

Ben kept smiling, kept nodding, tilting back on his chair, looking away from Isaac for a few moments before he spoke. "That is the thing though, isn't it, Isaac? It's always different for everyone. You learn the same sorts of things at school and then you learn more when you leave. I'm a big believer in learning constantly, trying new things – wider learning. It's amazing what you can learn from other people. You know what I mean?"

Isaac gave a slow nod, then another, a smile forcing itself onto his face. "Sure thing!"

Ben spoke again, his tone a little more serious. "Have you been learning anything in your spare time, Isaac?"

"I'm working with COBOL, trying to do some basics."

"Oh, that's interesting. We're not really using that, but it's good that you're working out the fundamentals."

"I'm a quick learner," Isaac insisted. "So, I can pick up things quite quickly."

Ben glanced back down at the CV. He did not look up when he replied, "Yes, that's excellent."

"You know, learning the fundamentals," Isaac added, his voice shaky, "that's always good."

Ben nodded. "Yes, it says that … No, that's not here. Okay then."

Isaac began to shift his shoulders, his arms began hovering over the armrests.

Ben continued, “I'm a big believer in attitude and personal attributes being as important – probably even more so – than qualifications. I think that the things we do for each other reflect what we do to ourselves. I studied languages at university.”

Isaac flinched.

Ben managed to look up from the CV for a second when Isaac did this. He leant back into his chair, continuing his talk. Isaac bit his tongue.

“I did different jobs, travelled – on a budget, it wasn't a very glitzy time, I can tell you that. I worked in an admin office in Paraguay, did charity work in Australia, learnt coding in Berlin. Seeing how other people do things with their lives is such an important thing. Of course, that's a hard thing to get right. I volunteered when I was your age too. Threw my CV everywhere.”

Isaac was biting down harder on his tongue. He waited for Ben to continue and then muttered, “Right,” when he realised Ben was waiting for a reply.

“What about you, Isaac? What else have you been doing over these years? Some of these dates don’t match up. You went from working in a supermarket to a major IT position, quite a jump.”

“I was … My parents gave me money to get by on for a bit.”

Ben nodded his head a little. “Right.”

“I was working in a supermarket just for a bit, during the summer, just to get some … It was extra … but it wasn’t really for me, you know? I’m better working in IT. It was just, I had a point where nothing was happening for me.”

Ben looked at the CV again, giving another little nod. He scribbled something down.

Isaac piped up again. “My parents used to drive me up to Edinburgh when I was younger, days out and that. There were always going away places. They’re away places just now, abroad, charity work and all that. I did not really get involved, bit of a waste of time.” Isaac stopped himself.

Ben leaned forward, looking concerned. “I'm sorry?” he asked.

Isaac nodded, smiled and spoke again. “When I was younger, I travelled.”

Ben did not say anything but he nodded his head a few times. His smile did not return. Isaac tried again.

“With my—”

Ben held his hands up. Isaac stopped.

“Isaac, it’s fine. I’ve found sometimes it’s not really about experience or even the qualifications. I’m a great example of this. This job is a good entry-level role. You’ll get to learn a lot about what we do. You’ll be making teas and coffees and taking lunch orders.”

Isaac flinched, shaking his head. “Oh, I thought the job role was data entry. I thought it would be more hands-on.”

Ben did not smile or nod when he said, “It’s in the job description.”

Isaac nodded and smiled. “Great. Teas and coffees. Teas and coffees.”

“What have you been doing in your spare time, Isaac?” Ben asked. “I'm not asking for some sort of crazy answer here, I just trying to get a sense of who *you* are. This could be a great role for someone like you, Isaac – I’m just trying to help.”

There was a momentary tremor in Isaac's body which found its way into his voice. “I've always been good with computers. When I was younger, I'd be in my room studying and I'd watch films – movies, same thing, no? – and I'd look up things, and I'd help around the house sometimes.” His face was turning red, his arms starting to shake a little. “Well … it’s not right,” Isaac continued. “Because I'm not … I don’t need to learn anything to be good at anything. I can learn the language on the job, I don’t need to bore myself to tears listening to lectures about how I’m not hard-working – I’m doing fine.” He breathed out. He wasn’t making eye contact with Ben, instead talking to his lap. “I'm fine. I'm fine as I am. I'm a capable young individual – you said yourself, it’s not always a matter of qualifications, it’s about experience, and I can do that. I have actual social skills, plus it’s data entry, I can do that easily enough. If you need teas and coffees, I could do that for a bit but it’s not really what I’m here for you, you know? I’m here to progress, to get on with my life. That’s what I want to do. To move away and on from all of this …” Isaac stopped talking. He was sweating.

Ben waited a few seconds before responding. “Well, it’s good that you’re a confident individual.”

Isaac looked right at him, moving to fold his arms before letting his hands find the edge of his armrests, wrapping his fingers around them.

Ben was still looking at Isaac’s CV when he spoke again. “Yes, that’s good. Do you have any questions, Isaac? Anything you'd like to ask?”

Isaac said nothing.

Ben said, “Okay, well ...” The positive tone in his voice dropped an octave. “It’s good that you’re learning coding on your own. I think you should keep up with that. It’s difficult out there. I hope you find what you’re looking for. I think you need to be … a little more honest. With other people, yourself as well, maybe. I think that would help. Anyway, that’s all for now. Thank you so much for coming in, really. I’ll drop you an email later on, yeah?”

Isaac nodded. He got up and left. Ben did not follow him. As he walked through the office, the woman with the red hair was walking back to her desk. Isaac glanced at her face. She did not look at him. Isaac looked forward as they passed, eyes locked on the exit at the stop of the stairs.

He did not look at the receptionist on the way out onto the street.

Patches of rain splattered onto the grey paving stones in front of him, beside him, behind him. They kept falling. The sound of rain falling grew louder as he walked; the rain kept coming, constant, everywhere. Isaac kept walking. He ignored places of shelter, places to stop and find his bearings, to get dry. He kept moving, walking in a straight line with his head down, his thin jacket becoming heavier, water seeping into his shoes. Water was dripping through the jacket and down onto his shoulder blades, leaving patches of dampness against his skin.

He needed to make his way back uphill, through the centre of town, across Tollcross then to Bruntsfield. Isaac watched a bus pull up to a stop ahead of him, a queue of people lining up to get on it. Isaac stormed past it. He walked uphill. After a few minutes of making his way uphill, the same bus swept past him.

He blew air into his cheeks and filled them up. His hair was now flat, soaked with rain and water dripping off the tips. His eyes scanned across the steamed-up windows at the back of the bus, heads turned away from him. He moved himself to avoid hitting three men on the pavement. Isaac shifted to the left, turning his body to squeeze between the left two. They stopped as Isaac moved past them. Isaac did not look back.

He came up to Queen Street. To the untrained eye, it is just the back road of the New Town, with entirely straight, black metal fences linking across the buildings, but with windows high enough for the occupants to look down on the thoroughfare outside. Queen Street is Edinburgh's best memorial to a time long past. The old money, slave money, all those things. It is far less populated than the more archaic exhibitions further into the centre. No signs for any nearby attractions, bar the road signs telling traffic how to leave it. Very old money indeed. On one side, the old tenements contain small offices for expensive-looking businesses with obscure titles and purposes. On the other side, lines of vast trees gated in by black fences provide private parks for the few residents in the area.

Isaac kept his head down, focusing his vision on his feet. There was nowhere for him to take cover. He came to the next junction, with the next available road up to George Street to his right. He stopped, shaking his head. He took his phone out, searched the contacts, stopping when he came to Cullen's number. If he kept walking along Queen Street, he would be further and further away from home.

"Fuck you, Cullen, you shit."

He paused, looking at the phone, then jerked forward for a second before turning right, heading towards George Street, uphill again. He kept the phone in his hand as he walked, his head bowed as water dripped off his hair.

It was not just Isaac who was caught out by the rain. A short blonde woman on the other side of the street soldiered uphill, the shoulders of her grey suit damp with rainwater, her broken umbrella poking out of a large handbag slung over her shoulder. She powered forward, not quite breaking into a run but moving at a pace far faster than Isaac's. Isaac tutted to himself, his eyes glancing at her legs.

She ripped the umbrella out of her bag and opened it. One section of the canopy was at an odd angle, and she slowed down to force some of the metal stretchers back into place, then held the umbrella over her head. It did not quite work, but well enough to keep her dry. Her pace quickened as she got to the top of the hill.

Isaac looked away, moving to cross the road. A cyclist

wearing a large, fluorescent yellow jacket and riding on a large bike with lights came quickly along George Street. Isaac had taken a step out into the road without looking, and he jumped when the cyclist shouted at him. The cyclist turned his head, his white helmet mounted with a small camera, and slowed down to shout something. But Isaac did not look at him. Instead, he walked quickly away from the cyclist and made his way inside a coffee shop on the corner.

There was a large queue and the staff behind the till were moving around quickly. The noise of the staff at work drowned out the strummed soft chords coming out of the speakers, loud enough to be heard while being impossible to pay attention to. It mixed in with the sound of several conversations happening all at once across the shop.

Isaac shivered as he came in, taking off his jacket. Ahead of him was the queue of people fidgeting as they waited. A young man wiped his steamed-up glasses with little success. A young parent ripped a chocolate biscuit out of the hand of her young daughter, bending down to remonstrate with her. The little girl shook her head as snippets of the mother's violent whispers reached Isaac's ears.

Isaac took out his phone, wiping water off the screen. He went through the names. Lyle was going out until late and was not answering his calls. Will kept texting Isaac about helping with some sketches he wanted to make, sending Isaac some examples. Isaac deleted his most recent one. He looked up Cullen's details again. Without hesitating, he pressed the call button. It rang out after a few rings, going straight to voicemail.

"Um …" he said into the phone. Isaac did not say anything more for a few seconds. "Do you want to just … hang out? We don't need to go anywhere, or anything. Just … I don't know." He paused. "I'm not working. Fuck it, you're the only one who knows about the not-job, so I can barely talk to the others now. My pals. Whatever. Fuck."

He hung up. The woman with the young child glanced over at him before grabbing her child again and leaving with her order. Isaac felt the weight of his wallet, a wad of cash squeezed into it. He looked at the items on display, the cakes and sweet buns.

There wasn't anyone at the till when Isaac went to order. One staff member stood alone, sorting out a row of cups, her back turned to the front. Her shoulders were tense, her hands wiping something out of a mug. In a daze she turned back to the till, her blue eyes scanning Isaac's features for a second before going back to work.

The barista was obscured by the till, leaning over to see Isaac as she started speaking. "What can I get you?"

He looked up at the board, his eyes moving to the woman's thin neck. He whispered, more to himself than to her, "Can I get a ... latte?"

She tapped some buttons on the till screen.

Isaac felt the money in his wallet again. "A large. I want a large one."

The barista looked back at him. "Sorry?"

He spoke again, louder. "Large latte, please."

She paused, typing in on the till, not looking up when she spoke up again. "Sure."

"I want the largest size," Isaac insisted. "Don't want a small any more. Largest you have. And a muffin. I want a blueberry muffin. And some nuts. And that cake slice."

The barista looked right at Isaac, her fingers tapping away on the till. "Well … sure, can I get anything else for you?"

Isaac was nodding, pointing at the glass. "The biggest one. That's what I want."

He paid for it in cash, too much cash, the barista pushing a collection of notes back, staring at Isaac as he left the counter. Isaac didn't even pick them up. She watched him, muttering under her breath, "Good for you, I guess."

Isaac settled down on a stool right by the window, coffee dripping onto the saucer and on to his heavy tray. He fumbled with the muffin's wrapper before ignoring it and going straight for the cake. Through the window, he could just about make out the outside world through the steamed-up glass. The foot traffic was congested on the corner, people slowing down and stopping to let others past, looking ahead of them and waiting for their turn to go.

There was an old man muttering next to Isaac, small lines of patter bursting out of his swollen red cheeks. Without prompting, he spoke to Isaac, his mouth staying open after he finished his question. "It's cold out there, isn't it? Wet, wet, wet!"

Isaac did not look at him when he answered. "Yeah, sure is."

Isaac ate his cake slice in one go, barely chewing on it as it entered his mouth. He coughed a little as it slid down his throat.

The old man spoke again, moving a little closer to Isaac. There was a whistling noise coming from the gaps between his teeth. "Aye, they get colder and colder with every year. You used to get more snow too; like, heaps of it, right up to yer ankles. Back then you had no cars – you could park on the street, aye, just up here. No coffee places, not as warm. Some trams – mind trams? Although they're bringing those back now."

Isaac continued to look away. "Yeah."

The man spoke again, a little firmer this time, a little faster. "They get rid of it all, but they just want to bring it all back. Doesn't make sense to me. Bloody council. It's worst during August."

"Everyone knows that."

The old man kept his mouth open. "Aye, that's how it was," he said. "Was much better back then."

Isaac turned to him. "You, know, I broke up with my girlfriend in one of these." He gestured to the coffee shop around them. "She kept going on about the fucking class struggle, spent years learning about it at university and then just … Just one of those things; like, you knew she would think about it when you were out shopping, looking at things to buy, or she'd mention politics to her friends – her shit friends. They would mention something and they'd all start yabbering. Christ. Big on sharing stuff, she was always big on sharing stuff. Used to eat a lot too, which I suppose was ironic. Not ironic, whatever ironic means. But I ended it in one of these places. Fuck, she was boring."

The old man did not say a thing for a few seconds as Isaac sipped his coffee. The man spoke again. "Sorry, son, what was—"

Isaac shook his head. "No," he interrupted. "I can remember thinking something funny, like it'd be funny just to break up in a corporate … like, a chain place, like one of these ones, this brand actually. I broke up with her in one of these. Thought … like, she'd gone on and on about the evils of capitalism, all that, but she'd only ever read about it in books. So, I dumped her in one of these. Now she's got a proper reason. I guess it was funnier at the time. Big on marches – that's where I met her, you know? One of those lefty ones."

"Sorry, what was that, son?"

Isaac was not looking at the old man any more, only looking ahead, out the window. He kept going. "The view was better, the place I did it in. You could see out into the road. More students about, younger people, like, more single people, *better* single people. Was a good thing to think about. Fuck, some of them, man. I don't remember them wearing that kind of stuff, you know? Better than your old fucking life, much better. It's a … I think there's a life ahead of me that I can have now. I can actually have a life now, money from somewhere. I hate using computers, I can actually do what I want now. Fuck, yes, I can actually do what *I* want now. Fuck my parents. Bastards."

The old man was shaking his head, leaning forward to listen to Isaac. "Sorry, son, my hearing's not so good, you'll need to speak up."

Isaac turned his head towards the old man, gazing into his mouth, his front teeth at bent angles, pushing into each other. He leant forward, whispering, "Always about the fucking council, you fucks. It's always the council fucking things up for you, but then you vote them in and then you fucking moan about that too. As if you get to fucking own it or whatever, but it's your own fault, it's your own fucking fault. You think I've got something clever to say to you? Nah, I just know you're projecting your own failings under your breath all day. You're just projecting – you know what that means? Fuck *aye* you do. Me, I've got a pal with money. I'm going to use him then go, get out of here. I won't be talking about this shithole to myself all day. Yeah?" Isaac, a smirk on his face, blew into his coffee. "Yeah. I'm great."

The man did not respond, moving away from Isaac, leaving his coffee cup unfinished. He took his time getting up.

Isaac tutted, shaking his head, muttering to himself, "It's all there. It's going to happen to me. Everything's going my way." He sipped his coffee. He whispered to himself after a few seconds, "I know I'm great."

No one took the old man's place. Isaac's phone burst into life. Cullen was texting about another job.

CHAPTER SIX

Isaac took a moment to breathe mid-sentence. He had been talking for several minutes without stopping and was beginning to stumble. Cullen did not say anything in the brief pause. He had his hands in his pockets as he walked, his eyes scanning the sky above them, the clouds moving with the wind.

Isaac picked up where he had left off. "He doesn't stop talking about himself. It's like … It's endless chatter about what he's going through. But it's obsessive, you know what I mean? He just won't let things go. There was a day yesterday where he left stuff in the sink; I told him about it, and he starts banging on about how he washes dishes at work."

Isaac paused to breathe again. Cullen briefly jumped in. "Sounds pretty serious. Have you tried to cheer him up?"

Isaac kept going. "I'm actually trying to avoid him now. If I know he's about in the flat, I've started keeping to myself now, like there's something I need to do – I mean, I find stuff to do. Obviously, I have stuff on that's not this, you know. He never asks about anyone else, then apologises, saying that he needs to stop talking about himself. I mean, it's horrendous that we can't have normal conversations. Talks about his work not going well, not what he wants it to be. Properly fixated on it."

"You faked yours."

Isaac was silent for a few seconds before he responded, "And so have you, with all this, but at least *we've* done something."

Cullen looked away from the sky, his eyes focused on the pathway ahead of them; a shortcut between two houses with high brick walls, enclosed enough that the sound of their shoes on the ground echoed a little. "I suppose it is something, Isaac."

It had been raining during the day. Isaac was walking exactly where Cullen walked as they crossed a muddier section of the path, their footprints merging into one. Isaac kept talking. "I mean, then there's Will, who's just moody all the time now, really snippy. Keeps going on about people he works with, moans about them."

"Do you actually like these people, Isaac?"

"I mean, I kind of … Well, they don't have proper friends of their own at all. I was there when no one else was, years ago. I was the glue that kept them together. They'd be boring without me. You really want to hear all this stuff, Cullen? They're a pretty dull bunch who just moan all the time about stuff."

They were back into a suburban area with a wide road that curved upward in the middle, the pavements narrow, ice sparkling in the amber street lights.

Isaac's words were becoming slurred and breathy, the heavy bag on his shoulders beginning to tire him out. Cullen did not alter his pace at all. Isaac breathed out more words, tensing and relaxing his shoulders. "You could just cross the road here, man. It'll be faster."

Cullen remained on the pavement. Isaac moved onto the

road. He planted his foot on some ice and fell onto his back, his fall broken by the bag on his shoulders.

The night sky looked brighter from this position, the street lights across the city gripping the overcast sky, the clouds turning a dull shade of maroon. Isaac did not move. A muscle in his right calf was cramping up. He did not move his hands, his arms.

"Christ, give me a hand," Isaac called out.

Cullen had disappeared from sight, turning the corner away from him. Isaac muttered, "That's … What an asshole."

He got up slowly, planting his feet as he walked. He saw Cullen in the far distance, still walking along the pavement at a steady pace. Isaac's gaze moved downward, watching his feet, planting them carefully. The ground was icy in sections, frost-covered for the most part, the ground sparkling in the amber colours, light hitting parts for a split second before vanishing forever, over and over.

Isaac lost sight of Cullen but found his way back to Cullen's house. The front gate had been closed. Isaac muttered to himself. "You could have at least … Come on." He crossed the front lawn, the frozen blades of grass cracking under his feet. He sneezed as he went inside and muttered to himself again. "Could at least put some heating on. Any heating on."

Cullen called down from upstairs. "Did you close the front gate behind you this time?"

Isaac's shoulders slunk down. He lowered the bag off his shoulders and left it by the front door, moving into the kitchen. He turned on the plastic kettle and opened one of the kitchen drawers. There were letters to previous tenants left unopened. He reached to open one of them.

Cullen had come back downstairs without making any noise. "What are you looking for, Isaac?"

Isaac flinched as he dropped the letter. He replied with a

louder voice than Cullen's, his tone of voice a little more pointed. "I was … You never have anything stronger. You know? It's a bit sad, that's what it is. Just waiting for the kettle to boil."

"You don't need to watch it boil. You bring the bag up first; I start counting. I'm not bringing it up this time, or any other time."

Isaac said nothing. They both stood in the kitchen for a few seconds. Cullen left to go upstairs while Isaac watched the kettle boil.

Isaac tended to his own drink before Cullen's. He grabbed the edge of the teabag with his forefinger and thumb as it floated to the top, dabbing it in and out then lifting the teabag out and dropping it into the sink.

He left the kitchen with his mug, climbed the stairs and went into Cullen's room. Cullen was sitting down with his legs crossed, his back to the wall. His eyes were closed. "You didn't bring the bag up."

Isaac shrugged. "I was going to do it in a second."

Cullen snapped back immediately. "Were you just watching the kettle boil?"

Isaac took a drink first before he spoke. "I was going to bring it up after. Do you think I was going to leave it down there all night?"

"So, it's still sitting by the front door?"

Isaac put his mug down quickly, the tea splashing onto the carpet. "You mean I'm not allowed to have a break? I'm allowed to be a mule for you, but I can't stop for a second? Brilliant stuff, Cullen, great man management. I never hear a word of thanks. Thanks, Isaac. Well done, Isaac."

Cullen did not say anything.

Isaac picked up his tea, took a swig and put it back down. His shoulders fell. "Christ, really?" He went downstairs, picked up the bag and took it back upstairs, dragging it up the stairs, hitting each individual stair on the way up.

Cullen spoke before Isaac got through the door. "Close the door behind you; keep out the draught."

Isaac pushed at the door, which dragged along the carpet. He did not close it. Isaac sat down on the cushions, his legs straight and his back against the wall. There was a sliver of cold getting into the room. "You could always put the heating on for a bit," he said.

Cullen shook his head. He wasn't paying any attention to Isaac anymore. He had begun to empty the bag, placing watches, jewellery and small valuable items in one pile, money in another.

Isaac watched him, not touching his drink. "So, you can't even stump up to buy a heater, can you?" he finally asked. "No wander you're so cranky all the time, Cullen."

Cullen didn't look at him. He was still counting, the bag to the left of him, the money to his right.

Isaac watched the money pile up for a few moments, then spoke up. "Cullen, how long are you going to—" Isaac stopped himself. He tried again. "Are you going to be doing this forever? You've never mentioned what you're doing with the money."

Cullen did not look up when he replied, "I'll know when to stop."

Isaac leaned back against the wall. He closed his eyes, yawning, before he said, "I know, it's just we've been fairly busy the last few weeks and we've never … It's always somewhere strange and half-abandoned. I don't know how you do it."

"As in what? How do I find these places?"

"Yeah, I can't figure it out."

Cullen stopped counting his money for a second. He looked up with a smile on his face. "Good."

"Excuse me?" Isaac asked, his eyes remaining closed.

Cullen went back to counting. "You need boots," he said.

Isaac opened his eyes. "Why?"

Cullen tapped his fingers on the money, a contented look on his face. "If you wore actual boots like I do, you wouldn't fall on your arse so much."

Isaac shrugged. "You keep walking quickly."

Cullen started on another pile of money. "Did you never work out how to walk on ice? You grew up in the country. You grip with your toes."

Isaac shrugged again. "I know how to walk on ice."

"So, you know how to—"

"It's not difficult at all. People fall down all the time, Cullen."

Cullen continued to count. He muttered, "Right then."

"It's about getting back up again."

Cullen paused his counting for a second, looking away from the money, up towards the light. He breathed out as he said, "I guess so."

Isaac remained silent for a while, drinking his tea, before he said, "It'd be better if we could go out in nicer weather."

Cullen shook his head and said, "Folk aren't out on nights like this, nor are they looking out the windows. It's comfortable. It's what people pay for, they like comfort. Comfortable means watching TV on a leather sofa, pretending to listen to jazz and shouting at your kids to go to bed."

Isaac smirked. "So, you like being uncomfortable then?" he asked.

Cullen fiddled with notes as he replied, "I like having little in the way of distractions."

"You mean you can't handle having distractions—"

"I'm trying not to draw attention to myself," Cullen cut in. "I'm just focusing on myself, working on myself, that's all."

"So, then what?" Isaac smirked. "You just focus on yourself forever, is that it? You're just going to pop out the ground and then everything will be back to normal?"

Cullen looked up at Isaac when he replied, "I'm just working on myself, that's all."

They sat in silence for a while.

Isaac eventually said, "So, we're going – you're going – to keep doing this for a while?"

Cullen's hands were reaching for something in his backpack. He stopped. He turned back to Isaac and said, "I don't know, actually."

Isaac snorted. "You don't know? So, you could just stop doing this any minute?"

"I mean, there's been police reports out about some robberies. We're being careful, we're staying out of the way – more importantly, we're not creating any patterns. That's the key thing. Each house has been a little bit different, not that you'd give a shit anyway."

Isaac was shaking his head. "For crying out loud, Cullen, I'm just asking if we can keep doing this, that's all, didn't ask you to get so stressed about it – that part of you hasn't changed. Did you manage to avoid trouble when you were abroad?"

Cullen stopped what he was doing. One of his hands snapped shut and curled into a fist, his fingers trembling. His eyes looked down at this hand, a little away from it, as if something was about to fall away from it, fall to the ground. He spoke slowly. "I've got no ties to what I did abroad."

"Why is that, Cullen? Why don't you have anyone following you?"

Cullen went back to his work, talking without looking up. "I paid a debt. I got given the chance to leave and I took it."

Isaac lowered his voice. “What happened to the people you were with, Cullen?”

Cullen put his hands down again, stared at the ceiling. “I lost my money way out east, had no idea what to do, fell into a gang of pickpockets and learnt some things. That was it. No big crime syndicates, nothing horrendous – I got out of it, got a clean break.”

“Just pickpockets?”

“Yes, Isaac, just pickpockets. There’s no grand criminal conspiracy here.”

Isaac breathed out a sigh of relief. “Good, so it means we’re safe then. So, there’s no one coming after you then. I was just checking. No big gangsters, no mob boss or anything. Cool. That’s good.” Isaac closed his eyes and folded his arms.

Cullen shook his head, grinding his teeth. When he spoke up his voice cracked a little. “You’ve never asked about me. Or even how this works. The only thing you’re worried about is that there’s a slight chance that you’ll get in trouble.”

Isaac rolled his head forward and rubbed his tired eyes. After a few moments, he yawned and said, “Nah. I don’t care about it. I’ll be fine no matter what happens.”

“You’ve never asked what I look for, how I’m looking for anything. You’re just asking about the connections all the time. You’ve not even asked about what else I’ve done, how I’m feeling, anything … It’s just the money you’re after.”

“So what? It’s not my fault you just vanished and reappeared again, then just turn up and start robbing places. Fuck, man, it’s you that’s got the communication issues here. I’ve progressed in my life, I’ve changed – I’m great now. You think you’re better than me because you steal from places now?”

“Oh, come on, Isaac,” Cullen said, raising his voice, “you’ve not actually changed at all. It’s maddening but then it's – Christ, I don't know – comforting? I don't know everything that's happened to you through the last few years, but I don't know how you can't change at all."

"What do you mean?"

Cullen paused. He lowered his voice again. "Remember I started doing 'Chemistry Facts' when we were walking down to class in the mornings, remember? I'd talk about old scientists and things about the elements, and you would just not stop asking questions. Then you'd act like you were fucking better or whatever …" Cullen trailed off.

"That chemistry stuff, Cullen, was dull—"

"I had to start doing that," Cullen interrupted, "because you kept ripping into people we lived with."

"Cullen, you're just talking over me now, you're out of order."

"Then don't you dare say that—"

"You need to simmer down, Cullen!"

"Actually, fuck off, Isaac. Fuck right off with that—"

"You're always overreacting," Isaac snapped, continuing to talk over him. "I mean, you left university and then the country! You vanished into thin air and then you're amazed that I'm asking so many things!"

Cullen twisted his fingers and did not look at Isaac, looking instead at his hands. He replied with a whine, "Can you just not be so critical all the time, it's obvious you're being—"

"You don't think that I can think," Isaac interrupted. "Like, I can't form my own opinions. You think I need—"

"Your questions aren't good enough. It's just brute force, and you're just waiting for me to get angry or give up, so you can feel better about your shit self."

"You're not acting like an adult. You ran away!" Isaac shouted.

"You faked – you're faking – a job, Isaac!" Cullen shouted back.

"Don't say that!" Isaac hissed.

"You completely made it up! I figured it out within minutes on that shit website you threw together. You don't think anyone else will work it out?"

"Don't say anything then – that's none of your business." Isaac was stammering now. "You … You're shouting, you can't even keep your nerve. Really weak, Cullen."

"Absolute rubbish, Isaac. It's crazy what you've done, you'll be found out!"

"And you won't be? You'll just be breaking into things forever? I mean, Christ, I don't even know why you picked me, if this was going to be such an issue for you."

Cullen smirked. He had a stack of money in his hand and a grin on his face. He said nothing.

Isaac filled the silence. "So why me? Why did you contact me?"

Cullen was still smiling. "I bet that hasn't even crossed your mind until now – why I went with you instead of someone else."

Isaac shrugged. "I'd assumed you'd explain it after a while."

"You really do have strange expectations about people," Cullen said. "God, even back then, it took me so long to realise it, man. It's impressive how far you're taking the fake job thing. I wasn't checking – not obsessively. Every time I had access to the internet, which wasn't that often where I was, I checked up on you."

Isaac shook his head, interjecting with, "Which is stalking – you've been planning this for so long – it's creepy."

"It's – no, I don't want to get into it. I mean, there are definitely people out there who would be more suited to this line of work, don't you think? I get you to carry the bags and talk every now and again, that's it. I could be doing more now, could be paying you less."

Isaac shook his head.

"Because this is probably the last time we're doing this, Isaac. Honestly, I can't keep talking to you like this."

Isaac said nothing. After a few moments, he snarled a response back. "Have you known this all along? Is this why this time is the last time? You fuck off for a few years then act like you're something just because you're some shady fucking criminal. Like you always were, you Irish fuck."

"That's terrible, really off – you don't know what you're doing."

Isaac kept shaking his head, talking loudly, shouting over Cullen. "Hurry the fuck up, Cullen! I'm waiting. I'm fucking waiting! I'm waiting, Cullen, I'm waiting. That's what I'm doing."

"Waiting for what?"

Isaac spluttered back, a whine in his voice, "I'll tell you. It's … two things, it's two things. I'm waiting for this whole thing to go bad for you, so I can be far, far away from you when this goes wrong. I've got my part, my money – I earned that money, fair and square."

Cullen was shaking his head. "You carried a bag and fell over a lot."

Isaac lowered his voice, rising to his feet, and said, "Do you know what the second thing is?"

Cullen shrugged. "What second thing?"

"The second … I meant the second thing that's keeping me here."

Cullen paused. He waited for Isaac to continue but he did not. "What is it, Isaac? What exac—"

"It's … What, sorry?"

Cullen paused. He tried again. "No, you interrupted, what did you want to say? What is it?"

Isaac muttered, "The second thing?"

Cullen nodded. "Yes, Isaac, what is the second thing? You can't just—"

Isaac leant forward and said, "I'm waiting for you to count my *fucking* money."

Cullen smiled and went back to counting his money. His smile faded after a while. When it did, Isaac retreated back to the corner of the room. He closed his eyes and let his head sag against the wall. He did not fall asleep, opening his eyes every few minutes to check on Cullen.

Cullen tied an elastic band around a stack of money and threw it at Isaac, the money landing in front of him. Isaac reached over put the cash into his jacket pockets. As he did so, Cullen spoke with a quiet tone. "Your flatmate, Will, is in pain. You need to talk to him about what he's going through. It's not enough to just let him go like that. He needs help, guidance. You don't need to tell him what to do, just … give him a chance, Isaac."

Isaac was already moving to leave. "Maybe me being a dick to him will inspire him to vanish for a few years," he said.

Cullen shook his head and replied, "You shouldn't leave him alone. He isn't happy. People who feel that low just keep circling the drain, round and round. You need to help him. Christ, you've been friends with him for years, then all of a sudden he goes through a bad patch, and you just don't care?"

"Cullen, I'm not responsible for anyone." Isaac pointed at Cullen for emphasis, his other hand buried in his jacket pocket, around the money. "I don't need to be. He's been an absolute arse to me, then he decides he needs to be fucking cool with me again when he needs a shoulder to cry on? Course. Just like you, you arsehole – I'm not responsible for you, Cullen. That's always been the thing, isn't it? You were crying out for someone to look after you all those years ago.

Not my fault that you couldn't manage on your own. I'm glad you left. Hated everyone else in those halls we were in, but at least they weren't you, you prick."

"I have to warn you—"

But Isaac turned away, continuing to talk as he left the room. He spoke louder as he walked down the stairs. "I'm never talking to you again, you wee … Fuck off, then …"

His hands sank into his pockets, gripping onto the large stacks of money. He held onto them for dear life.

He made his way down to the front door. Isaac did not close it behind him on the way out. He left the gate open as well.

CHAPTER SEVEN

Lyle had been on the sofa all afternoon, sending and receiving messages to and from old friends – including the old friends from abroad he had been emailing back and forth. His boss had sent him some long messages that he had not read.

He'd been doing this sort of thing for the last few days. He had booked some time off work and had not ventured back home to see his mother. He did not speak to anyone in the flat; no one asked how he was. He had slept on the sofa the previous evening and hadn't moved since then, staring out of the window, waiting for the winter sun to rise.

Lyle looked up from his phone when Isaac entered the room that afternoon, huffing and puffing as he dragged in shopping bags. Lyle stretched his neck to see what was in them. "Why did you buy all that beer?"

Isaac was still breathing heavily when he replied, "I just thought ... thought it would be good to go out. We've not been out in a while. Will … We're … Give me a second – lots of stairs – could use a hand."

Lyle looked over to the empty space where Will had been sitting earlier, sketching Lyle. Lyle had done him the courtesy of not moving around, letting Will draw him without asking him any questions. Will had left a mug there, half-empty, along with his notebook, scraps of paper ripped out of it, a pen left with its lid off.

Lyle bit the inside of his lip. He looked back to Isaac and said, "I'm not really feeling up for it, had a hard day. I was thinking we could speak to him properly. About how he's doing."

Isaac responded forcefully but kept his pace slow. "Oh, come on. We can go out like we did back in the day! Back in the day!"

Lyle put down his phone. His boss had texted again. He stared at the notification. "Don't think I could manage it," he said.

Isaac opened up one of the beers, nodding his head, not looking at Lyle as he spoke. "Aye, but what's wrong with a little throwback night out? Just like back in the day?"

"Where do you want to go?"

Isaac shrugged. He was smiling. "We should go ... We should go wherever."

"Don't you normally want to plan things out?"

Isaac's voice softened. "What do you mean?"

Lyle sat up on the sofa. "Last time you got pretty stressed at Iona's, and that – about no one going downstairs to the taxis when they were parked outside for five minutes."

Isaac was shaking his head at the mention of his ex-girlfriend's name. "I mean, that's unfair," he said. "They were taking … Whatever, it's us! The three of us! Like old times." He picked up a beer and threw it at Lyle, who dropped it on the ground.

Will had been standing in the hallway listening to them talk. He had finished wiping away tears from his face, breathing out to clear his airway.

He'd been drawing more than he'd been spending time on the internet. His drawings were always of the same thing –

the shape of a man cast in shadow. The more developed of his drawings showed facial features with fangs and lizard-like eyes.

He'd not been to work for a few days now. His parents had called him during the afternoon. They had been called because Will was refusing to answer the phone calls from his boss at work and had been called up as his emergency contact.

Will had cried all afternoon afterwards.

He took one last breath before walking in, talking loudly to announce himself. "So, what were you guys talking about?"

Lyle said, "We were just talking about you, actually. We wanted to talk about something."

Isaac paused, not looking at either of them. Then he said, "Should I put some music on? I'm going to put some music on. Lyle, do you still have those speakers in your room?"

"No, they're out in the hall by my door."

Isaac got up, speaking quickly. "Great, I'll get them. Sorry, be right back—"

Lyle cut him off. "Do we really need the speakers brought in? It's just the three of us."

Isaac and Lyle held each other's gaze.

Lyle's phone rang, the number for his boss flashing on the screen. The sound broke the silence in the room, but Lyle never looked at his phone, talking over the ringing. "Are you bringing your laptop through?"

Isaac muttered, "Yeah, obviously." He left the room, shaking his head. As he stepped into his bedroom, he looked at the pile of clothes on the bed, most of which were dirty. He rummaged through the pile, sniffing at some items of clothing. He called out into the room, "God, fuck off, Lyle," then threw some of the clothes at the window with some force.

He opened up the music player program on his laptop,

which took a while to whirr into life. He went back through to the other room, and the tinny music was loud enough to drown out most of the noise that Lyle and Will were making. Will was frowning and nodding at something Lyle was saying.

Isaac yawned. The light coming from the windows was a shade darker than it had been, and he watched the shadows on the walls for a minute, his hands twitching a little. Isaac looked back at his flatmates without saying anything.

Lyle was still talking. "I don't think it's always a matter of chance that you meet people like that, you know? It's always like they're supposed to be there at whatever time in life you're living."

Will nodded and replied, "I don't know – it's random though, isn't it? It's not something you plan out. In your head, it's … I don't know the word."

Lyle was smiling, nodding as well, saying calmly, "You're fine, take your time."

Will paused as the music changed to a long, drawn-out guitar opener. He started again. "I think it's—"

"Fuck are you guys talking about?" Isaac interrupted.

Lyle looked at Isaac. "Some work drama."

Isaac took a drink.

Will turned his body towards Isaac, looking up at him. He said, "How's work been with you? Are they still making you do those night shifts?"

Isaac frowned and replied, "Not doing those anymore. Had a … Well, I'm not doing them anymore. Don't need to. I'm better than that. I'm great now. Much better."

Lyle and Will did not ask any other questions about it.

Isaac spent a good thirty minutes on his drink. He did not join in the conversation and finished his beer without saying anything. Will excused himself after finishing his drink, asking the other two if they wanted another.

Lyle moved closer to Isaac, who was busy scratching his nose. He whispered, "Isaac, do we really need to go out? I'm worried about Will. He's got some stuff on. Maybe we should just stay in."

Isaac was shaking his head. "Yeah, I figured. That's why we need to get him out and fired into someone!"

Lyle whispered again, watching the door, "Isaac, I don't think that's what he needs at all right now."

"Right now he needs a temporary solution, something to get him through just now. Like, are you just going to talk to him all night? Make yourself feel better about your life and all that."

Lyle shook his head, his voice rising above a whisper, still watching the door. "Or we could talk to him and figure something out. We can't just … It's not just like the same thing that works for you, you always try to go out when—"

"I have no idea what you're talking about," Isaac snapped. "I'll turn the music down. Look, once he's loosened up a bit, he'll figure himself out and he'll be back to normal again. Like, he's always going round and round in circles, and you're just letting him feel sad all the time. You know how he likes to self-flagellate."

Lyle took a drink. Isaac finished his and went over to the box of beer. He carried back two, offering one to Lyle, who was busy on his phone, ignoring another new message from his boss. He muttered, "My boss keeps texting me."

"You're far too focused on that job. I think you've always been like that. You're a waiter. You're good at all that people stuff, it's a straightforward gig. But then you barely ever look after yourself and do nothing with your life. I've told you that already. I thought you hated that chain restaurant."

"It's not a chain restaurant, Isaac," Lyle snapped.

Isaac raised his eyebrows, holding up his hands. He whispered back, "Yeah, you used to work in one. And then you just kept doing it, didn't you? It's still the same thing."

Lyle looked back down at his phone. "I know what I'm good at, Isaac."

"You know what I mean. You're always pissing about *not* doing the things you're supposed to do. You keep going on about my cash payments. It's a mess. Fuck, man. No wonder Will's getting worse, you half-ass his personal stuff too. Where is he?"

Lyle opened up the messages on his phone. He did not look back at Isaac when he said, "He's phoning home. He's had some stuff on with his mum. He wants to quit his job. You need to talk to him tonight about it."

Isaac took a drink. "Sure. At least you're off work tonight."

Lyle put away his phone, not answering his boss's texts, and replied, "Yeah."

"Where is it you work again?" Isaac asked.

"George Street. I work there now."

Isaac nodded. "I thought you worked in that place on Nicolson Street."

Lyle shook his head. "Few years ago, yeah. The pizza place, the chain one."

Isaac paused, looking away for a few seconds. "Thought that was last year you worked there?"

Lyle rubbed his nose. They both took a drink in silence.

Isaac finished his beer and grabbed another from the box. Lyle began to thumb through his phone again.

Will came back into the room, his tight-fitting top unironed. He took another beer from the box. He took a long breath and kept his eyes on the ground as he came over, not looking at the other two as he sat back down. He spoke out loud to no one in particular. "I guess we're going out then."

The trio made a mock cheer together, but Lyle looked

over at Isaac and said, "We could make it a quieter night, yeah? I still feel knackered."

Isaac shrugged and muttered under his breath, "It's not like you've got anyone else to talk to."

Lyle moved over to Isaac's laptop. He started typing and called out, "Throw me another beer. Do you have anything on your laptop that isn't shit?"

Isaac shook his head as he said, "This album is a classic. What's wrong with the classics?"

Lyle scrolled through Isaac's music quickly, never stopping to rest on any of the titles. He replied, "There's nothing wrong with the classics, it's just that other bands have made new things in the last five years. There's nothing on here – where's my laptop?"

Five minutes later, they had all switched positions. Lyle had moved to the armrest of the sofa, his portable music player playing some loud dance music. Will was laid out on the sofa, talking out loud to the ceiling.

"Those weekends, man, when we had just moved up from London, we'd go up to Inverness and it was … Even then you could tell it was just so weird seeing a family like ours in that part of the world, you know? Like, you could tell folk were staring all around us, but you'd actually talk to them and they'd relax like normal. But there were always people at the back. See, you could feel it as a kid, the eyes watching you, nothing being said. The silence when you entered a room. It's hard to describe."

Lyle nodded and replied softly, "I think I understand."

Isaac took a drink, looking at his phone.

Will nodded, continued talking. "Like, you could tell there was this edge, you know, but then you didn't know. I mean, people were friendly enough, like, there wasn't anyone bothering you. You could hear them not talking, hear them not looking at you, hear nothing at all, but you *knew* they didn't feel something – or felt something, I don't know. You'd hear them drop into Gaelic a few times and you *knew* that was about you. It's annoying to have to present yourself, to be … something like that. But then you talk to people, then they're fine, they're chatty, there's nothing wrong. Maybe it's fine now. The land itself – the mountains – it's great."

Lyle waited for him to keep going before saying, "We've kept talking about that – it's supposed to be nice. I've been meaning to get the bus up – would be better if we could drive."

Isaac did not look up from his phone. After a beat, he shook his head.

Lyle looked over at Isaac once Will had finished. He watched him for a second. Lyle asked, "Isaac, where are we going?"

Isaac shrugged, still not looking up from his phone. "Don't know, Cowgate, somewhere there."

Lyle shook his head. "That far out? We could probably find a pub that's closer, text a few people."

"Nah, into town's better," Isaac insisted. "I think folk would be more up for it if it's a bigger night." He took a drink, still looking at his phone.

"Who are you texting, Isaac?" Lyle asked.

Isaac was looking at the last text he had received from Cullen a few nights ago. He had not texted him since the argument. There had been some responses from his ex to his previous texts. He still had not looked at them. "No one, no one you need to know about."

Lyle and Will looked at each other. Will said, "I mean, we should go through a few more of these first. It's early, it's cold outside."

Isaac raised his voice over the music. "Yeah, but we can afford to get in somewhere now. We're not students anymore." He put his phone away and sat up more. "What about Dylan? Should we invite him?"

Lyle and Will both shook their heads at the mention of his name. Lyle said, "We're done with Dylan now, Isaac."

Isaac's shoulders slumped. He moaned out loud. "Aye, but he's good for … you know."

The song ended. The next song had a quiet intro. Isaac muttered under his breath, "Fine. Shitebags." He went back into his room, picked up a dirty checked shirt off the floor and threw it to the side of the bed. He went into the wardrobe and took out a red, long-sleeved shirt. He reached for his desk but stopped. His laptop was still in the living room. He went back into the pile of clothes, pulling out socks and underwear. He examined an old pair of black skinny trousers for wear and tear. There was a white-looking stain around the crotch, the fabric around the knees looked creased and there was mud on the hems. His shoes were the same ones he had worn for the last few months, black trainers with white stripes, mud around the edges of the sole.

He moved onto his knees, pushing his head into his duvet, straining his neck downwards, pushing downwards, harder, opening his mouth. The music in the living room had changed from what Isaac had put on, something with a breakbeat sound vibrating the floor in an offbeat rhythm. Isaac screamed, his hands pulling at the fabric of the trousers, knuckles white in the darkness of the room. The sound was muffled under the sound of the music.

"Absolute fucking, all of them, all of them, all of them are shit … Fuck sake."

He breathed out. He glanced at the door before going under his bed again. The money was all there. He'd spent the afternoon counting it, over and over. Enough to let him live here for a few months, at least. Enough to let him be comfortable for a few months. He could move out if he wanted, find somewhere else. He could do anything he wanted.

He muttered to himself, "Fuck it, it's one night. Just one decent night, just one."

He left the bedroom and went back to the others, wearing something a bit more presentable. Will was laughing at something Lyle was saying. They were both quite animated.

"Mind how you couldn't stop setting the fire alarm off in the flat for, like, a week? Nearly got chucked out of the place!"

Will giggled. "I know!"

Isaac opened another beer and sat back down, not joining in with the laughter. He waited for them to finish. "When was that? I don't remember."

Lyle and Will looked over at Isaac. Lyle continued the story. "You weren't there. Remember how I had that French exam but then *suddenly* there was that massive party upstairs, remember? So, I went up to check …"

" …and you didn't come back," Will continued. "So, Mark went up, then I went up!"

Lyle laughed. "Yes, brilliant! Such a good night."

Will said, "I was so drunk during that exam."

They drank again at the same time.

Isaac looked away and out the window. From where he was sitting, he could not see much. He took a long drink.

They left half an hour later, out into the night. As cold as it was, their insides were warm from the alcohol, their steps lighter, the street lights brighter. Some sort of invisible energy pushed them forward, faster. They strolled under the looming shadow of the castle, down through the Grassmarket, past the expensive pubs and restaurants. They took their time, their breath visible in the cold air. The pubs were busy, but filled with an older set of locals. They moved towards the Cowgate and the sound of shouting and high heels on the pavement, and they went into a dingy rock music pub they'd been to a few times over the years. It was dark and their shoes stuck to the floor. They went up to the bar and got their drinks in.

Isaac shouted over the music. "Mind when this place used to have a jukebox? It had tons of pop hits on it – you could throw tons of money in and play chart stuff, wind up all the goths!" Isaac laughed to himself.

They found a booth at the back, cast in shadow. They sat down and all drank in unison.

Isaac spoke up again. "Fucking hilarious, man. They really didn't like it."

Will looked away from them, his eyes lighting up for a second. He turned and shouted over the music, "Sorry, guys, back in a second."

Lyle watched him leave. Isaac took out his phone and checked through his messages. Lyle shifted over to Isaac just as the music changed to something quieter, slower-paced.

"Isaac, why don't you want to talk to him?"

Isaac glanced up. Will was chatting to a woman by the bar. Isaac stared at her chest. He spoke without looking away. "He's talking to someone just now."

Lyle was sitting across from Isaac. His hands were wrapped around the glass. He said, "You know what I mean."

Isaac tutted under his breath, still staring at the woman. She was laughing at something Will was saying. Isaac growled, "Why do I need to talk to him? It's not like … I've never had to before. He's always been able to sort himself out. People really like him, for some reason."

Lyle kept his drink in his hand, spinning the plastic glassware on the table slowly, his phone on the table near it. He glanced at the black screen, but it did not change. He spoke up. "He hasn't, Isaac. He's always struggled a bit."

"It's not like I can constantly drag him up all the time," Isaac snapped. "He always goes on about … his damn art all the time. Why did he study art if he knew that it wouldn't get him anywhere?"

Lyle shook his head. "That's not fair."

Isaac watched the woman put her hand on Will's arm. "Life's not fair." He said this with a smile, taking a drink. "Why can't he ever stand up for himself? I'm bored of having to do everything for him. Didn't you say he was only just getting by? If he can't afford it, why doesn't he move … I mean, if he can't afford it, why doesn't he get his shit together?"

Lyle tensed up. "Isaac, you know it's not …"

The woman was whispering something into Will's ear. Isaac raised his voice, saying, "I'll talk to him later. I'm just saying that I think it's a bit pathetic. It's not a 'be a man' thing, it's simple human stuff. He just doesn't try, it's like bad things have only ever happened to him. Like, he doesn't say anything until we're here, then he has a few drinks and suddenly he's so interesting and chatty."

Lyle did not look at Isaac. The phone had gone off again. Before he opened it, he said, "Come on, Isaac, it's …"

The woman had left Will, who was still at the bar, waiting around. After she left, his shoulders sank a bit, his face pensive. He looked animated again when a member of staff handed him a drink. His expression fixed into a smile.

Isaac watched all this and then looked at Lyle and said, "He just can't do it. You can see from the outside that he can't do it. He talks about it all the time. I've never seen him do anything. Have you? I've never actually, you know, actually seen him do anything? He does need to grow up."

Lyle looked away from his phone, straight at Isaac. "That's not – you know that's not on, Isaac."

"I'm right. You know I'm right. He's so – like, he just won't talk about it, never talks about anything. He's doing this to himself, you know that. You've talked and talked and talked to him, at him, but he doesn't get it at all. Then everyone feels sorry for him because he's …"

Isaac stopped. Lyle did not say anything; he kept looking at Isaac. Isaac looked away, back towards where he last saw Will, who was gone. Isaac muttered under his breath, his face red, "I'll be back. Where is … See, he wanders off."

Isaac went to the toilets, taking his drink with him, and looked at himself in the mirror. The bass sound of the club upstairs was making the walls shake. He picked at some errant hairs sticking out across his pale face. There were some on his cheeks too. He brushed his hair down, splashing some water on it. He spat into the sink.

"Fuck off, Lyle."

He gripped onto the edge of the sink, looking away from the mirror, down into the sink, staring at the drain. He muttered, "Can you both just fucking be up for this? Stop turning this into a pity party, for crying out. You all just need a fuck, none of this." He breathed out of his mouth. "Just a decent night out. Just want one. After Cu … that fucker … I want a night out, not a fucking sit-down thing – actually being out, actually being on a dance floor. Fucking tired of sitting around and just *fucking* talking."

He finished his drink and dropped the glass into the sink. He left the toilets and headed straight to the bar.

The booth they had been sitting in was full, Will and Lyle sitting with some other people Isaac did not recognise. There was no space for Isaac to sit so he stood at the edge of the table. One of the new people nodded at him. Isaac did not look at him.

Isaac could not hear the conversation over the music, which was loud and heavy. The inside of his ears vibrated with the sound of a double bass pedal being pressed over and over. One of the new people had his eyes closed and was nodding his head in time with the drumbeat.

There was a woman with them who was sitting next to Lyle. He was whispering something in her ear. She glanced at Isaac. Isaac stared at her as she talked back to Lyle. She looked away towards Will and began to laugh, covering her face. She was laughing at something Lyle had said, along with Will. Isaac said to Lyle, “What was that?”

Lyle turned to Isaac. He said nothing. Lyle turned back and continued talking. Isaac muttered under his breath, “Fuck off, Lyle.”

There was no reaction. No one heard him over the music. The conversation continued as before. Isaac looked at the woman again, taking a drink. The man next to him turned his head to Isaac, speaking into Isaac’s ear, his glasses sliding down his nose.

“It’s Isaac, isn’t it?”

Isaac did not look at him and did not turn to him when he replied, “What?”

The man spoke again. “Your name’s Isaac, isn’t it?”

Isaac shook his head, still not looking at him. “I can’t hear a word you’re saying. You’ll need to speak up.”

The man tried again. “Sorry, I didn’t mean to …”

Isaac shook his head, still not looking at him, and said, “No idea. Can’t help you.”

The man looked away, with his half-finished drink raised to his lips and his other hand in his pocket.

Isaac looked at the drinks of his friends, already nearly finished. He moved forward, placing his hand on the corner of the table.

Lyle went for his jacket. Will watched him and they got up to move. Isaac drank his own drink in one go. They stepped out into the Cowgate and met with sounds of conversation on their left and right from separate smoking areas for different venues next to them.

They filed onto the road, a taxi whirring past, couples

walking hand in hand, groups of students in one direction, older people in the other. All either drunk or on their way to be, passing through to other pubs, other clubs. A history never written or remembered, a proper Scottish tradition told through bad hangovers, stolen glances and broken things.

The cold wind always went one way and the three of them went with it, further into the Old Town.

Isaac spoke up when they got away from the crowds on the road. "Who was that girl?"

"Which one?" Lyle replied.

"The only one. I've never seen her before."

"She's engaged to one of them now," Will said.

Isaac did not answer for a few more seconds and then said, "Really? Really though? Can't see that happening." He looked across at a group of women walking down the street in the opposite direction.

"He's pretty settled. Works high up at a bank, I think," Will added.

Isaac spoke loudly as the women passed close to them. None of them turned round to look at him as he said, "Well, that's great, isn't it? Bloody great."

"Where are we going?" Lyle asked. "We've just walked past a few places. Isaac, where are we going?"

Isaac did not answer. He turned back to look at the group of women. Lyle and Will kept going and Isaac caught up with them just as they turned towards a pub on the corner.

"Let's go in here; it doesn't look busy," Lyle said.

Isaac walked behind them, complaining loudly. "Why would I want to go into a place that's dead inside, Lyle?"

"Because I – we – want to sit down for a bit, Isaac."

"Oh, great, that's great then. Brilliant."

They were met by warm air and muted candlelight, small round tables with chairs around them. When they entered, the clientele turned to face them as they brought cold air in from outside. In the far corner, a pair of men sitting by the window stared at Will as he walked up to the bar.

Will spoke quietly to Lyle. "Let's just have a quick one here."

Lyle muttered, "Actually, Isaac, you're right, not here."

But Isaac was already ordering a round. Will found a table on the opposite side of the bar from the men, near a group of four older women. When Isaac turned around with the drinks and saw Will, he groaned, "Christ, why are we sitting over there?"

Lyle took his drink from Isaac and said, "I think we're better over there."

Isaac looked around: the men in the corner were still staring at Will. Isaac said, "I mean, there are booths over there which are free. That one in the corner."

Lyle was moving over towards Will already, and he said to Isaac, "We're only staying for one. A quick one."

The women next to Will's table were laughing loudly at something. Isaac shook his head as he sat down, biting the inside of his lip.

Will excused himself to go to the toilet. Isaac took a drink, watching Will leave. When he'd turned the corner, Isaac snapped at Lyle, "Oh, *now* you don't want to sit down? I don't get what's got into you guys at all. It's like we're, I don't know, in slow motion now. Like we're not on the same page."

Lyle had his phone out. He spoke without looking up from it. "You mean, we aren't on the same page as you."

"Why can't you be?" Isaac snarled back. "We've managed decent nights out before. You've got your work things, but then you're always out with folk. You don't like it when I talk about your job? Like, you, your life, is just hanging out with people and handing them food, that's all you do."

Lyle's phone vibrated, lit up. He opened up the message quickly. It was from his boss. He read it and muttered, "I mean, it's rude."

"I don't get why you stay there," Isaac snarled again.

Lyle had put his phone down the moment Isaac opened his mouth, and he spoke loudly enough that the women near them went quiet for a few moments. "I'm sleeping with my boss, Isaac. You happy? He's a retired rugby player, has two kids and an ex-wife. You realise I've got more going on than you?"

Isaac did not look at Lyle for a few moments. He took a drink then said quietly, "Fine … I guess? I don't know what you want from me here. Far too much information."

Lyle bit his lip then turned back to Isaac. "Why can't I talk about this with you?"

Isaac took a drink, a long drink, staring at the far side of the table where Will was meant to sit. He put his drink back down again and said, "What you get up to in your spare time has nothing to do with me."

Raising his voice again, Lyle said, "It's actually a fundamental part of who I am, it's … *Come on*, Isaac!"

"It's got nothing to do with me. You just need to …"

"You're quite good at pushing people away," Lyle said. "Are you still texting her?"

Isaac did not answer.

Lyle whispered to him, "I know you still text her. All those nights out by yourself, coming back in from the cold."

Isaac shook his head. He looked over at the group of women. "Those folk – they're talking too loudly."

The women in the corner were again laughing at something. One of them moved to let her friend out of the booth, and Isaac shifted in his seat to edge away from them. He was not in their way. Then he said, "You should just leave your job or something. You could work as a waiter in Spain again."

Lyle was shaking his head. "Yeah, I could work as a waiter in *Greece*. Isaac. That's where I spent my year out. You are the fucking worst."

Will was making his way back from the toilet. Isaac looked over at Lyle and said, "Sleeping with your boss is a bad idea, you know that?"

Lyle shook his head and said nothing.

Isaac and Lyle both looked in the direction of Will. One of the older women from the group next to them had gone up to the toilets and had stopped him, putting her hand on his shoulder. Will put on his happy face again.

Isaac leaned towards Lyle and muttered into his ear, "I mind when you didn't talk to anyone at all – tiny wee kid not trying to go out and meet anyone, living in your room all the time. I had to drag you out to things the first time we met, remember? After a few months you started doing your own thing – fuck, man."

Lyle snapped back, "I was just saying, Isaac. It's awful, the stuff you come out with."

Isaac nodded and grinned. He said, "You always let folk like that push you around. Like you don't stand on your own two feet at all. Can't look after yourself. You've worked at that restaurant for years, so what now? Are you doing it for more shifts? This is how you're getting ahead? Just quit your job, for *crying out loud*."

They were both still looking at Will, at the woman not letting him go.

Lyle said, "You don't get to tell me what to do, Isaac. Christ, the stuff you say is vile, vile. Even when you're not saying anything, I know you're thinking about saying it, making yourself feel big–"

"Like, what do you actually want to do?" Isaac interrupted. "You hate the job so much."

Lyle put his head in his hands. He groaned. "Christ, my life isn't just my job, Isaac – I do hate it, right? I do, so stop going on about it."

"But you've never left. And you're just going to date the boss now? Get married?"

"Fuck – you harp on and on about how much I must hate that job and how I should quit. Then I do something for myself and then you get annoyed! Do you ever get bored of laying into people all the time? Aren't you tired of being like this?"

Isaac stared at his empty glass on his table. "I do what I want. I'm not that bad a guy. Everyone thinks that … but I'm not. I'm fucking great. You just don't like it when people argue back at you. I'm just being honest. I'm telling the truth. You're letting yourself be pushed around all the time and you don't do enough."

Will finally managed to pull himself away from the older woman. He came back to the table, tripping over a chair leg as he did so. He was sweating.

Isaac turned to Lyle and whispered, "If you try to cheer up Will again …"

Lyle seemed to say something else into his drink. Isaac watched him, then muttered to himself, "Yeah, you do that."

The other two stayed silent as Isaac began to speak. "You know how we used to do that thing where we used to get fired into women – and men, right – but a while back, remember? Not that far back. I mean, we can't really do midweek nights out anymore, because I work – I work, that's fine, a proper job now. It's not like that now, but it was better then, back when the women were up for it. Where did they all go? Everyone who was out was more up for it. It wasn't like it is now where everyone just hides in their room and stares at their phone. Who wants to sit in all the time? That's the worst part of it. The fact that we could go out tomorrow, the day after. We could, we all could, we all bloody could, but then we just fucking sit down and just fucking talk about tedious, crap stuff. There's no movement, no nothing, just fucking patter that you all need to hammer around like some mallet hitting some peg. It's crap. I don't get it, I honestly don't."

Isaac's face was red from talking. Lyle and Will finished their drinks at the same time. The three went outside.

Lyle was tapping on his phone, moving away from the other two. He deleted the texts and photos from the boss in one go. He started writing out a message to some other people, his face a picture of concentration. "Sorry, guys, I'm going to bail. I've been invited somewhere, some women I know."

"Oh, fuck off then," Isaac said.

Lyle paused then said, "Friends of friends, some people I knew way back when. You guys get home okay, yeah?"

Will was still trying to get into his jacket, more focused on looking at Lyle. "Are you good, man?" he asked.

Lyle did not look up from his phone, but he said, "I'm good. I'll see you later," and left.

Will waved; Isaac kept his hand in his pockets. They watched Lyle leave up a side street. Lyle's phone was ringing and he answered it.

Isaac tutted. "Couldn't wait to leave, could he?"

Will rubbed his nose. He spoke normally, saying, "Should we get a drink somewhere, Isaac?"

Isaac took his hands out his pockets, moving his arms into the air. He raised his voice. "Nah, let's go clubbing. We're just round the corner from our old haunt, mind?"

Will closed his eyes quite slowly, then reopened them. He muttered, "It's a bit of a dive. I'm not really up for it."

Isaac turned with over-dramatic emphasis, arms out wide.

"Which means that it's high time we went back in, doesn't it? Cheap drinks, cheaper women."

"I don't know, I'm not really in the mood."

"Nah, don't be daft, this is *exactly* what you need. You think about dumb shit too much. You think all the time. You don't try to get out of your head and do things. Getting fired into someone is just what you need."

They were already around the corner. "Are you seriously —" Will began.

Isaac interrupted him. "Will, sorry, but what was wrong with that pub in there? You were in there for a second, then you wanted to leave. You're really flaky recently, fuck sake."

Will looked at Isaac, who was turning away. Will followed him up the hill, towards a queue lined up at the side of the dark street, the remnants of a bassline vibrating out from the club. Will kept his hands in his pockets, looking up at the night sky. It was cast in a thin mist that glowed from the lights of the city. He looked up as he said, "I just keep hoping that things will work out the way they should, is all. It's just difficult just now, nothing's quite right. It'll get better though." He paused then said to himself, "It has to get better …"

Isaac swung his arms up again, tilting his head upward to the sky, adopting a mock voice of an evangelical priest. "The world curves of the … Fuck, towards … Fuck, no. The universe curves towards something."

Will finished the quote for him. "'The arc of the moral universe is long. But it bends towards justice.' Jesus, Isaac, that's a … Never imagined you'd have ever remembered anything like that."

Isaac lowered his hands, looking at his friend in quiet surprise. He spoke with a mock pride. "I know things, Will. Lots of things. Martin Luther King said that. Great guy."

Will smiled, looking ahead towards the slowly advancing

queue, young men and women huddled together, the imposing frame of a bouncer. “Yeah, it was originally ... not Martin Luther King. Some priest said it back in the American Civil War, but it’s a good quote.”

Isaac didn’t say anything for a few seconds, but then said, “Oh, right – so he did say it then?”

Will nodded. “Not originally—”

“So, he used it then,” Isaac interrupted.

Will breathed in through his nose, out through his mouth. After another beat, he replied, “Isaac, he did not come up—”

“But he said it, that’s the thing.”

Will’s shoulders sagged. He breathed out a response. “Yes, he—”

Isaac shrugged, interrupting again. “Weird how you know all that stuff and yet you don’t do anything with it. So weird.”

Will remained silent.

They were behind a group of women a head shorter than them. One of the women looked over at Isaac, who turned his head to look towards Will.

After a few minutes they found themselves at the front of the queue. The bass sounds felt louder and louder. The bouncer at the door wore a thick black waterproof jacket. He stared down at Isaac and Will as he passed back IDs to the two men in front of him, letting them pass with a word and without a smile. He looked old. He began speaking to a colleague behind him, in the smoking area. A few people were across the street; women in pretty dresses sat on the kerbside, talking quickly at each other.

Isaac and Will waited their turn to go into the club. Isaac looked over at the bouncer, who was still talking to his colleague. Then he looked back to Will and started speaking again. “What’s his name?”

Will looked dead ahead, whispering back to Isaac, “Sorry?”

Isaac said, "The guy who said that thing first."

"Which guy?"

"Don't be stupid. That guy who said, 'The arc of justice …' What was his name?"

Will did not respond for a few seconds, closing his eyes and opening them again. He started talking slowly. "You know, I can't honestly remember. American Civil War history isn't actually a strong suit of mine. Theodor—"

"Theodore Roosevelt?" Isaac interrupted.

"Not him, someone around that time."

"Then who? Who would have said that?"

"Isaac, I honestly don't know."

"Well, it's obviously not Roosevelt."

"I didn't say it was Roosevelt."

The bouncer stared at Isaac, who stayed quiet for a few seconds. When the bouncer went back to his conversation, Isaac continued, "So you don't know who said it?"

Will sighed. "Isaac, what do you—"

"Like, Martin Luther King said it," Isaac interrupted again. "So, I was correct."

Will, eyes trained on the bouncer, said, "Not originally, he didn't."

"But you don't even know who said it in the first place! You know I'm wrong, but you don't know the answer? What's the point of that?"

They said nothing else. The group behind them, a mixed group of men and women, were getting louder. Isaac looked behind him.

Will kept looking at the bouncer. He muttered, "Do you still text her?"

Isaac was still staring at some of the women behind them. "Who?"

"You know what I mean."

Isaac continued staring behind him. "I'm not texting her."

“You sure?” Will snapped back. “You spend a lot of time on your phone.”

The bouncer, finishing his conversation, asked to see their IDs. The pair handed them over. The bouncer looked at Isaac’s blank expression, then back down to his ID. Isaac looked back at Will, who still looked dead ahead. The bouncer was still looking at Isaac when he passed the ID back.

Isaac went straight in without waiting for Will, squeezing past the queue for the cloakroom which spilled out into the entrance, pushing past a group of tall men in polo shirts to head inside. He squeezed into the entranceway to the club, the remnants of an old cellar carved open. Groups and individuals passed by Isaac to head outside, or towards the bar in front of Isaac, or to the left towards the dance floor. They merged into each other, moving slowly, patiently making way for people with drinks in their hands and not standing still for long enough to get in the way. A group of short women walked in front of Isaac, pairs of small drinks in their hands. He watched them move, eyes glancing at them in turn. They didn’t look at him.

Isaac went to the nearest bar to get a drink. There was not much of a crowd around it. The closest barman was serving a tall blonde. Isaac looked over at her then looked back at some of the other staff behind the bar, focusing on an older-looking woman with short hair and pierced ears, near the till, her eyes watery and distant.

Isaac tutted under his breath. A clear-looking drink in a tall glass was within his reach, just to his left. It looked half-full. Without looking around again, he picked up the drink and downed it in one. He put the glass down in a fluid motion, slowing only to place it on the shining grey metal sheen of the bar.

No one looked at him. He tutted again, louder this time.

He searched for his wallet. Leaning against the bar, both of his arms resting over it, he looked at the amount of money in his wallet. He smiled and looked back over at the blonde woman counting her change.

One of the bar staff came over. Isaac shouted his order over the music. The barman leaned back a bit from his shout. Isaac did not apologise for shouting; instead, he leaned forward and opened the wallet again. The barman glanced at the notes and did not look Isaac in the eye again.

Isaac took his drink and left, pouring the change and cash into his pocket, his wallet in his other hand. The weight of the change dug into his leg and he limped a little, adjusting himself to compensate, to let him walk with comfort. He kept stopping in the middle of some groups of people to adjust his trousers.

He turned around and moved back through the entrance. Will was not there. He went towards the first bar. Will was not there. He moved towards the dance floor, a large space which he could look down upon. He watched a group of tall women in the far corner talking to each other, moving around. He glanced at the back of the dance floor, then to the front, not making eye contact with anyone.

Will was not there.

He made eye contact with the woman who had looked at him in the queue outside. She looked away and said something to her friend. Isaac moved away, muttering into his drink, "Come on, Will, grow up. Come on …"

He moved towards a second room; a bar was lit up in the far corner. Again, he didn't make eye contact with anyone, his head glancing between heads, at the invisible midpoint of conversations he was not a part of. There were seats at the side, all taken. No Will.

Isaac turned around, around, on a spot in the middle of the floor. Some drink fell out of his glass as he turned, spilling onto his fingers, which were gripping the glass with some force. He took a drink.

Will was not there either.

Isaac moved faster, not running but building pace, his free hand twitching, his other gripping the glass. He went into another room, a smaller space with a smaller dance floor, tight and packed with people. Pairs of women were dancing together, men standing looking at them. He moved around them, shifting against them, moving them out of the way. He was biting the inside of his lips. "Bunch of absolute fuckers … Just a night out, I want a night out, just one. After all I've done, the shit I've put up with, do this for me. How hard is it …"

He was shaking his head and muttering; groups moving past him kept their distance, people sitting down watched him as he went by. He moved faster, back towards the main dance floor. Finally, he found Will there.

Will's eyes were closed in concentration, his mouth all smiles and arms all moves. He was dancing with two women a head taller than him, doing a marching movement in his arms perfectly in time with the music, tilting his neck side to side. He was completely in time with the women, completely in time with the people around him.

Isaac stood and watched him. Will did not look at him, totally into his own thing. Isaac turned his head to look at the women. One of them looked at Isaac, then looked at her friend.

Will saw Isaac and embraced him, before heading away from the dance floor like nothing was wrong. Isaac looked at the two women, who waved at Will and went back to their own thing. The old song faded into the new.

Will smiled at Isaac, shouting over the music. "Hey buddy! Where'd you go?"

"I was looking for you! Fuck sake, you need to keep up!"

Will did not frown. He was still smiling. He shouted back, "You found me! It's all good, man."

Isaac shut his eyes for a moment and started again. "That's not really … Who were those girls?"

Will was laughing. "Fuck knows."

"Dude, you shouldn't have left, could have—"

Will was still laughing when he interrupted. "Nah, mate, needed a drink! Wahey!" He had both hands in the air and was moving away from the dance floor, away from the mass of people.

Isaac made a sharp, slow intake of breath, one that almost made him grow two feet; his chest out, fingers on his palms open wide. He took Will by the shoulder. "Okay, mate. Listen. We're not gonna pull if you act like that."

Will kept laughing. "But, honestly? I'm good right now. Real good! I'm just trying to be, Isaac. We're not going to figure everything out."

"So why not—"

"Have you ever tried dancing by yourself?" Will interrupted.

Isaac screwed up his face and shouted back, "What?"

Will's voice dropped a bit and he spoke faster than he would normally do. "Used to do it all the time down south in clubs. Didn't need to be … Not trying to impress anyone. Back when I was a teenager!"

Isaac took a drink. He said, "Aye, but …"

Will was looking past him, his eyes focused on something in the distance. "I feel great, actually."

Isaac spoke quietly, a slight whine in his voice. "No, there's … It's like Dylan used to say: there's always a moment in the night where the women outnumber the men by a bit. There's a tipping point where it's just a … Come on, the window's closing—"

Isaac kept looking around as he spoke, and people were

looking over at them. Will screwed up his face when Isaac was talking. He interrupted loudly, saying, "Isaac, what the hell are you on about?"

Isaac looked away. The whine in his voice was gone. "It's fine, you try and get some girls over. I'll get more drinks."

Will held his arms up triumphantly, chanting in a sing-song voice, "Drinks, Isaac! Drinks! More drinks, more drinks, more drinks!" He stepped forward and past Isaac, towards the larger bar. Isaac watched him go. Everyone in the queue for the bar looked forward, men standing with their hands in their pockets. Will did not look at where the nearest spot to the bar was. He stood behind two people, who split to let some people out with drinks. They moved forward and Will moved forward with them, closer to the bar.

The music changed to the piano chords of a dance track Isaac did not recognise. He took a swig from his finished drink and did not taste anything, the smell of it filling his nostrils. He gripped tightly onto the glass. The crowd at the bar did not seem to shift, spreading to let people out but with more people joining all the time. A gap in the crowd appeared to Will's left, but he did not move to it. Then people were leaving the bar with their drinks, and Will naturally sank into the gap. He started talking to a tall man in a cap near him. They laughed about something, both talking rapidly to each other. A group of women at the bar began to leave with their drinks, hands held high above their heads to make room for everyone else. Everyone let them pass. The crowd around them flowed forward. No one looked back. There was a little bit of a crush, but everyone kept their hands to themselves. Will was laughing loudly with the man in the cap. A woman close to them, just to the right, turned her head round. She was smiling, looking confused.

Isaac shook his head. "Come on, hurry up …"

Everyone waited, united in want, an exact want at that

moment in time, waiting next to each other, waiting in turn. Isaac's grip tightened even more around his glass. He looked around for somewhere to put it down. Some people brushed past him, and he turned and shifted his shoulders slightly. He stared at a pair of them as they walked past – two women in short skirts. They did not look back.

Isaac looked back over to where Will was standing. He was at the bar now, side by side with the man in the cap and another woman. They were talking to each other and doing shots. They all ordered more drinks, and Will moved away from them with a pair of drinks, smiling as he went. Everyone let him out and everyone moved forward.

Will handed over a drink to Isaac. "See, Isaac? Didn't take long at all. Was a bit of an adventure, if anything."

Isaac shook his head. "Probably should have got more. Queue's massive. Didn't think about that, did you?"

Will drank without looking at Isaac. They stood around in silence, Isaac looking at Will as if he was about to say something. Finally, he said, "Will, who were you with?"

"No idea! Just friends you meet on the way. It's all fine, Isaac, all fine, all completely fine. I've not felt this good since – like, since a long time."

Isaac looked away at a woman passing by. Then he said, "I think we should go talk to some people, or something like that. No more hanging about."

Will took a drink and started moving away. "So good, just want to dance now! Those shots were *needed*!"

Isaac called after him, "What about those guys you were talking to, the guys from before – those girls you were with?"

Will turned back for a second. "What? Isaac, it's just the two of us, let's go dance! Dance! Come on, dude!"

They moved towards the large dance floor. It was packed too. Areas of it that had been empty when Isaac had first been in were full of young men standing in circles. They were glancing over at groups of women dancing next to them, trying to make eye contact. The men outnumbered the women.

Isaac scowled. "The window! If fucking Dylan was here … Come on, Will."

Will could not hear him over the loud, pumping music. He made his way through the crowd, Isaac moving behind him. He found a decent-sized space near the far wall and drank half his glass in one go.

Isaac tried to catch the eye of people around him. It was the same everywhere – women in groups, men around them. Isaac and Will were far away from everyone where they stood. No one paid any attention to Will as he moved his arms, his legs, with more energy than anyone else. A group of tall women to the left had their backs to them. Further on from them was a group of women outnumbering a pair of men.

Isaac glanced over, saying, "Dude, we gotta get over there."

Will started laughing. The song ended, the DJ catching the mood in the room and playing a Motown track, one faster and with more pace. The next one was even faster. Isaac looked at Will, who shimmied and moved with everyone else. He leaned over and said to Will, "I think we should go talk to people."

Will shook his head, wagged his finger and flexed his hips.

Isaac tried again. "Will, I mean it, we should go talk to people. Come on, it's—"

Will interrupted, forcefully this time. "Nah, just dance, stop talking!"

Isaac looked at a group of guys in the corner. One of them was dancing with a taller woman, her figure well-built, her moves more pronounced and professional. The man's friends watched on, bobbing their heads.

Isaac looked around the room again. No one was looking at them.

Will leaned over to Isaac and said, "You can talk to me, you know. About anything, anything at all. You're a dick, but you don't need to be."

Isaac did not look him in the eye. He looked over at the DJ booth. The DJ was an attractive blonde woman with headphones. Isaac watched her work. She did not look up.

"Why can't you talk to me, Isaac?" There was almost a squeal in Will's voice.

Isaac looked at his drink, finished the rest of it. He looked Will square in the eye. "Fuck off, Will," he snarled back. You're always like this. Can't even get you to do anything."

Will stopped moving, looking back at Isaac. "Isaac, calm down. Why can't you just be fine? I know you're going off on one. I'm not doing great, but I'm finding ways to cope, just fucking dancing, drawing. I've cracked it, Isaac, I'm drawing all the time now, I've found a way back into art."

"Listen, let me … fucking tell you. It's like you're on some weird little online forum about … fuck, I don't know what you like, fucking paintings or whatever. You and your weird pals online talk about paintings all the time, your favourite shitty brushstrokes, your little French Monets or Kadshitskis or whatever – and it's all pish. You'll never see it any other way because you'd rather have folk tell you that what you're doing is fine. And that's fine, then you just – do nothing, Christ …"

Isaac walked away, moving between crowds of people. He did not look back at Will. Moving was difficult. People were standing in circles to dance. The floor gripped onto his feet without ever feeling stable. He went back to the bar.

The queue around the bar was a mass of people. He stood and tried to peer over it. He managed to walk into someone trying to get to the dance floor. The man was shorter, drink in hand. He grinned and patted Isaac on his shoulder as he passed him, not looking for trouble. The people around him glanced at Isaac as he went by. Isaac did not look at them, moving away out of the room, back towards the entrance, back to the bar he started in. More people were entering. Groups of women, all dressed up.

Isaac let out a silent whine, unheard under the music and noise and chatter. No one looked at him. He turned his head and saw Will trying to follow him. Isaac kept moving. He looped back towards the dance floor. He looked over at the crowds, and Will's face appeared between the mass of moving faces, the lights, people cheering and singing along. His smile was gone, his eyes trying to reach Isaac's face.

Isaac stared at him for a few seconds. Will walked forward. Isaac kept facing him and walked backwards, away to the left, towards the bar. He moved faster, past people standing at the bar. He picked up a drink which had been left on an unoccupied table. He pushed through, a rap song blaring, everyone getting every second word. He moved through more crowds. He did not turn his head.

He looped back through towards the area near the main bar. The man in the cap from earlier was sitting near here, talking to the woman that he had met at the bar, along with two of her friends. Isaac looked away, muttering. He looked behind him. Will was not there. He moved quickly, back towards the entrance.

Near the entrance, a man and a woman were talking to each other. Everyone walked around them. The man slowly moved his hand through her hair. Isaac looked at the woman's expression of concentration as she gazed into the man's eyes.

He muttered to himself, "Everyone leaves me alone."

More people were filing in, and a lot more women than

men. Isaac shook his head. As he stumbled away, he took out his phone and started writing texts to his ex-girlfriend.

He went outside. The noise of the nightclub could only be felt through the vibrations from the walls. Isaac made his way up the hill, his head down. It had started raining, water flowing down the length of the hill. In the dark, the water appeared to make the same movements over and over, forming the same shapes. Rain fell onto his phone screen but he continued to text, not looking up as the amber street lights made the clouds above glow in yellow and red.

Will had not followed him out. He was inside a toilet cubicle. He was breathing hard through his mouth and there were tears running down his cheeks. He kept his feet against the cubicle door to keep it shut. The lock was broken. Outside it people were banging on the door, and Will couldn't keep them out.

CHAPTER EIGHT

The bus station was busy. Groups of tourists took up space with backpacks and rows of suitcases. A queue for the Glasgow bus extended round the corner. It was raining heavily outside, the noise of it muted by the chatter further down the long concourse and the glass separating the large coaches from the waiting passengers. Rows of seats lined the length of the corridor, and scattered amongst them were older patrons, waiting patiently to be called. Younger people stood around in groups, huddling together. Rain scattered against everything outside in waves, caught by the wind. It had been raining all morning.

Isaac's hair was still wet from the walk over. He sneezed loudly and a few people turned around. Phlegm brushed against the tips of his fingers as he moved to cover his mouth. His teeth felt warm. He had not cleaned them in a few days.

There was a slim red-headed woman sitting across from him. She was looking away from him, legs folded, her body turned towards the glass windows, towards the bus nearest to them. One of her tights had a tear in the seam running down her leg, near to her feet, snugly kept in small leather pumps.

A small red suitcase stood up on its wheels in front of her. She had not looked up when he sneezed.

Isaac continued to stare at a space in the floor just in front of her. He pressed his tongue against the back of his teeth, rolling it left to right, left to right. His hands were stuck in his jacket pockets, his fingers curled into fists.

He glanced up at the woman's tights. She did not notice him.

Isaac tutted. He took out his phone. It was low on battery. He had one new message from Cullen – the first one for a few weeks. He looked at the notification but did not open the message.

Although there were lines of large coaches lined up next to each other, the closest one to Isaac looked nothing like any of them. It was a small single-decker bus. The driver was not inside.

There was a smell of cigarette smoke coming from a few feet along, the driver standing out of the rain and away from his bus, away from sight – the spot littered with cigarette butts. The front of the bus was covered in dirt, its white paint hidden behind mud, lines on the glass kept in a perfect curve by the windscreen wipers. The bus driver was standing in the archway of the stance. He was tall and wearing a short-sleeved white shirt, which looked perfectly ironed. The belt of his trousers was near his belly button. He smoked a cigarette, paying no attention to Isaac, the woman, or anything living around him. He was looking up at the rain falling near him, his other hand in his pocket.

The rain continued to fall.

People filed past Isaac, further down the station towards the busier stands, the Glasgow bus slowly filling up. The sound of the rain picked up suddenly, held by a gust of wind so that it dragged along the hard concrete outside. A large coach pulled away, the driver slowing to give a wave to the driver smoking outside, who removed his hand from his pocket to wave back. The coach continued, leaving the station, turning left and out onto the main road.

The man threw his cigarette onto the floor. He moved towards the door. Isaac turned his head to the right, his line of sight looking past the woman. He walked towards the bus, head down as he went through the doors.

The driver pressed buttons into the ticketing machine with one forefinger at a time, bending his neck to push his head forward, eyes dead ahead at the machine. Isaac paid with the wrong change, muttering his destination to the driver, managing to get the sound out properly after a second go. He had not spoken to anyone for at least a day.

The driver passed the ticket back with a smile. "There you are, son. You might want to get a weekly saver – saves you just buying individual tickets all the time."

Isaac did not look at him when he moved away. He made his way to the back row of seats, taking a seat near to where one of the 'STOP' buttons hung from the poles.

The bus began to vibrate as the engine started up. The driver kept the doors open as an older woman approached with a walking stick. She silently climbed on, a wide smile on her face as she leaned the stick against the door, watching her feet as she pushed a hand onto a railing on the inside of the bus. When she was on, she fumbled around with a large handbag by her side.

Isaac pressed his head against the side of the bus, the glass vibrating heavily against his head. He watched the woman's hands, her shaking hands, as she counted the money. She talked with the driver quietly, the man leaning over to talk to her in turn. Isaac rolled his head back. He checked his phone. He looked at the icon showing multiple messages, then put his phone back in his pocket.

The older woman took a seat near the front of the bus,

grabbing the seat and helping herself down. She looked up at Isaac along the way with a smile. Isaac was staring back into the bus station, trying to seek out the red-headed woman. He could not see her from where he was sitting.

The bus pulled away. Isaac looked back into the station. He managed to make eye contact with the woman but looked away when they locked eyes. The bus turned onto Queen Street, making its way out of the centre of town, further south.

The bus rattled around, taking its time to move through the city. The traffic began to lessen as it left the centre but became busy again as it moved towards the city outskirts. The distance between the houses began to thin out, further and further, inch by inch. The rain battered against the windows, raindrops dragging down the pane, over and over.

The bus came to a roundabout by the city bypass. It kept left at the roundabout while the majority of traffic was turning right. Once it was able to move, the driver put it into gear and thrust forward, along a road that led away from Edinburgh.

The bus got stuck behind a line of cars moving slowly down a single-lane road, passing near a school. The afternoon winter sky was turning darker, the rain easing off. There was a grey colour in the air, the surroundings a muted shade. They were out of the city, fields in the distance to their left and right, large metal power lines crossing above them.

Isaac tried to sit up straight. He closed his eyes every few seconds, the sound of the bus constantly in his ears.

The bus started moving faster, faster still. The rain began to thin out. The overcast sky dwarfed everything below it, fields and low hills. The bus pulled onto a dual carriageway and turned off at the first junction, the driver making a jerking movement with the wheel because the junction had appeared suddenly.

Isaac had his head away from the window now. The older woman sat upright in her seat, her stick planted into the ground.

There was no traffic on the road now. Ahead of the bus lay a collection of houses, all grey-roofed, single-storey. They sat in four rows, the road running between them. Beyond them, to the south, the land remained flat, with the road heading towards a forest of evergreen trees.

Isaac pressed the button on the bus to stop.

The bus did not slow as it approached the stop near the rows of houses. Isaac pressed the button again and rose from his seat. The driver braked sharply when he saw Isaac approaching the front. The bus ground to a halt. There was no sign to say where they were. There was a glass panel for the bus timetable attached to the bus stop, but it had been left empty.

Isaac stepped out, not looking at the driver as he left, not saying anything. The bus made a guttural sound as it dragged itself away. Isaac was on his own, his hands stuck in his jacket. The bus drove on.

Behind Isaac, the dual carriageway was distant but still visible, small shapes of cars running left and right, vague sounds from their distant engines audible to Isaac.

His parents' house was here, at the end of the small collection of identical houses. Isaac stopped for a second on the short walk down to it, looking into the windows of the nearest house. The television was on. Isaac glanced at the flashing screen for a moment. A car drove past on the main road, shattering the silence.

At his parents' house, the front garden was a mess of thick green grass which rose in clumps at the edges, creeping across the edge of the pavement. There was little in the way of plant life, nothing in the way of anything to look at. The curtains on the front windows were closed.

He took out his keys and opened the door, which swung open with some force. Piles of letters had collected at the bottom of the stairs. He stepped over them. They were cast along the long entrance hall, letters from this year, from the end of the last. Bank letters and circulars, catalogues for summer clothing sales. Isaac went straight to the bathroom at the end of the hall without closing the front door behind him. When he was finished, he did not wash his hands. On his way back to close the front door, he stepped on the letters and picked up a few postcards from foreign locations, countries in the Far East. Isaac glanced at the handwriting, the bright images on the front.

His parents had been travelling together for some time, having left their jobs behind. There was no indication in any of their letters that they would return home any time soon. Isaac muttered to himself as he glanced over images of sandy beaches and hopeful faces. They looked happy.

He turned into the kitchen. Nothing was laid out. There were cans of soup in some of the cupboards. He took out a pizza from the freezer, putting it into the oven, picking out a beer from the untidy pile of them in the fridge.

The fridge had a photograph on it held on by a black magnet – his parents standing on a beach on a dull, stormy day. The sea was writhing with rage, his parents clinging onto their jackets, clinging onto each other. Isaac was the one who had taken the picture. It had been taken when he was much younger, and the photo had faded a little by being exposed to the sunlight over the years. His parents were not looking at Isaac or at the camera. They were looking at each other.

He unhooked the photograph and began to tear it to pieces, bit by bit, his hands shaking as he did so. He left the torn pieces on the floor.

He went to the small living room. He did not turn on the

lights. The remote was left pointing away from the television on a small table. It was where Isaac had left it the last time he was here, close to a photograph of him and his parents at the beach. He was younger, his hair lighter, his smile wide, looking off camera as his parents stood behind him.

He put his feet up on the sofa and turned on the television. The screen came to life and showed the same programme that the neighbour had been watching, the noise of it loud and tuneful. Isaac muted it, watching the people talk noiselessly on screen. A guest was invited on whom Isaac did not recognise. He was young and male, from a reality dating show. The women fussed over him, all shiny grins and young faces. Isaac pressed his tongue against the back of his teeth again. His gums felt sore.

Half an hour later, Isaac had finished his pizza and his beer. He looked out the window, looking far into the distance, across the fields to the forest on the hill, the one by the road extending far out to the left. Isaac had never been out to those woods. He had been told to explore them when he was younger, told to go outside. He had stayed in his room.

He changed the channel. There was a pile of DVDs in the corner, most of them still in original packaging, by the TV. He had bought them a few months ago.

He turned over to a cartoon on one of the children's channels. He watched it the whole way through with the sound on, muting the adverts when they were on.

He got up again later, leaving to go upstairs to his room. It was the same as it was when he was a teenager. There were no posters or pictures on the wall. The cupboard was made of cheap MDF, the desk and chair hidden behind it to the left so no one could see what Isaac was up to at his desk.

Isaac had never wanted to decorate his room. When he had left to go to university, his mother had decorated anyway, covering one wall in wallpaper with a pattern of white roses bunched together, repeated over and over on a black background.

There were other piles of clothes on the floor. He picked up some of them and took them back through to the kitchen, putting them in the washing machine and letting it run.

He returned to the living room, stepping over his dirty plates to lie on the sofa. There was a wine stain on the sofa, a sharp red colour. When he was younger, he had screamed at his mother over dinner being late and had slapped the wine glass out of her hand. He had sworn at his father and stayed in his room for that weekend, emerging on Monday to go to school. His parents never raised this incident with him. His mother had never cleaned the wine away. Isaac glanced at the stain for a few seconds before taking a nearby cushion to cover it.

He opened a new text message from Cullen. It said that there was one more job. He was messaging because it needed two people – it was risk-free and, potentially, huge.

Isaac started writing out a long message to respond. He typed for a solid minute, his thumbs brushing over the keys, only stopping to correct spelling mistakes.

He stopped suddenly, closing his eyes. "Ah, fuck off." He put his phone down and did not pick it up again.

The television was now showing a documentary on Scottish clans, the battle between the Stewarts and the Campbells. Isaac changed the channel. The television did not have many channels to choose from. He watched a quiz show for a good half an hour, not reacting to any of the questions being asked and answered. The woman asking the questions was blonde.

Isaac ground his teeth, his tongue pressed against them, pushing hard. He closed his eyes. There was a sound of applause coming from the television. He muttered to himself, "I don't need anyone. I'm fine here."

Later, he went upstairs. He went back into his bedroom, into the dark. He fell asleep on top of the covers, still fully clothed. In the dark, the flowers lost their shape, became something else. They looked like gaunt, pale faces, the indentations of their skulls underneath piercing through the skin.

CHAPTER NINE

Isaac felt the errant stubble on his chin. He had been drinking by himself for the last few nights and had not showered. He was currently lying back on the sofa, staring at the ceiling. Lyle had just come out of the shower, his face clean-shaven and towel wrapped around his body. Isaac asked, “So, where is this party we’re going to?”

Lyle looked back at Isaac. He was in the kitchenette, getting a glass of water. “It’s a party I got invited to. Some old friends of mine, got in touch with them a while back. They’re loaded, so it should be good. Have you got something smart to wear?”

Isaac curled his neck forward, eyes squinting at the ceiling light. He sneered. “Smart?”

“Yeah, you need to brush up a little bit, make an effort.”

Isaac paused before he answered, “I mean, I’m always making an effort.”

“You know what I mean. It’s … This kind of party isn’t what you’re used to.”

Isaac spoke again as Lyle drank. “Just because I’m not used to it, doesn’t mean I can’t do it.”

Lyle spat out water into the sink.

Isaac got up from the sofa, stretching out his arms. He yawned as he asked, “Why are you drinking so much water?”

“I’m not feeling well. I’ve been out so much the last week. And the two we’re meeting tonight are … They stress me out, really stress me out …”

Isaac opened his mouth but then closed it quickly. He did not interrupt Lyle as he rambled on.

“You’ve no idea. It’s not as if I like half of them. It’s enough that – it’s enough, it’s enough, it’ll be enough—” Lyle’s hands were shaking.

Isaac cut in. “Didn’t know you were going out earlier, you could have said. I had the week off this week, last week – two weeks. You could have said something about going out. You’ve barely been here. Just left me out again. Typical.”

Lyle wiped water away from his mouth. He stared into the sink. He grabbed two glasses, a wine bottle, and bottle opener, leaving them out on the kitchen top.

Isaac broke the silence a few seconds later. “It’s just rude, not inviting me out, that’s all. Is the shower free? Not sure. Will normally takes ages, you know, with the crying and all.”

Lyle muttered, “Think you should check for yourself.”

Isaac got up and walked over. “Excuse me?”

Lyle relaxed his shoulders, releasing his hands from the sink, walking back out of the kitchen. He did not look at Isaac as he left the room, calling back, “You should look for yourself.”

Isaac stood still, staring at where Lyle had been, out into the dark corridor. He called out after him. “That’s still rude, Lyle!”

Isaac went back into his room. He breathed in, holding his breath for five seconds. Ten seconds. Fifteen seconds. He breathed out hard through his nose, then in and out again. He screwed up his fists, bending his knees. He pressed his curled fists against the sides of his head, pulling his chest up. His body strained, his gut shifting as he sucked it in, the skin bending against itself. He did this slowly, forcefully. He did it three more times and stopped after that. His heart was pounding.

He got dressed. He had bought a suit a few months ago. His ex-girlfriend had picked it out for him.

Isaac went back to the kitchen, took a can from the fridge and sat down on an armrest, looking up to stare at the ceiling. He opened the can, put it to his lips, tipped the contents straight down his throat. He sat in silence for a while.

Will came into the room, also wearing a suit jacket. "Isaac, do you know where we're going?"

"Will, do *you* know where we're meant to be going?" Isaac snapped back. "I haven't seen Lyle all week, and he's acting weird. Has he been drinking all the time?"

Will grabbed a beer and sat down. "I thought he was with you ..." Isaac shook his head at this. "You were away for a bit. He mentioned this party a while ago to me, said I should come along."

"Fuck, never mind," Isaac sighed.

They sat in silence and looked at their phones.

After he had finished his first beer, Will left and brought his laptop in, setting it up to play music. Isaac took another swig from his can. The first song Will put on had a quiet intro, then a breakbeat cut in after a few seconds. Just as the first person started rapping over the music, Isaac turned to Will, talking over the words that were sung.

"Where have you been the last few days? You've not left your room or anything."

Will kept looking at the laptop. After a few seconds, he turned the music down, turning back to Isaac to talk. "I've been drawing. Well, I'm trying to. It's tricky trying to pick it up again. I've found drawing people is a bit better – actually, I'm getting used to it. I spent ages online, looked up modelling – like, wargaming? I used to do it a lot when I was younger; it's what got me into art."

"What, with the little men and the dice and things?" Isaac screwed up his face.

"Yes, that thing – I loved it when I was younger. Couldn't really afford it so I did a paper round. It got me into art, properly, was a gateway for me."

"Right, so you're going back into your childhood. Now that you're an adult with an art degree, sure, it's a big scary world. Run away from your problems. Solid pick there."

"I was just looking it up, that's all." Will took a drink.

Isaac shook his head. "It's not really something you do as an adult, though, is it?"

"I remember it was … like the theatre of the mind, you know. It was like I could paint all those models – I spent hours putting it together, getting glue stuck on my fingers, all that – and it was like I was giving them life. I didn't even like the gaming part of it. I just liked having things which I made in my hands. Like, nothing existed before. It was all mine."

"Theatre of the mind – like you were a God," Isaac said. He did not screw up his face this time.

Will shook his head, taking a drink. "No, because it's all fair – it's dice and measurements. You go up against someone who's done all the same things that you have – they've bought the models, they've picked out an army, they've done all the same things that you have. Then it's about movement and the roll of the dice. That's what it's all about."

Isaac sat up more, looking over at Will. "This is the weirdest thing I've heard you say, Will – and you've said and done some weird stuff over the years. So, you really went all in for this stuff as a kid?"

Will shrugged. "I mean, I did it for a bit. It's just a bit of fun, Isaac."

Isaac shook his head. "So why are you so interested in it now?"

Will opened his mouth to speak but he was interrupted by the entrance buzzer going off.

Isaac sat up, and his eyes immediately snapped forward in the direction of the sound through the wall. He lowered his voice and said, "I didn't know we had people coming over. We never have people over."

Will tensed his shoulders up a bit, breathing out. "Okay, it's fine."

Isaac looked back up at him. "Is it fine? No one's told me anything. Why aren't people telling me anything?"

Will looked back through the doorway just as they heard Lyle's footsteps heading towards the intercom. "It's friends of Lyle," he said. "He's mentioned it to me a few times. Old friends from years ago, I think."

Isaac waited until he heard Lyle pass the doorway. "He's never mentioned them to me."

Will said nothing, sipping his drink.

Isaac spoke again. "I … I said I did not know other people were coming. Lyle never mentioned them to me."

Will kept his eyes on the doorway. One of his fingers was fiddling with the top of the can. "Well, they are now."

They both listened to the front door opening. There were excited squeals coming from the corridor.

Isaac whispered, "I don't like that you didn't tell me anything about this. Why are you like this?"

Will kept watching the door. He breathed out a response, his shoulders tense. "It's not a competition, Isaac."

Isaac tried to readjust himself on the armrest, sitting up a little. "You're right about that."

Will did not respond. He looked away from the doorway, towards Isaac. Isaac looked towards the doorway, ignoring him.

Two women with blonde hair and short dresses came into the kitchen. One was taller than the other; the taller woman walked in front, her friend kept close to her back.

Isaac looked up towards the taller one, offering up a hand without moving from his position. "Hey!"

They did not react to him; instead grabbing the glasses that had been left out on the counter. Isaac put his hand down. Will spoke up after they had opened the bottle with the opener that Lyle had laid out. "Hey, ladies, how are you? I'm Will. This is Isaac."

The taller one waved back. The other held onto her drink for dear life.

Isaac spoke up. "You can sit over here if you like. I was talking to Will about his art, how he was—"

The taller said, "Oh, you're *that* guy? Lyle was saying – sorry, one sec."

The two of them looked over. Isaac opened his mouth to speak but Will spoke first. "Yeah, I was trying to … Sorry, I'll move up. What are your names?" He moved over on the sofa, far enough that he ended up sitting on the edge. The two women spaced themselves out evenly. Isaac did not move to let them past, his eyes glancing down at their legs. The taller one said, "Oh, thank you so much."

They all took a drink at the same time. The music cut out, but a new track started quietly. Isaac shot a glance at Will. He lowered the can from his mouth first and said, "So, Will was telling me about – what was it you were talking about, Will?"

Will paused. The two women looked at him. He spluttered out, "Oh, I was talking about work. Just how my week was going."

"Yeah?" the tall one replied. She was smiling, her teeth showing. The other friend did not open her mouth.

"Yeah, he works in a call centre in town. Complaints and stuff," Isaac said firmly.

Will nodded slowly. "Yes, that's what I do."

The two women said nothing, and they all drank in silence again until the quiet one spoke up. "I like this song."

Will nodded as he replied, "Yeah, it's good. He's class live. I've seen him play down south."

As Will started talking, Isaac took out his phone. The two women were paying attention to Will, ignoring Isaac. He stared at the screen. He had received another message from Cullen earlier. Another text about the job – the big job. The one with the potentially life-changing amount of money.

Isaac made eye contact with the quiet woman, who had glanced over at him for a second. "So how far away is this place?" he asked.

No one else spoke straight away. The two women stared at Isaac. The taller one responded, and Isaac switched his gaze to look at her when she spoke.

"Sorry?" she said.

Isaac waited a second. Will did not say anything. Isaac tried again. "The place we're going to. Where is it?"

The taller woman replied. She wasn't smiling this time. "The address was on the invitation."

Isaac shook his head as he replied, "There was an invitation?"

Will waited a second before jumping in. "Sorry – Isaac's our flatmate, he didn't know about this."

The taller one nodded. The quiet one said nothing, turning her body to face Will. The taller one said, "So is he invited?" She paused before she added, "Okay then."

No one said anything after this. The music played on, and they all drank in silence. Isaac took out his phone to look back at Cullen's message. His face was red.

Lyle came back in. He was wearing a grey suit jacket with black lapels and a black shirt with matching trousers. He wore black leather shoes which Isaac had not seen before. Lyle glanced at Will, then the two women. "Hey, guys!"

The quiet one became more animated. She said, "Lyle, you look great, *darling*!"

Lyle shrugged. "I mean, I guess so. Who even says *darling* nowadays?"

Rain started to batter against the windows.

They drank in the flat for a bit longer. Isaac did not move from the armrest, watching the mouths of the people talking around him, not following the conversation at all. He stared at the shadows moving on the wall behind the women. The room was warm. He yawned. No one was looking at him. He drummed the top of the can. A droplet was stuck in the section between the lip and the top. He pressed at it with his finger, poking it with his fingernail.

They made plans to leave. Isaac got up first, standing in the corridor for a minute by himself. He moved back into the living room when no one followed him. He went into the fridge and started taking beer out of the box which Lyle and Will had bought. He stuffed cans of beer into his jacket pockets. No one else took anything.

Isaac took his time walking down the stairs. He could hear the rain battering the ground outside. Isaac hung back as the others went down and whispered to Lyle, "Are we walking?"

Lyle screwed up his face, not bothering to whisper, his response echoing round the close. "No, not in this weather. Plus, it's miles away. What would be the point of that?"

Isaac whispered, "Well, how far away is it then?"

Lyle shook his head as he said, "We'll take a taxi."

Isaac bit the inside of his lip and replied, "No need to make a song and dance about it." He attempted to put his hands in his jacket pockets but couldn't – the beer cans were taking up all the room.

Will stepped out into the road to flag down a passing taxi. The quieter woman tried to work out an umbrella; the taller one stood in the doorway. Lyle and Isaac stood and watched Will. Isaac muttered, "This is weird."

The quiet one managed to open her umbrella, the foul Edinburgh wind pulling at the black material.

Lyle said, "What's weird, Isaac?"

Isaac shot Lyle a look. He went back to watching Will, who was still struggling to flag down a cab. Isaac responded in a loud voice, "Well, we don't normally do this, do we?"

Lyle said nothing.

Isaac continued, "I mean, you've never had people round here before. I know you don't like having them round here. I don't get to meet your friends. Why have they come round here?"

Lyle shrugged. "They wanted to see me before we got there."

"Got where? You aren't telling me anything. That's weird. Stop being weird."

Lyle was smiling as he shook his head. He watched Will and did not look at Isaac. "No, Isaac, there's nothing weird about that. Like, nothing at all. You're being far more argumentative than normal."

Isaac looked away. "You could have said that they were coming."

"What would have happened if you'd known? What would have changed about you?"

Isaac said nothing.

Lyle turned back to Isaac and asked, "What were you expecting, exactly?"

Isaac muttered, "It's just weird, is all."

Lyle kept looking at Isaac. "You know what *is* weird? The fact that you're the one with all the money – much more money than me and Will – but you never take taxis anywhere.

You always walk, you always make us walk. You could easily afford it, but you don't. You've never offered to pay. Not once."

Isaac turned to watch the pavement. The rain was flowing down the street, waves of water flowing downhill, his feet not blocking anything off. It just went around him. He did not look at Lyle when he said, "Then why all this? If *you* can't afford it, Lyle, why aren't we taking the bus?"

Lyle looked back to Will, who was becoming exasperated, standing close to the road. No taxis were coming.

Isaac spoke up again. "I'm just asking questions."

Lyle muttered, "Yes, you're just asking questions."

Isaac turned to him. "What's wrong with just asking questions? I can't help it that I need to know things. Like, how we're all suddenly going out now and how you're all acting weird."

Lyle closed his eyes for a moment. The wind calmed for a second. He breathed out and started, "Isaac—" but Isaac cut in straight away.

"I'm just asking questions. What's wrong with that?"

Lyle said nothing.

The taller woman craned her neck under the umbrella her friend was holding. Isaac turned his head to see them walking over and a taxi coming up the hill with its light on. Isaac immediately strode forward and stood in front of Will. As the taxi pulled round to pick them up, Isaac glared at Will, who wiped water off his face and said nothing.

The other three stayed safe under the umbrella, staying on the pavement. Will was already moving to guide the women inside, opening the door for them. Lyle moved to get Will in, and Isaac walked around the other side and went in by himself.

There were enough seats for everyone, but it was quite cramped, with seats facing each other and a small amount of space between them for their feet to go. Isaac sat in one of the seats with his back to the driver. He looked back at the driver. The driver was turning his head, out to the right to look into the passing traffic. When he drove, he kept his eyes in the rear-view mirror, staring at Will. Will shifted in his seat, looking away from him, looking out the window.

"Is your hair supposed to feel like that?" The taller woman had tried touching Will's hair.

He moved further into his corner. "Yeah, please stop doing that," he replied.

She reached out again and said, "It feels—"

Lyle reached forward and took her hand, saying, "It's bloody awful out there, isn't it?"

There was a general murmur of agreement, and the woman lowered her hand.

Isaac did not look away from the closest window to him while Lyle and Will kept talking about the state of the weather. The taxi slammed on the brakes on the run-up to a red light, and everyone exchanged glances after this quick manoeuvre. Isaac turned his head away from the window to stare at the driver. The driver looked straight ahead, not looking in his mirror. Everyone else exchanged more glances.

Isaac turned his head back to look out the window. It was hard to see out now that it was steamed up from condensation. The taxi's movements were sharp, turning left and right, the engine revving louder as it headed up a hill. They stopped at a set of lights, right next to a waiting bus, the whirr of the engine next to Isaac's side of the taxi. The women started talking and Isaac looked over, but he could not hear what they were saying.

The taxi moved on. The taller woman was speaking to Will. "We met Lyle at … Where was it, Athens?"

The quiet woman answered, "I thought it was Zante?"

The taller one replied, "No, not Zante. That was one of the islands."

Lyle was sitting next to Isaac and was staring out of his own steamed-up window, a mess of lights and lit-up shop windows on his side. He replied, "It was Crete."

The taller one pointed at Lyle and snapped her fingers. "Yeah, that was it! You were on your own and you were so, so quiet all the time."

Lyle kept looking out the window. "Yep, that's what it was."

"So did you guys travel around there?" Will asked.

"Yeah, over a few islands, then back to my parents' place," the taller woman said. "But I think we were going to cut back in and go through Eastern Europe with a bunch of people from Brighton that we met, but we left them because they were a bit *needy*, you know."

Isaac looked over. "How do you mean, *needy*?"

The tall woman spoke, a little slower this time. Isaac looked away when she looked over at him. "I mean, they were very demanding of our time, wanted to know what we were doing all the time, sending us messages when we were out doing things, without leaving us alone, you know? *Anyway*, we needed to get away from them all. We – with Lyle, obviously – we nearly went to Cyprus, but the beaches were better in Egypt."

Lyle looked over at her. He spoke apologetically. "I ran out of money."

"Oh, but we offered to pay, *darling*," the tall woman said. "It wasn't the worst thing in the world, the offer was there – you were so damn proud."

Lyle went back to looking out of the window. He muttered under his breath, "I'd run out of money well before Crete."

The tall woman did not notice this and continued to talk.

“We got so drunk on that first night, remember? We stayed up to watch the sunset on that weird beach that was so remote. It was so quiet! Just us, the only people for miles. You carried me home. What was it we were singing?”

Lyle didn’t answer and she tried again. “Something from the eighties, wasn’t it?”

Lyle shook his head, muttering out a response. “No, can’t remember.”

The taxi lurched to a stop at another set of red lights, the driver shaking his head. Isaac looked backwards through the front window. It was hard to tell where they were. The taxi had headed further north into Edinburgh, a part of town he had never been to, past where he had had his last interview.

There were lines of residential housing, like the kind Isaac had been to with Cullen.

“Big houses,” said Will. Isaac looked over at him. Will was peering upwards through the window. The women were on their phones. “Big fuckin’ houses,” Will muttered.

They had crossed into a more expensive part of town. The buildings became more spaced out; higher hedges and thicker; larger cars, either white, silver, or black – nothing else. There were lights on. Tall and wide windows were lit up but hid behind taller, thicker bushes with clean lines. The occasional metal fence obscured everything behind it. The pavement and parked cars started to pull away, the streets wider without warning.

Isaac looked away from Will, who still looked upward, eyes not resting on anything, wiping the windows down, his mouth opening and closing. He did not say anything more.

Isaac looked over at Lyle. Lyle was still looking back out the window, his head resting against the taxi, as if he were trying to sleep. His eyes did not move or focus on anything in particular – just staring out into the cold.

Isaac looked back at the women, who were still on their

phones. He spoke out loud in the silent taxi. "Hope this road keeps going, eh?"

No one looked at him.

Isaac went back to looking out the window.

The taxi pulled to the left, near a high white wall. The taller woman looked up from her phone and said to the taxi driver, "No, sorry, it was just … The entrance was just back there. Could you turn … Actually, never mind."

The quiet woman pulled her purse out. "I'll pay for that," she said.

The tall woman looked at her friend after seeing the total price, then whispered, "Nineteen fifty."

The quiet woman shook her head, whispering back, "Give me a minute, give me a minute, hang on ..."

The taller woman reached for her purse as well, a thin black thing with a silver trim around the opening.

Will went for the door, but his head turned quickly as he heard the jangle of coins.

The tall woman was shaking her head. "Sorry, I can't see. Can someone put a light on?"

Exactly one second of silence passed and the interior light of the taxi came on. The quieter woman opened her purse and went through it. The three men on either side of the taxi stared at the purses, not looking at each other, doing their best to ignore the gaze of the taxi driver.

The engine kept running. No one said anything.

The quiet woman kept her palm flat as her friend counted through her money, putting a five-pound note down, then five individual pound coins. Then she pulled out a stack of twenty-pence coins, placing them around the pile of pound coins. She bit her lip as she looked into her purse, screwing up her eyes and leaning her neck forward.

Will reached for the door handle, glancing over at the driver. The driver was staring at them.

Will whispered, "I think one of us could pay for it. It's just a twenty-pound note."

The tall woman tutted, counting out a pile of coppers and placing it into the quiet woman's hands, who then put all the money into the hole separating the passengers and driver.

They got out of the cab in silence, and the driver pulled away without counting the money, leaving them by the side of the road, the rain falling steadily onto the pavement. Will and Isaac began to walk back towards the entrance they'd missed; Lyle waited up with the women.

Isaac looked back at them as they walked quickly through the rain. "We should try to let them get ahead of us."

Will kept shaking his head. "Think he wants to chat to them for a bit."

"They're an odd bunch."

Will did not react at first but, after checking they were not in earshot, he said, "I think they're used to a different life-style. But yeah, weird."

Isaac looked at a sports car parked by the side of the road, an old classic car with a retractable roof. He looked back at Lyle, walking between the two women, his hands in his pock-ets. "Why are they talking to him again?"

"What do you mean?"

"As in, why have those girls started talking to him again?"

Will shook his head, looking around for an entrance. "Well. I don't know. Sometimes friends lose touch, doesn't mean that what they did before is just … I don't know. It's history, isn't it? You spend five minutes or a few weeks with someone and you think about them, the stuff they do to you – stuff they do to themselves."

Isaac paused before he replied, "Uh-huh."

Will continued, "It's what friends do. You learn stuff about them, subsequently stuff about people, stuff about yourself." He looked at Isaac for a second, before looking back forward.

Behind them, the three stopped walking, their umbrella torn asunder.

Isaac breathed out of his mouth. "Yup. You've been drinking again. That's some pithy stuff there, Will. What's up with you lately? Always in that sketchbook. What exactly are you drawing?"

Will was already turning his head away when Isaac started talking.

They walked on through the rain. No puddles formed on the pavement – the ground was flat, with no unevenness or blemishes in the pale street light. There was nowhere for the rain to settle. Isaac kept looking at the ground to avoid the rain hitting his face, sharp cold droplets hitting his skin.

They finally found the entrance, and a pathway took them towards the corner of a large house, the front door hidden by a row of columns reaching upwards.

Will blew out a whistle. "Fuck me."

Lyle had caught up with them, the women walking behind him. A thumping noise could be heard coming from inside. As they walked past a window, Isaac glanced inside and saw a mass of people inside. "Christ, there are so many …" he muttered to himself.

They made their way inside. Isaac did not spend time looking at the women in short dresses moving across the floor, their dresses in gold sequins and silver flair or their small black skirts and tanned skin and clear complexions. He did not look at the swatches of red hair in a sea of blonde cuts, the thin frames that they all had. When he walked in, he was looking up at the ceiling. It soared upward, carried on rich white walls and gold trim, possibly twice the height of his own room, maybe three times as much. He stared at a chandelier with its light flowing through the glass, the sight of it hurting his eyes, a spider web of blue and red choking his blinking eyes. He turned around again, his wet feet squelching against the tiled floor.

The others were already moving. Lyle had been introduced to someone and was led away. Isaac and Will followed him a few feet behind, outside of the circle which was forming around Lyle. The man Lyle was with was a head taller than Isaac. The women had been dragged off and were laughing with a group of large men around them, drinks in their hands, walking into a room with more pretty faces and lingering eyes.

The man with Lyle spoke in a Scottish brogue, but there was a lot going on in the background – female chatter down one hallway, the clatter of glasses down another – and Isaac missed what the man had said and could not find his way back into the conversation. The man wore a dark navy suit with a gold tie. Isaac stared at the pocket square – it was a gold colour, which matched his tie, and had a navy-blue border, which matched the suit. It kept its perfect triangular shape as he turned to face his guests. He had a thick beard, which looked well-groomed. He was laughing, drowning out the conversation immediately around him, as if he were singing an old song. He glanced over at Lyle when he laughed. Lyle had been looking at him the whole time without smiling.

"… so yes, make yourselves at home," the man said.

Isaac tried to manoeuvre himself so he was part of the semi-circle which had formed around the tall man, but there was no room for him. He hung around behind the backs of his friends. He sneezed, his hair still wet from the rain outside. A few people turned around to look at him before turning back to the man. Isaac brushed his hair flat with his hand. Two women in shiny cocktail dresses walked past without looking at him. Isaac glanced at them but said nothing.

Isaac reached inside his jacket and pulled out a can. He opened it and the can foamed up immediately. He placed the can to his lips. There was not much else for him to do. His friends were busy talking, so he would have to move to the edge of the semi-circle to even listen to what was going on. He took another drink. A group of women and a tall, muscular man walked past, still talking. Will was talking loudly, something about his sales job. There was so much background noise that Isaac couldn't make it out.

The tall man left them to speak with another new crowd of people coming in. Lyle looked away to Isaac's right. He walked away and Will followed. Isaac turned to look at the crowd who had entered. There were six of them, men and women, all pleasant to look at, all smiling and dressed up and standing around the tall man. Then Isaac looked at Lyle, who was walking up the stairs without looking back.

Isaac followed Lyle up the stairs, catching up to him. "Do you know where you're going?"

Lyle did not respond. Will had fallen just behind them, looking up at the ceiling. "Cornices, look!"

Isaac turned around to ask, "Will, what are you talking about?"

Will pointed upward at the ornate designs running along the edge of the ceiling. Isaac brushed his hand along the banister as they walked up, not letting go. It was a wide staircase, the banister a deep dark brown, well-varnished and smooth. He did not let go of it.

Will pointed up again. "Up there, in the corners."

Isaac didn't look. He turned around to follow Lyle.

"Isaac, look!" Will said.

Lyle looked up, then ahead. A group of four women were coming down the stairs. There was room enough for everyone to pass by each other. Isaac glanced at them and suddenly spoke when they came close enough. "Will, I have no fucking idea what you're talking about."

Will said nothing. The women coming downstairs looked at him. Isaac continued to berate him. "You're always saying something stupid. Honestly!"

Will looked at his feet the rest of the way up.

The stairs came up to a landing; another set of stairs at the end continued upwards to another floor.

Lyle looked behind him, checking for movement. He whispered to the two, "This way."

There was a room just to one side which was open – a large bedroom, probably just smaller in size than the flat they all shared.

Lyle breathed out as they entered, closing the door behind them. "We're going to sit here and drink. I've been here before. There's a mini fridge here. One second …"

Isaac stayed standing while the others moved to a sofa on the other side of the room. The bed was twice the size of Isaac's own bed, but even then it only took up a small portion of the room. He took a few steps forward towards it. He turned back to watch Will staring around the room. It was painted dark green and white. The bottom half of the wall was green, the top half white. There was no unevenness in the way it was painted – it was exactly half and half, the green a little lighter than the shade of the carpet, which stretched in from the corridor. Isaac looked at the white walls, then back to Lyle.

Lyle was sitting with his back against the bed. He called out to Isaac, "It's decent here, isn't it?"

Isaac turned to look at the door. He snapped back, "Lyle, where the hell are we? Where the hell are we, Lyle?"

Lyle raised his arms a little, opening one palm, a bottle of beer in the other, taken from the fridge. He pondered Isaac's questions for a few seconds before breathing out a response. "Calm down, Isaac."

Isaac wagged his finger. "Don't tell me to calm down."

"I got in contact with some old friends," Lyle said. "Awful people – but they have other, decent friends. As you can see."

The three of them paused as they heard footsteps running down the corridor. There were people coming up and down stairs, audible through the door. Isaac's ears pricked up at the sound of English accents – loud men talking over female chattering.

Isaac stopped pointing and Lyle lowered his hands.

Isaac said, in a quieter tone, "So, what? Your friends just turn up and you … you take advantage of that?"

Lyle looked away for a second and he frowned. He finally replied, "Well, it's not really like that. More of a … It's weird, actually – I just kept texting them, and they texted back. They keep wanting to drag me places."

"And what? They drag you places, then what?"

Lyle glanced at Will for a second before continuing. "I go drinking, I get talking to people. I think I made it up as I went along. I just kept … being places, going out all the time. I've been here a few times. It's been wilder than this – look, it's just been *better* for me, trying this out, doing new things. It's a bit mad."

Isaac drank the rest of his can in one go. He did not talk.

Will spoke up. "That's … great and everything, but are you good? You've barely been in the flat or anything."

Lyle took a long drink. "I know. I know, I know. It's … it's not forever."

Will looked confused. "What's not forever?"

"None of this. None of this is forever. We're drinking in a fancy house for one night, then we're … We're not doing this forever, I'm just having a mad week. That's all it is. Next week – it'll be better next week."

Isaac shook his head. "So, what? You had a mad partying week and didn't invite any of us?"

Lyle breathed out. "I'm cutting down drinking. I'm not stopping, but I'm cutting it down. I'm serious. I'm serious! I've hit the crest of a wave here. Turns out being social at work all the time pays off when you're with powerful people who want people to talk to."

Will opened his mouth to speak, but Isaac cut in. "So, one big week and it's all too much for you? You can't be arsed."

"No, it's them – it's all of them," Lyle insisted. "They do this because they can afford to. Not afford the drinking, it's all the other things. Their homes, their jobs, they're all there for them. They're all dicks to each other as well. Almost like it's something to do. I mean, I'm bored of it all, bored of it. The two that got me in here, they've used me for making drinks and being something to show off. I'm moving away from them and making better connections. But then … I can't spend crazy amounts of time with these people. They're – not awful – they're just this way, that's all."

Isaac was shaking his head. "Mate, you're rambling, why can't you use one word instead of talking? This is just … bollocks. Bollocks. Bollocks. So, you just turn up out of the blue and start being everyone's friend, right? What exactly do you offer to these people, exactly? What is it you give them?"

Lyle was silent. He stared at Isaac. He did not say anything.

Isaac opened and closed his mouth a few times. Will stood back. Isaac finally broke the silence. "I'm serious. What is it, exactly? Why you? What makes you so special, huh? What is it?"

Lyle continued to stare.

Isaac looked away as he tried again. "What is it? What is it?!"

No one said anything. They all waited. One by one, they took a drink. Will sat close to Lyle, his eyes on the floor. Lyle kept staring at Isaac. Isaac looked away, moving closer to the wall.

After a minute of this, Isaac sat on the floor with his back to the wall, legs spread, across from Lyle. Isaac had finished one can and put it on the carpet, the light weight of it causing it to fall over. He left it there for a second. Something spilled out of it. He lifted it and tried to make it stand by itself. It came down again. Isaac lifted it again, angling the can upright. He watched it for a few seconds. He waited for it to balance. He raised his hands like someone patting a dog, palms facing down on the can. The can held on. He moved his hand and pressed the ground around the can, testing if the movement around the carpet would do anything to it. Nothing happened. The carpet was immensely firm. The can remained upright.

Lyle was sat on the bed. He looked over at Isaac. He called out, "Do you want a bin for that, Isaac?"

Isaac continued to stare at the can. He shouted across the room, "No."

Lyle waited a few seconds before replying, "Isaac, what are you doing?

"I'm doing whatever the fuck I want."

Lyle shook his head and looked back to Will. "Amazing."

Isaac did not look up. "What's wrong with that?"

Lyle did not look back, still looking at Will. He said, "It's been five minutes. You've been doing that for five minutes."

Isaac took out his phone. It fell out of his hand. He picked it up. No new texts. "It's not been five minutes."

"All right, Isaac."

"You're wrong, Lyle." Isaac raised his voice. "It's not

been five minutes. You can't just throw out numbers like that, can't just make things up." He opened another can.

They all sat drinking. Two men, tall and thin, poked their head through the door then turned without really reacting to the three.

Isaac had his phone out, typing another text to his ex. Will called out across the room, "You're not texting Dylan, are you?"

Isaac looked up, dropping the phone on the ground, shouting across the room, "Are we serious – is that definitely over and done with? We're just ignoring Dylan forever?"

Someone outside the room was laughing. The music had been turned up somewhere and there was chatter through the corridor. There was a crowd of people coming upstairs; something was happening. Isaac watched the door but no one came in.

Will sighed, sounding exhausted. "Yes, Isaac. Yes, it is," he said. "We aren't speaking to him – he was always shit to be around. Like, ever so mildly racist. I mean, fuck, he's horrible to women. I was trying to be cool about it – me and Lyle decided it. That's what happened."

Lyle nodded. "Exactly. Exactly! Look, we're getting older now – we don't need to hang around with people like him. We're moving on, we don't need to sit down and talk to him about every single thing he's done wrong – we aren't in a court of law or anything."

"So, we're not going to have a discussion about it?" Isaac snapped. "What about free speech?"

Will and Lyle looked at each other with strained expressions. Will finally said, "There's not much to discuss, Isaac. What's the point of talking about free speech when we've been over the arguments before? Who actually benefits from that? I'm trying to get fucking … I'm miserable, all the time, and you act like it's nothing—"

Isaac cut Will off mid-sentence. "Don't see why we're sitting in this room. We should go out there." He reached for another beer in his pocket, opened it, took a swig, and put it down next to the other can. He picked up the other already open one and took a long swig.

Lyle pleaded, "Isaac."

Isaac held up his finger. "The one thing we could agree on is that Dylan could get out there. Like, he'd walk into a room and start talking to people."

"Oh *wow*, he has some social skills," Lyle said. "We did not invite him, Isaac, because he's a bad fucking guy."

Isaac waved his hand for a few seconds as he drank, spitting beer out as he talked back. "Yeah, because we rocked up to this room and hid in the corner. No one knows who we are. We're just that awkward bunch of people hanging about in the kitchen, or the bedroom, or whatever."

Will and Lyle looked away from Isaac. Lyle breathed out. "Well, we're not though," he said. "We're just taking a break, that's all. There's a lot going on downstairs. It'll get quieter."

Isaac nearly started talking again but he stopped. He took another swig of his beer. It was quickly empty. He looked at it with puzzlement. "It's just weird. That's all." Isaac felt for the other beer. He picked it up, felt the weight of it. There was not much in it. His lip was quivering.

Will muttered to Lyle, "It's better that he tries to get the hint." They both looked over at Isaac.

Isaac said, "We should go. Let's go talk to people and quit all this negative shit."

Will said, "Isaac, do you maybe just want to … talk a bit? We're a bit worried about you. It's just, you won't ever talk to anyone – it's a bit odd. Where are you going all the time?"

Isaac was already up. He left the room, not waiting for the others, not taking his drink with him.

Lyle and Will watched him leave.

They waited for him to go.

They started talking to each other. It wasn't a long conversation. It didn't need to be. Lyle told Will his news, told him about his future. They drank to his success. It had been one of the few conversations they'd had in months that wasn't about Isaac, a fact that both silently understood.

Isaac looked behind him for a moment. There were roars of laughter upstairs. Isaac paused, as if someone was about to come out of the bedroom, pull him back in. He turned away. He stared at the stairs that kept winding up, chatter and noise, a mess of conversations that he couldn't pick up. He needed to pee. He moved for the banister in front of him, looking down at the ground, then back up. The staircase kept rising and rising, round and round.

He turned to move downstairs. The entrance hall was now empty. He took a left. Another empty room, then the kitchen in the next open space. It was completely out of step with the ornate stylings of the house. There were white tiles on the floor, black on the walls, clean silver counters and ovens. It was empty, bar for two people, a dark-haired woman in a colourful dress and another man, two inches taller than her, with large forearms and a blue shirt. Isaac muttered an apology and left them to it.

As he left, he turned around, watching them talk. Isaac could not see her face. He muttered another apology and moved.

There was no sign of a toilet.

He kept walking. He went back around in a loop, back into the entranceway, back into the room next to it, back into the kitchen. The pair he had left were now kissing. Isaac moved away quickly, his shoes still wet enough to make a sound on the kitchen floor.

He went back into the entranceway and paused. He moved slowly back upstairs, back towards the noise, back towards the room they had been in originally. His two flatmates were not there. His drink had been left alone. Isaac went into the walk-in bathroom that was in the bedroom. When he finished, he sat back down where he had sat before, a little more upright and alert than before. He placed his hand on the wall. When he took his hand away, there was no imprint, no indication that anything had ever been there at all. He sat there drinking, looking at the doorway then back down to where his can had been.

He finished his can and threw it over the bed. It hit the radiator and made a noise.

Isaac looked around the empty room. He cried out, "I should have been here. Here all along. Fucking Lyle!"

He stood up, moved out of the room and upstairs. He reached into his pocket for his last can.

He was met by a man and a woman slowly walking downstairs, holding hands, not saying anything. Isaac watched them until they reached the corner for the stairway, then he kept moving up.

On the next floor were more rooms. Two women giggled as they nearly bumped into him, their laughter more muted as they moved off. Isaac glanced after them. Neither of them looked back.

There was a sudden cheer, whistling, laughter and clapping from one room on the left, and Isaac walked over to the doorway. It was blocked off by two men looking into the room. Both were bulky and large, quietly standing next to each other without talking, both still. They did not react to what was going on.

There was no way to see what was going on inside with the two men in the way. Isaac got on his tiptoes but couldn't see. There was an extended noise from the crowd in the room. Isaac stared down at his feet, back to the ground, his shoes bending. He reached as high as he possibly could without falling forward.

He stared at the back of the heads of the men in front of him. They did not react. They did not look at each other. There was no sense of what was going on inside.

There was a lull in the noise and the sound of someone with Will's accent saying something, then the sound of laughter further into the room. Above the heads of the men, Isaac could see shadows moving against the ceiling, vague iterations of shapes that he could not make out, duelling with each other, caught in a frame in the high white ceiling. The noise of talking and cheering and laughing made everything indistinct and audible at once.

Isaac stood there for a couple of minutes. No one came out. He did not ask to go in. He spent much of his time staring at the backs of the two men, who never moved. Neither of them was drinking. The voice which sounded like Will's was not audible. A few people passed behind Isaac. Isaac did not move to let them past, so they had to squeeze past him. He moved off down the corridor, finishing his drink. He ran a hand along one of the walls, the stone cold and flat. There was not a loose flick of paint, nothing. At the end of the corridor was a window that took up the tall height of the corridor. Rain and wind battered against it, the shape of a tall tree moving, the light of an amber street light behind it.

He was still holding the empty can in his hand. He tripped up a little, just as a couple were leaving a room; two women quietly holding hands, moving in single file past Isaac without raising their heads.

There was a room on the right that was quiet, the floor a fresh dark timber which did not look polished, did not look worn. It looked alive. A thin red rug lay at the centre of the room. The room was lined with books, thick volumes that were grouped together by colour, rows of red, rows of blue, small gold lettering on their spines shining in the light from a thick green lampshade.

Isaac stepped into the room. There was a woman sitting by herself reading a book on a sofa. There was an identical one across from it. Isaac ignored her. The curtains were drawn. Darkness filled the four corners, oddities cast in shadow – a globe, a writing desk, a closed wooden cupboard.

Isaac went up to the bookshelves. On closer inspection, the blue books consisted of history – Scottish and English, volumes covering ten years each, all equal in their size and shape. The red books concerned something about 'Natural' Philosophy. He tutted.

Isaac turned to look at the woman. His eyes stayed on her for a few seconds. It was someone he had met before – the barista from the coffee shop. The book she was reading was a thinner volume. Its cover was white with black lettering, some sort of pattern on the front, maybe an animal, maybe a person. It was hard to tell; her hand covered part of it. It did not have the same quality of the other books, the same age or conformity to it. It did not belong to the library.

Isaac looked back at the bookcase. He said, "I don't think anyone's ever read any of those books, far as I can tell."

She did not respond.

He continued to talk. "I'm scared to try and take one, in case the whole thing topples over."

The woman did not look up from her book when she replied. Her words were slow and clear. "I guess you won't know what that looks like until you yank one out, see what happens."

Isaac held his hand over a book from the eighteenth century – it was dated on the spine, not on the cover. A collection of studies on ethics. He tutted. He reached towards it, spun his head back towards the woman. He said, "Nothing happened. Do you think if I pull the right one, a door opens up?"

The woman did not look up. "What would you want to find behind the door?"

"What?"

She looked up. "The secret door. What would you want to find behind it? Anything at all, anything you could imagine." She blinked a few times.

Isaac turned back. "I don't know. I don't know. That's a strange question."

She gave Isaac a strained look. She turned a page – not forward, but backward. Her voice remained calm. "It's not a strange question at all."

Isaac shrugged. "It's a bit weird, that's all. Doesn't mean anything. What do you think? What would you find?"

The woman frowned. "I don't think I'd know until I opened the door. I mean, you can't really know what you want until it appears in front of you. Sometimes that stuff happens out of nowhere. You can't help that it happens, but you keep going anyway."

Isaac glanced at her. She turned another page. Isaac looked back to the books, up to the rows at the top, just as preserved as the ones on the bottom. He said, "So, you're just kind of moving through life, waiting for something to happen."

She shook her head as she read. "Nah, not really. What would you want to find?"

Isaac screwed up his face a little. "Money, definitely money for me. Which isn't … It's what comes with it, that's the thing. Security and that. Money buys things that *lead* to happiness. I could move out of my flat, finally, get around better people, people with places like—"

"Like this?" she interrupted.

Isaac started walking around the room, examining the

books. The colours turned from green to black, fine leather, not a blemish in sight, the gold writing engraved perfectly throughout. He muttered to himself, "I mean, why not?"

The woman turned another page and continued to talk. "It's just a party. It's none of the other stuff. The squabbles over money, the failed marriages, kids in rehab. Why are you here then, if you don't know anyone?"

Isaac looked at her, staring at the back of her head. He looked back at the doorway. They were still alone. He spoke up, a little slowly. "I came here with some people."

She waited a few seconds, turning the page. She replied in the same concentrated tone as before. "Same. So, where are they just now?"

He was walking round to the other side. Geography, geology. The bookcases were tall, with three shelves that ran above Isaac. There was no way of reaching up. "They're being … I live with them. They're just not the same now. It used to be … better? In a way. I don't know what's happening with them. They just snap at me all the time now, like they know something I don't."

"Why do you think that is?"

He came back to where he had started. He stared at the woman, who didn't look up. He took off his jacket and made his way to the sofa across from the woman. She did not move. But she did turn a page. She smiled a little, her eyes still scanning the pages.

Isaac looked down at her bare knees, one stacked on top of the other, her legs crossed over. Her raised foot was swinging in time with the faint sound of music in another room. He looked at the bookshelves closest to him. He said, "There's no fiction. Like, there's all this stuff that's here, right?" He gestured with his hands, making his fingers wave. "But then there's nothing to actually read. It's all just reference material that's out of date. So much of this is useless anyway."

The woman glanced up from her book. "I disagree – there's value to all of it. Just depends on where you find it."

Isaac pointed at her book. "Then why are you reading your own book?"

The woman closed her book, keeping her place with one hand. "I always bring books with me. I like reading."

Isaac screwed up his face. "You carry books around with you?"

She did not respond. She just stared at him.

He muttered to himself, "I wouldn't say it's annoying."

She kept looking at him and said, "Bothersome?"

"It's not really something I can relate to."

"What do you mean?"

Isaac shrugged. "I don't read that much. It's always people that read a lot who talk about reading a lot, like they're better than people that don't. Like I'm missing out or something. It's—"

"So, you feel like you're missing out?" she interrupted.

They locked eyes for a second. Isaac looked away. There was noise from the corridor, people chanting something, moving downstairs. Isaac turned his eyes to the doorway leading to the world beyond. "No, I'm not missing out on anything. You can just do what you want, it's …whatever."

She gave a small smile. "Well, that's decent then. I've always thought there was something … snobbish about saying that kind of thing. Like seeing people do something well, all by themselves, is somehow bad. It's just a sort of judgement on yourself. You have to let people live their life, if you want to do it your way. It swings both ways. You have to let people have a swing, to see how far they can get. Learn some things on the way." The woman went back to her book.

Isaac tried again. "I just don't get it. There's some strange *fascination* people have about it. I mean, I read – everyone reads – but there's something exhausting about people who do that sort of thing. Like, they think they have … They don't have common sense, is what I mean. It doesn't make you special."

She did not say anything.

Isaac stared at the ceiling. He reached for where he thought he would have a can to drink, but there was nothing there. "Why are you on your own? Don't see you starting a book club anywh—"

"Sorry – you've mentioned the books thing already, but what's this about being special? I'm reading a book, that's all I'm doing. I'm not trying anything. You're just being rude."

Isaac closed his mouth, fell back on the sofa. The woman had put her book down and replaced it with a glass of champagne.

Isaac looked around him, his face red, muttering, "No, it's not that – did not mean that. It was just that there's more interesti … I'm more interested in more random things, like useless bits of information. Like with Medelev … no—"

"Mendeleev?" the woman offered.

Isaac waved his hand and carried on. "Yes, when Mendeleev developed the periodic table, he left some of it empty, empty for elements that he hadn't discovered, that no one had discovered, but for bits – things – that were there. He knew they were there, but not what those things were." Isaac tapped his pockets for his can, shaking his head. He kept going. "So, he knew there were chemical elements out there that hadn't been – yeah, he knew there were things out there – something below alum … No, was it copper? No, gallium, something below gallium – that sounds familiar, yeah."

"That's interesting," the woman said. She looked away.

"Yeah, things like that. I like that." Isaac also looked

away, muttering, "Yeah, I like that sort of thing. Bits of useless knowledge. Chemistry facts."

The woman shook her head. "Not that it's useless. It's interesting, that's what it is. Like it's …there's a reason."

Isaac stared at the ground for a few seconds before looking back at her. Words rolled out of his mouth. "You know, I learnt about that from a friend at university – my only friend at university, come to think of it. He talked about that one day, went on and on about it. I can't remember much about him now because it was so long ago and he just vanished out of the blue, but it's that one thing that I can remember him saying to me. Like, I remember it from time to time when I'm trying to do other things. I don't know what the reason is."

A group of people walked into the room, their intrusion drowning out Isaac's words. He turned to them with a look of frustration, and they promptly left when they saw Isaac and the woman on the sofas. Isaac watched them go. Two of the women were staring at him as they left.

When he turned around, the woman with the book was still looking at him. She pointed below Isaac, and said, "Try reaching under your seat."

Isaac leaned forward. He had left his jacket in an untidy, folded mess next to him and his movement forward made it fall off the sofa. He did not reach for it. He tapped around on the floor with his hand on the floor. He tapped left and right.

She watched him do this for a while. Then she said, "I recognise you from somewhere – you're seriously here on your own?"

Isaac groaned as he bent over. "Had an argument with my friends – hang on." He got off the sofa and onto his knees, now on all fours, reaching down and finding a plastic bag with some beer cans left in it. "Not my fault, they've gotten worse now that they're older. They've lost a step somewhere.

It's … They aren't trying hard enough any more at it, then they're surprised that they aren't that good at it. These things take practice." When he was back on the sofa, he snatched at one of the cans, ripping it out of the bag.

The woman neither spoke nor touched her drink.

Isaac said, "I'm sure I've seen you - I'm Isaac."

The woman raised her eyebrows for a quick second. "Diane. Might have been at work – I work in a coffee place in town."

Isaac nodded. "Nice to meet you."

Diane nodded. "My real name's Ariadne; don't like being called that, but there you go. Think my mum thought it would make me sound *sophisticated*." She put emphasis on the final word, screwing up her eyebrows and reaching for her drink.

Isaac joined in with her, saying, "My folks were like that as well. They're still travelling."

Diane nodded. "That's interesting. Have you ever gone abroad to see them?"

Isaac talked at the same fast speed as her. "Why would I want to hang around with my mum and dad? I don't see the point, really. I'm not going to scrounge off them. They've always been … They're boring. Really boring." He put the beer down on the table in front of him. His hands were shaking.

Diane watched him do all this in silence, watching his hands, the strained expression on his face. "Are you all right?" she asked.

Isaac nodded quite rapidly. He spluttered out, "Yeah, I'm good. I'm good all the time, really."

She paused and then nodded a little.

He picked away at the sofa with his free hand.

Diane was going back to her drink. Isaac saw this and said quickly, "I – uh – the cornices in here look nice."

She looked up, at the same time he did. The cornices were

white in contrast to the dark colours of the room. She put her drink back down. "They are nice. Georgian era, part of the original fittings in this place. That's good that you're picking that sort of stuff out. It's those little details—"

Isaac interrupted. "Nah, it's not. Don't care about that stuff."

She started leaning forward to listen to him.

Isaac took a swig and kept talking. "It just feels forced, you know? Like, I don't talk about this stuff. It's just things in the room; you don't learn anything about it just because you know random trivia. It's not like – it's just stuff that's good for a quiz. So why does it stick out? Like, I can't remember important things, things that get me jobs. It's not like we're doing a pub quiz or something – I can't – I don't need to make other people happy. I need to just get myself there, get myself sorted out, then everything will be fine. Once I've done me, once I've got that sorted, I'm good."

Diane nodded.

Isaac was getting louder. He slowed down, raising the beer to his mouth, hitting his bottom front teeth. Then he rambled on. "I mean, it's important to me. I want it, for myself. I don't care what people think. I'm allowed to have what I want – you know what I mean? I don't understand why it's so much bother for everyone else, like, my life needs to be commented on or something. I don't care – I don't really need it or anything. I don't need that kind of person in my life. Well, I guess so – I don't think I've had that issue specifically. I mean, I do feel out of joint sometimes with my friends. I guess I'm great a lot of the time, but I'm listening at least, you know?"

Diane took a long drink and nodded.

Isaac kept going. "I guess it's more … It's not like I'm lacking direction or anything. That's normal – normal enough, I mean. I mean … it's difficult when everyone around you is doing well. You want to be near them, I guess, you want to be near a strong port in a storm, some people – people who know where they're going, at least."

"What do you think they say about you?" Diane asked. "Your friends?"

"Don't know. I think Will and Lyle, they're—"

Diane straightened up at the mention of Lyle's name. "Oh, is it that Lyle? The tall one? I met him already, like, a week ago."

Isaac nodded and took a long drink. Diane kept going. "That's why … I think they mentioned your mate, Lyle – something about a new restaurant on George Street. Think they know – well, everyone knows everyone. I've met him before, actually, only in passing. You mentioned his name and it rang a bell. Think he's in with some guys who work in London. I mean, I'm in that crowd, I'm with that crowd. Sorry. I'm so drunk. He's a nice guy, Lyle. So, you live with him?"

Isaac thought about this for a few seconds. He muttered, "Yeah, he mentioned that was happening."

Diane was all smiles, taking a drink before she said, "He'll end up making it big, by the sounds of it. It's weird how Edinburgh works like that – it's such a small place, everyone knows everyone. I've had the same sort of friends since university; I met them because they knew people from back home. Do you know anyone?"

Isaac was looking at her feet, the can his hands. He spoke quietly. "No. I'm from a really small village in the Borders."

Diane kept smiling. "Oh, how lovely."

Isaac nodded. "Yeah, a properly small place, actually – on the outskirts of it, actually. Had to go to school in a place miles away. So yeah, pretty small."

"Sounds lovely. Do you go there a lot? Must be nice – you must feel quite determined, like you're meant to become someone. Small beginnings, sense of purpose and all that."

Isaac glanced at her, his eyes swimming between the darkness from the window and her blue eyes. He muttered again, "I guess that's true. But my folks are travelling now. Been doing that for ages. I don't speak to them. And I honestly don't want to – I think folk who travel a lot get pretty high-minded, but then they come back and forget who they're talking to. Like, my experience matters a little less because I'm not looking at old rocks or some shit. I'm a pretty productive guy in my down time. Can't manage to do what they do. Can't stand the holiday shit. It's when folk don't tell you what they're doing, then they don't bring …" He trailed off and stayed silent. There were cheers coming from down below – away from the room, far away from where he was.

Diane spoke slowly. "I know what you mean, Isaac. I get lost in supermarkets, my own house – I missed a flight to Greece once when I was in the departure lounge. Burst into tears, had to come home, missed a whole trip."

Isaac was shaking. He put the can down on the table with a jerk, his hands moving around. He muttered, "That's shit."

Diane had her glass of wine in front of her, staring into the glass. Isaac still stared at her feet. She kept talking. "Don't really know where to go sometimes. I don't know, it's like … where do my friends go when it's all done? Like, where are they all going to? I can't really – sorry, this is all very deep chat. It's like I can't stop relying on them, it's all very—"

"Lyle, fuck sake," Isaac spoke out loud, not listening to her, talking over her.

Diane looked up, startled. "Sorry?"

Isaac muttered to himself, "Once this is all over. I'll go home."

Diane kept looking at Isaac. "Don't think this party is ending soon."

Isaac closed his eyes for a few seconds, opening them to look past her, to the books around him, the warm glow of the lights, the ambience of the room. "When it's all done. I'll never see it again."

"Are you okay?"

Isaac was rubbing his face. He stood up, then tried to sit down again, before going out of the room.

Diane called after him, "Isaac?"

When he was out into the corridor, he leaned against the wall, shifting his weight on his feet. There was something forming at the back of his throat. He was leaning forward as he walked, or at least half-walked, nearly walking into one couple coming upstairs. He kept moving down without looking back. He leaned over the handrail as he walked downstairs, glancing at people coming upstairs. He muttered as they passed, "Fucking Lyle. Don't tell me shit, then."

He was back downstairs. He turned into the side room off the entrance hall. There were groups of people sitting around, men in suits with their ties undone, women sitting far into the corner, one woman in tears being consoled by her friends. Isaac looked at them all, their faces unknown to him, none of them looking back. Will and Lyle weren't there. There were some people singing around a piano to a song Isaac did not recognise. The noise of the singing became louder as Isaac moved away, the echo sounding out through the room, people turning their heads towards the music.

Isaac kept muttering. " … hands plates around for a few years and then gets a fucking free pass."

He was back in the entrance hall, and he went towards the front door. He had not let go of the beer can in the entire time since he had left Diane. He placed the can on the ground. The door was awkward to open. A large, thick doorknob proved difficult to turn, solid to the touch. He attempted to pull it for about a minute, only to look up and locate a lock higher up which was keeping the door closed.

The weather had worsened. Isaac walked forward onto the lawn. There was no sign of the path he had taken when coming in. He found it eventually. The chatter and music were gone now.

He walked home in the rain by himself, texting his ex-girlfriend over and over.

CHAPTER TEN

Isaac had been sitting at the bus shelter for some time. Tree branches cast shadows along the ground in the distance. The wind had slowed down but came in bursts which swept at Isaac's feet. There was no one around. His hands were in his pockets, curled into fists. His mouth hung open, and he watched the cold breath leave his mouth and disappear into the night.

The bus stop was down a suburban street in the south of the city. Isaac had walked there, as per Cullen's instructions. Isaac had the timings wrong and had left too late. There was no sign of Cullen. The roads glowed the same amber colour from the street lights, all bar one; a light across the road had turned red, burning out from old age. Isaac stared at it for a bit.

He curled his toes and tapped his feet on the ground a few times. A car was approaching and stopped at a set of traffic lights. He looked away from it, down the other side of the street. The wind was carrying the rhythmic tap-tap of the car's engine downwind. Isaac pressed his feet down, tapping them on the floor.

Isaac stood up, gave a long breath. He sniffed, snot

forming in his nose and dripping down into the back of his throat.

He went to leave. He moved slowly at first, his hands still stuck in his pockets, hunched over a little, staring at the ground. He turned left, with the wind at his back. He did not look ahead of him. He pulled his hood down as much as possible, a symbolic gesture more than anything else.

The sound of the car became more laboured as it approached. Isaac moved further to the left, away from the road. He turned his head right but did not fully turn around to look at the car.

The car passed Isaac. It was a small vehicle, an older model. After moving a few feet forward, the yellow indicator flashed on, the brake lights came on. The car pulled closer to the pavement, just past Isaac.

Isaac didn't look at it. He quickened his pace. His heart was beating against his ribcage. His shoulders were hunched.

The car moved again, slowly, the engine whirring steadily, winding down as it reached Isaac's side again. The window whirred down. The face of the man inside was cast in darkness. The man shouted from the car, "It's me." The voice belonged to Cullen, talking over the noise of the engine.

Isaac peered into the car, bending down.

Cullen continued, "You're half an hour late."

Isaac came closer and said, "I didn't know you had a car."

Cullen shrugged from behind the wheel. "What's that got to do with you being thirty minutes late?"

Isaac paused, but then he shouted over the noise of the car, "To be honest, Cullen, I'd thought you'd given up on me already. You've not—"

Cullen shook his head, talking over him. "No, sorry."

Isaac pointed his finger, shouting louder. "Don't interrupt me. You've vanished again with your weird—"

Cullen was still shaking his head. “Isaac, I can’t hear what you’re saying. Get in the car.”

Isaac got in the passenger side. The car was warm enough. Isaac turned to Cullen. “When did you get a car?”

Cullen was winding the windows down manually. “Just something I’ve borrowed. Put your seat belt on.” He had turned his head right, looking down the road. He waited until Isaac had put on his seat belt, put the car in gear and turned the wheel, going back onto the road and carefully accelerating.

Isaac spoke quietly. “Stolen?”

Cullen kept his eyes on the road.

From Isaac’s view, the front of the car was all plastic: hot air blasting out from sets of small round heaters, the radio set-up with a CD player. The clock was an hour out of time. Cullen’s hands were steady on the wheel, his eyes checking the rear-view mirror.

Isaac did not look away from Cullen. He asked another question. “So, you just found it?”

“Stop talking about the car.”

“Why can’t I talk about the car?”

Cullen waited a second before spluttering out, “Okay, why do you want to talk about the car?”

Isaac looked ahead at a set of traffic lights. Cullen slowed down. There was no one else around. Isaac said, “Because we just walked everywhere before.”

“It would have been a bit obvious driving around in one car all the time, don’t you think?”

Isaac muttered, “We could have done a few jobs with a car, at least when I was there.”

“And you vanished. You wanted out. What have you been doing in that time?”

Isaac looked out the window. They were heading further south, to the outskirts of the city. He muttered, “Nothing.”

Cullen nodded. "Fine, then." He picked up speed as they approached the bypass. The dark outline of the Pentland Hills showed up against the night sky, lights on the dry ski slope.

Isaac began to speak again but without ever looking at Cullen. "I'm not sorry. You're different, Cullen, you're really different and, to be honest, I don't like you. I've never liked you; you're kind of a prick. Prick. That's what you are. I can have the money, I'm fine with the money, but I'm better with you out … not being here."

Cullen smirked before he responded. "You said you liked the money?"

Isaac turned his head. Cullen hadn't looked away from the road. Isaac snapped back, "Yeah, I do."

"You'll like where we're going then."

Isaac examined Cullen's face. He looked self-satisfied, like he had won a bet. Isaac looked away with a frown. Isaac tried to take off his jacket, but it was difficult with the seat belt attached. He started by unzipping the jacket but struggled with the zip. He still had to get his arms out of the sleeves. He tried pulling the left sleeve away by using his right hand, but that made no difference. He leant forward in order to give himself some space, but it was still awkward.

Cullen sighed. "Isaac, do you want the heat turned down?"

"No."

"So, you don't want any help?"

"No."

Cullen smirked again. "Okay."

Isaac waited a few seconds then said, "I don't need help. I'm great, thanks."

"You could have taken it off before."

"I'm fine. This takes a minute," Isaac snapped.

"Okay, Isaac."

Isaac looked over at Cullen with a glare. "You're being weird."

Cullen sighed again. "I'm not being weird."

"You steal for a living."

No one said anything for a while afterwards. The sound of the heater felt louder; it was at the forefront of Isaac's senses, the hot air reaching a point in front of Isaac's face and going no further. His eyes were watering.

Cullen nodded. He did not look at Isaac and muttered to himself, "That much is true. Not forever, though. Not forever."

Isaac stopped fiddling with his jacket and tried to get the seat to move back instead. He reached to his right side, moving close towards the gearstick by accident. Then he turned to his left side, reached under the seat and found a lever. He pulled it and the seat immediately moved backward, carried by the forward momentum of the car, leaving Isaac with his legs sticking out in front of him.

Cullen did not look across. He was looking at his rear-view mirror, at a car that was behind them.

Isaac moved the seat forward again with some deliberation. He turned back to Cullen and asked a question. "Where are we going?"

Cullen did not respond. Isaac tried again. "Cullen, I'm only asking because you've not got a satnav. Is there a map? You need directions?"

Cullen still did not respond.

Isaac looked out the window. He slapped his thighs, doing a quick drum roll and using the passenger door as a symbol. Isaac muttered, "I had better shoes for this."

"Better shoes?"

Isaac moaned out a response. "No, not shoes, boots – bought new hiking boots last week. Went to a proper shop to get them. Like, really, really thick. Really warm to wear. They give me an extra inch in height, probably."

Cullen turned to Isaac for a second to say, "So why aren't you wearing them? I told you it was far away, outdoors."

Cullen turned back to the road. Isaac hadn't looked away from the window, but he now turned his head to examine Cullen. He did not say anything and looked away.

Cullen smirked and said, "Great stuff."

Isaac drummed on his knees again. He shrugged and said, "I didn't think you were being real with the job."

"You didn't answer my texts."

"So, you weren't worried?"

Cullen watched a car speed past them. He didn't alter the pace to keep up. "I have no idea what you get up to, Isaac."

Isaac nodded. "I've been up to a lot. I've started seeing someone."

Cullen raised his eyebrows. "Really? What's her name?"

Isaac looked out into the night, the trees lining the side of the road a thick mass that blocked out everything before them. He talked a little loudly, sitting up. There was a smile on his face. "Well, it's early days. Met her at a party. Name's Denise. Should be better with a bit more money, though."

They were pulling out of the city, moving west along the bypass, the road curling northwards. They passed a long road with signs for the airport appearing. Isaac watched the signs as they passed, occasionally looking up at the dark sky. Nothing appeared in it.

Cullen asked a question. "Have you been texting her a lot?"

Isaac was continuing to stare out the window. "Hmm?"

"Have you been messaging her?"

Isaac said nothing for a few seconds, then, "No, not like that."

Cullen nodded and asked, “When are you seeing her next?”

Isaac shrugged. “I don’t know. I don’t know.”

Cullen smiled.

Isaac turned to Cullen. “Can I put some music on?”

Cullen was still smiling. “No,” he said. He was firm. He pushed the accelerator down steadily, the small car straining under the pressure of rolling on, faster and faster. He talked over the noise. “What’s her name?”

Isaac had looked away by this point. He did not respond.

Cullen tried again. “The new girl’s name, again?”

Isaac stared at the moon vanishing behind some clouds. “D– It’s De …Deirdre.”

Cullen nodded. “Cool.”

“It’s going well.”

Cullen smiled. He muttered, “I’m sure it is.” He was slowing down. There was a truck in front of them. A car sped alongside them, driving well over the speed limit, its engine blasting out a guttural roar as it passed. Cullen sighed, checking his mirror for anything else. “Isaac, can you just get some sleep or something?”

“What? Why do I need to sleep?”

Cullen indicated right and made a safe manoeuvre to go past the truck. “Because it’s a long drive. We’ve got a few more hours to go.”

They were approaching the Forth Road Bridge, the dark edges of it shooting into the sky, the lights of North Queensferry in the distance glittering across the Forth.

Isaac groaned. “What? Oh come on, Cullen!”

The front window was beginning to steam up. Cullen turned up the heaters even more.

Isaac looked over at the Forth Rail Bridge. The water below was a thick black shade, with no sign of any movement across it. Isaac muttered, “Haven’t been out here before.”

"Where's the furthest north of Edinburgh you've been?"

"I went to Glasgow, remember?"

"Glasgow's not north of here."

"I mean, obviously," Isaac said. "I've just never been up here."

"You're from Scotland and you've never been up north?"

"No, I'm from the south," Isaac snapped. "The south of Scotland. So, I have been north. I'm in the north now, aren't I? Scotland is the north."

Cullen made a clicking noise with his tongue. "Incredible."

"That's not fair. I don't have a car."

Cullen laughed. "But you've never been on a train or anything?"

"I didn't move around when I grew up. I got moved school but to somewhere further south. I've been on holiday, Cullen, to campsites. Have you been camping?"

Cullen sighed. "No, I have never been camping."

"No, your parents paid for you to leave uni and then you just vanished or went crazy or – whatever, whatever the fuck this is. Whatever."

Cullen smirked. "Great stuff, Isaac."

Isaac folded his arms.

Cullen looked over at Isaac for a second. "Why did you move high school, Isaac? I remember now – you said about it during the first week you were at uni. You were drunk and you seemed angry about it."

Isaac shook his head. "I don't remember."

Cullen nodded. He replied, "I know, you were drunk at the time."

They were on the bridge now, the sound of the tyres making a noise on the bridge elements, beating in a steady rhythm, pha-dum, pha-dum. When they passed over it, the noise vanished and the road remained. Isaac looked around him, back across the river towards Edinburgh.

Isaac said, "Had some issues with someone there."

"Bullying?" Cullen asked, speaking a little quieter.

Isaac shut his eyes, turning away from Cullen. "Yeah, that was it."

Cullen took his eyes off the road and gave Isaac a hard stare. He muttered quietly, so Isaac could not hear him, "Who was being bullied, Isaac?"

Isaac didn't say anything.

As they drove on, there was nothing to look at and fewer cars. The moon seemed to glow now without anything to drown it out, but it kept being obscured by dark clouds.

Isaac forced his eyes shut, unable to keep them shut naturally. He fidgeted uncomfortably. Every now and then he would open his eyes to find that only a few minutes had passed by, Cullen only ever looking ahead into the night. At some point when his eyes were closed, they had turned off the motorway and were driving down single-lane roads. They drove through villages and past isolated homes.

Isaac had managed to keep his eyes closed for his best time yet, a good fifteen minutes. His head had just begun to swing back for a moment, sleep taking him, when the car made a swift turn to the left, which made Isaac move forward. The headlights had already been turned off before they stopped. Cullen had taken the key out of the ignition. He was looking to the left. They had parked in a lay-by.

It was hard to make out their surroundings. Isaac's eyes began to adjust to the lack of light, the shape of the world outside the car becoming clearer in the dark. A thick gust of wind rattled the car for a few moments but died down quickly. The car maintained some of its internal heat, but the temperature was dropping quickly. Isaac stuck his hands between his legs.

The lay-by overlooked an expanse of land covered by woodland on the other side of the road. The vague shape of a track wound through the trees. Even with the moon covered by the clouds, it was still possible to make out the shapes of mountains. The lack of colour made it all one entity, shapes of rock and wood growing out of the dead earth, a lone house an intruder upon the land.

Cullen was reaching for the back seats of the car. He said, “This is a holiday home – I’ve been looking at a few, tracking some addresses and details and that. This one’s separate – it’s not a holiday home for rent but it belongs to someone. Someone who isn’t currently here.”

Isaac was looking outside. The cold was forcing him out of his sleepy disposition. He stared at his shoes.

Cullen plucked his bag from the back seat. He continued, “The guy had mail about a few other homes he owned, including this place here.” He pulled out of the bag something that looked like a woolly hat. “It’s not rented, it’s not occupied. Folk with second homes that they can’t fill – rates are so low that they just buy houses and then rent them out. But no one’s renting this one. Who wants to live in remote Scotland deep into winter?” He pointed down towards the visible section of the farmhouse.

Isaac did not follow his hand; he was now staring at Cullen. “Cullen, what are you—”

“No one, exactly, that’d be stupid,” Cullen continued. “It’s just a second home. Just way out in the sticks, no real address. It’s remote enough that it won’t be checked all the time, but these guys are rich enough that there’s going to be something lying around.”

Isaac began tying his shoelaces but did it incorrectly, so undid the double knot, pulling his foot up higher to make use of what limited light they had. He made a movement to reach for the light between him, but a sudden shift in Cullen's shoulders as he moved his hand made him flinch.

"Anyway, it's easier now that you're here," Cullen said. "I'm glad, in a way."

Isaac screwed up his face for a second. "We're friends now?" he snapped back.

Cullen nodded and sighed. "We were friends before."

Isaac looked over to where Cullen had been pointing. He could see nothing in the darkness. He muttered, "By association."

"That's not true."

Isaac kept looking out the window. "They always told me in the flat that you found me dull."

Cullen looked at Isaac, but Isaac did not look back at him. "That's not true," Cullen said.

"You kept trying to speak to other people, back in Freshers' Week, you stopped talking to me. Mind when we met that girl, what was her name – Caitlin, or something? It was like you forgot I existed." Isaac blinked a few times. He looked down to his trainers and began fiddling with the laces.

Cullen had taken a pair of boots out of the bag and was changing footwear, the car creaking as he moved his seat back to give himself more room. "You made a big deal about how I couldn't stack dishes properly."

"Oh, come on, you did stack them weird! Like, how were they ever meant to dry like that? You never even cleared the soap off them! Wasn't my fault she found that stuff weird. It was all the other weird stuff that I told her about, that's what did it."

"Don't do an 'oh come on' to me," Cullen said. "You just needed to make me feel bad to feel good about yourself."

Isaac shook his head. "Oh, do shut up."

Cullen waited a few seconds before speaking again. "You like making people feel bad."

Isaac smiled and shook his head. "No, don't be daft."

Cullen breathed out. "You used me," he said slowly, not looking at Isaac.

"So what? You're using me now! Did you just want a turn? You've gone mental, Cullen, with all this stuff. Should have fucking died out there instead of all this."

"You'd be poor and unemployed without me."

Isaac waited a second before talking back, turning back to Cullen and looking at him in the eye, through the dark. "The people in that flat didn't like you that much either, Cullen," he ranted. "You were always weird, so weird and clingy. Remember how you brought in those game models, remember those? Those wee army men? You tried to sign up to a club or something, make weird wee friends. Christ, if I hadn't brought that up in front of everyone, you might have actually joined up with them. Fucking hell, you were almost in tears. You were such a ditz, honestly. Had to make your insecurities known to everyone all the time, like you were waiting for someone to be your dad." Isaac was grinning now. He had managed to tie his shoelaces in one go, pulling them into a double knot. He was still grinning as he shook his head. He made a large tutting noise.

Cullen threw some of the items from the bag onto the dashboard in front of Isaac: a pair of leather gloves and what looked like a hat, but on closer inspection was a balaclava. He pointed to them and said, "Put that on. When we get down there, check round the back."

Isaac stared at them. "Jesus, that's a bit much, Cullen."

"Why is that something you're concerned about now?"

"I ain't concerned about anything, you prick!"

"Great."

"You daft prick."

"You get really angry when you're nervous," Cullen responded calmly, pulling on his balaclava.

"Oh, you can get fucked," Isaac snapped back, spitting as he spoke.

Cullen responded calmly again, taking his time. "Like everyone else is to blame for your shitty life."

Isaac put on the gloves with a rasping, flailing motion. He dragged them on to his fingertips with one hand, pulling them down with an exaggerated motion, out of frustration. He tutted again, putting the balaclava on without looking for the eyeholes. He was blinded immediately, the taste of wool on his lips. He felt around for the eyeholes, placed his fingers into them and dragged them across his face until they met up with his eyes. He adjusted it again, feeling his hair twist underneath it. He put his hands down, then raised it again to adjust it, his hair shifting again.

Isaac said, "My life is fucking great, thank you. Fuck off." He gripped his hand into a fist.

Cullen was already moving, flicking the light switch. When he slowly opened the door, the light did not turn on. He moved the door very slowly.

Isaac followed suit. The gloves were not insulated enough to make his hands any warmer, but they offered some protection. The balaclava made his cheeks itch.

Isaac turned to Cullen, who was scanning the road. The car was hidden from the road. Hidden enough that cars passing by would only see it if they strained to look. Even then they would only see its outline but not the number plate. There was no clear path down, just a crash barrier protecting that side of the road.

Cullen had already walked around the front of the car and was at the barrier, placing his hands across it, taking one leg over it, taking his time to find his footing and lowering himself a little. Isaac followed him. Cullen had taken his other foot over successfully and was beginning to descend the slope. Isaac leaned over and attempted to find his footing in much the same manner. He landed in something that felt muddy, his shoe sinking into the mud.

The way down was marked by grass, rocks and plants. Isaac watched Cullen and tried as much as possible to follow his footsteps. The moon showed itself through a gap in the clouds, making the outlines of branches and bushes visible at short distances. Isaac took his time getting down, planting his feet with more difficulty than Cullen, who was already nearly out of view. The balaclava was making him sweat, his cheeks growing warmer. He scratched his nose. He ducked quickly as a low-hanging branch nearly hit him in the face. He lowered his head under it, raising his hands to his head as he did so.

He got to the bottom to find Cullen waiting for him. It was impossible to read his facial expression, his black balaclava drowning out the look in his eyes. His arms were by his side. He motioned Isaac to follow him. Isaac blew through his mouth, his breath hanging in front of him and rising into the night sky. Now that he was at the bottom, he spent a moment glancing around, watching for movement in the night – for Cullen. He moved slowly, attempting to catch up without acting hastily. The land was entirely still. The wind did not come. The chill in the air would have been worse for it.

Their movements were deliberately slow, Isaac taking a beat between each movement to glance around, his ears training on anything and nothing. Cullen's route was slower still. He moved his legs quickly but slowed to plant his feet softly into the ground, not letting the impact of his movements create any noise. Isaac did his best to follow in the same fashion. But then he stepped on a twig, the noise of it cracking under his foot, causing him to stop. He took a few more tentative steps, his shoes sinking into the mud on more than one occasion.

By the time they were nearer the house, he was breathing

heavily. It was a single-storey cottage with grey stonework. The outline of the black roof drowned out the moonlight above it. The lights were not on. Around to the left was a driveway and a dirt road leading away from the direction they had come. There was no car in sight. A single door lay ahead of them, cast in shadow under the roof. There was no concrete nor paving stones around the cottage, the forest engulfing everything up close to the door. There were no fresh-looking footprints. The door was firmly shut.

Cullen turned and slowly motioned to the right of the house with his head. Isaac did not move. Cullen pointed at the side of the house with his hand. Isaac understood. Cullen turned back around and approached the door. Isaac hesitated and moved forward, turning a little to the right. His foot got stuck again, in something that was more of a puddle than it was mud. A cold sensation shot through his foot and up his ankle. Isaac raised his head to the night sky, curling his fists, his mouth closed.

Isaac moved towards Cullen, who was bent down in front of the door. He had taken a crowbar out of the bag and pushed it against the side of the door, forcing it open. Cullen stopped for a few moments and pushed at the door. It swung open. He stepped inside, moving his hand into his outside pocket. He pulled out a torch and turned it on. Isaac paused and followed him in, taking his time to pass through the doorway.

Cullen was already busy inspecting the interior of the cottage. A window lit up the end of a thin corridor which had two doors on the left of it, two on the right. The first door was open and Cullen went into the room. Isaac did not move for a few seconds but then followed him in, taking one long, deliberate step inside, loud enough for Cullen to hear. The torch flashed back to Isaac's shoe and then back inside.

The torch was now being pointed at a myriad of items in

storage – things covered up with white sheets. Then Cullen moved on to the next room.

Isaac followed him in. He found Cullen inspecting the room in much the same manner, torch shining on more objects, ornate-looking items.

"It'll take ages to get through," Isaac said in a whisper.

Cullen turned around quickly – very quickly – at a speed which made Isaac jump. He whispered, "How secure are we?"

Isaac hesitated before he answered, "What do you mean, how secure are we?"

"Was there anything round the back?"

"What do you mean?"

Cullen turned off the torch and crouched lower. "Did you go around the cottage to see if anyone is there?"

Isaac nodded. "Yes. We're fine."

Cullen nodded back.

Isaac moved towards an ornament on the mantelpiece.

Cullen did not watch him but called out to him before he got close to anything, "Isaac, don't touch anything. Some of it's fragile."

Isaac did not turn around, continuing to push his hand towards something on one of the tables.

Cullen moved up next to Isaac without him realising. He spoke with real anger in his voice. "Go outside. I'll call you in."

Isaac jumped back towards the door, back into the corridor. He went outside, putting his hands inside his pockets. He turned left, keeping to the side of the house. It was hard to make anything out that was a few feet in front of him, but the moon's light clipped the surrounding mountains, curved and cracked lines hanging in the air, solid and unmoving. He took a few steps forward, trying to plant his feet in the ground.

Around the corner of the house was a man slumped on a

bench. He was facing the vast expanse of trees beyond him, the mountains in the far distance. There were beer cans on the ground, under the bench, unevenly spread. The man had headphones on. He was smoking a cigarette. With no noise around, the sound of the nicotine burning inside it could be heard from several feet away, from where Isaac stood. The man took off his large headphones and let them rest around his neck.

He looked at Isaac.

As Isaac moved back, the man rose and came towards him. Isaac continued to walk backwards, hands in front of him, mouth hanging open. The man kept coming, round the corner, his hand hanging onto to the wall. Isaac turned and slipped in the mud. He lost his balance, his knee bending as he fell to the ground, making a liquid splash, the mud enveloping his lower leg.

The man did not move quickly but his eyes never left Isaac.

Isaac grabbed at the mud, but his gloves were thick with mud now, sloppy enough to make it harder to grip anything. He managed to turn onto his back, facing the man, who paused in his slow approach. The man reached into his jacket pocket and pulled out a knife.

The music from the headphones was audible now – something orchestral. In the dark, the man's features were indistinguishable. He was wrapped up with little skin to show. He walked forward again, heavy boots planting into the ground.

Isaac pushed his hands into the mud. With the man now standing at his feet, Isaac sank deeper into the mud. His hands were fully submerged.

The man did not say a word.

Through the mud lay solid ground, somewhere not damp from the weather. Layers of rock, crumbled into pieces, but pushed together into layers and layers, parts older than Isaac, older than us, older than anything.

The man stood over Isaac, planting his feet carefully. The man examined the knife, his hands shaking. The man put his foot on Isaac's thigh, slipping a bit, but forcing it down. Still he did not say a word. His eyes were pitch black and fixed on his prey. He lowered the knife to Isaac's stomach.

Isaac gargled, tears blocking his view, made cold by the night air. His arm reached out to grab the man. But the man was too strong and his parka jacket too hard to reach around, too hard to grip. Isaac grabbed at him anyway, trying to push him away.

The man pressed harder on Isaac's leg, making Isaac twist his foot. He put the knife to Isaac's neck.

Cullen's crowbar made a singing noise in the air.

It caught the man in the side of the ribs, and he staggered backwards, still clutching the knife. Cullen left Isaac in the mud, stepping over him without stopping, the crowbar raised. He swung again at the man's hand with the knife, the crack sounding like a branch breaking. The man made a pallid whining noise.

Cullen waited, crowbar raised, the same as before, his arm bent with the crowbar ready to swing. The man did not move, just stood coughing and wheezing. Cullen switched the crowbar to his other hand, curling his now-empty palm into a fist. He planted his feet and threw a solid punch, catching the man on the jaw. When the man's head moved again, Cullen threw another and the man fell to the ground.

Isaac forced himself upwards. His heart was pounding. He whined, "Cullen, what the …"

Cullen gripped the crowbar tightly, then released the tension, returning it to the inside of his jacket. He turned, heading away from the house.

Isaac opened his mouth as Cullen walked past him.

Cullen spoke quickly. "We need to go. We need to call an ambulance."

Isaac began to walk unsteadily, gripping at his stomach. He saw Cullen quickening his pace, hands putting something back in his pockets. He was now making his way back to the car, saying, "We need to go. We need to call an ambulance."

Isaac called after him, "What? What about the stuff? We need to leave him, can't have the cops come—"

Cullen called back, "There's no time. We need to call th—"

"What do you mean there's no time?" Isaac called out. "He's fine, he's not …"

Cullen stopped, turned back to Isaac. He repeated himself, carefully, quietly, "We need to go!"

Isaac threw his arms in the air. "The money!"

Cullen nearly walked into a tree as he shouted, "We need … Go, go."

"You didn't get the—"

"I just had to beat a guy to within an inch of his life, do you understand?" Cullen shouted. "Do you understand what I've just had to do? Do you understand? Why don't you understand? What is it about all of this that you don't understand?" He staggered away from Isaac, who was still looking at him.

Isaac spoke slowly. "Don't call an ambulance. Don't do anything like that."

Cullen stared back. He could not look away from Isaac, the blank stare Isaac was giving him.

They did not move. Then they began heading back where they had come from, back towards the car.

On the way back, a branch scratched Isaac's face, clipping the side of his cheek, close to his eye. He stopped for a second, pushing his hands to his face, his vision a mess of branches and unending darkness. Everywhere he walked, he found himself in bushes or mud or a mix of both, unable to keep going without stopping. But he did not stop again, despite the cracking branches, his feet being soaked in cold water.

They reached the car, Cullen first, Isaac dragging himself over the barrier afterwards. Then he reached for the car door. The cottage was far behind them, distant from the road. Isaac threw off his jacket with the car door open, Cullen already turning the ignition on. There was no one else on the road. Isaac strapped himself in with the jacket at his feet, hurling it on the back seat when Cullen pulled out into the road.

Cullen drove quietly, not turning the lights on. They followed the road, not turning back the way they came, only turning on the lights after they had driven far away enough from the turn.

They drove on much as they had before. The car kept the same steady speed. The world looked exactly as it did before, with the moon overcast and Cullen not gripping the wheel any differently.

Isaac was becoming accustomed to the darkness, and he could see Cullen's face. He was breathing hard. Tears were streaming down his face. He was shaking.

Cullen finally spoke. "He must have moved up at some point. These places are all empty. No one lives up here anymore. It's all second homes, places you go to in the summer."

Isaac, rubbing his face, said, "I don't—"

"You need to burn your clothes," Cullen interrupted. "Don't do anything for a few days. This is the end of it, Isaac. I can't find my phone. You need to call—"

Isaac just said one word. "No."

Cullen, whimpering, said, "It's over. I had to stop that guy. Please call, Isaac."

Isaac repeated himself. "No."

"He was just an old man, just a lanky-looking old man. A scared old man." Cullen's voice was shaking as he spoke. He didn't look at Isaac, didn't check his mirrors.

Isaac looked away.

Cullen said, "He was trying to hurt you. He was hesitating. He looked old and frail, Isaac – I don't know, Isaac …"

Isaac shook his head. "I don't understand … Stop interrupting me, you're always interrupting me! You're always doing this. I don't understand why you want me out here for *this*, why you get me out and insult me and just make me do shit, shit things."

"Because you never want to do anything good, Isaac," Cullen screamed. "You don't want to be good. You don't think you'd be worth something if you were."

Isaac didn't say anything.

Cullen continued to whimper. "You were always like that, even back at uni. I didn't think you'd have changed that much." Cullen stopped talking and kept driving. At one point he had to pull over, his hands shaking, wrapping around each other, turning over and over, fingers interlocking and moving and shifting.

Isaac did not do anything for the rest of the journey. He stared at his trainers. They were soaked with mud, now dripping onto the mat. They looked discoloured and worn, suddenly old, like they had never been new in the first place, as if they had been like that all along.

CHAPTER ELEVEN

Dylan had been talking for a few minutes, since he had sat down with Isaac. He had not stopped to drink. At points, Isaac sighed into his pint, trying not to interrupt.

Dylan used his hands a lot when he talked. "But it would be class, really. If you planned it out properly, did some training, got it to motivate you enough, you'd do well for yourself, like, really, really good for yourself, man. It'd be brilliant. Just b-rilliant. B-rilliant!"

Isaac nodded and took another drink. He opened his mouth to speak but Dylan carried on.

"I've been doing archery as a class for the last couple of weeks. It's class. I signed up for it because I was seeing someone that was into it – nice girl, nice personality, very cute – but I really stuck to it; ended up going every week and now I'm great at it. There's a community centre around the corner from my house and I go there – you know I'm living in the north, right? Way up in Sutherland. Really nice, quiet place. Quiet, but I'm managing it fine."

Isaac nodded. He was not looking at Dylan. His hands were gripping onto the glass, shaking, pressing smudged fingerprints against it. He held his breath, his eyes glazing over. He breathed out again, just as Dylan was finishing his last sentence. Isaac had tensed up like this a few times since the last job with Cullen. He looked at the half-full glass in his hand, and said, "I've heard of it, that's great."

Dylan continued to talk. "So, I've been doing bouldering too – it takes a bit of skill. I've managed to get some of the gear, which helps because the stuff that they have doesn't really work that well, you know? Cost a bit, but I've been doing it for weeks now and it's great, really great. My core strength has always been really good, and a few people said I'm a natural, which is great!"

Isaac nodded. "So, now you can shoot arrows and climb rocks?"

Dylan shrugged and smiled. He replied, "Which could come in handy."

Isaac took a drink. He wiped his face with the other hand. He looked across to the busy bar and back to Dylan. "You're really serious, aren't you?"

Dylan's expression did not change. "Yes."

They were in a pub close to Isaac's flat, a craft beer bar which Isaac had never been to. They did not serve pints. The beer was expensive, and the crowd was student-aged.

Isaac took another drink. "I mean—" he started, then stopped for a second. He continued, "So, if the zombie apocalypse happened tomorrow, you'd be ready for it?"

"Yes. I'm ready. Are you?"

Isaac shrugged. "I don't think it's realistic."

Dylan made a single chortle which was loud and made a few people some distance from them turn around. "Well, I know it's not realistic. Do you think everyone just wakes up and thinks to themselves that their lives will change dramatically tomorrow?"

Isaac stared into his pint glass.

Dylan answered his own question. "Exactly, I'm glad you

agree with me. Thing is, we're surrounded by zombies, every day – everyone just being so bloody ordinary all the time, not really waking up to the world. We need to be better, you and I."

Isaac took a drink. The beers were small but strong. It tasted of something close to chocolate. Dylan had bought it for him. Isaac looked back at Dylan. "Is it my round?" he asked.

Dylan leaned over to Isaac and whispered, "What would your special skills be?"

Isaac shrugged. "Don't know. I'm a hard worker."

Dylan held his hand up. He looked into the distance as he talked. "You'd need to be good outdoors. Can you cook? You couldn't do much tech stuff, not that you'd be great at that – fundamentally, you can do it, I mean … You know what I meant – it's not quite as useful when technology is gone."

Isaac raised his eyebrows, finishing the last of his drink before trying to speak again. "I've been camping once. Do you want another?"

Dylan kept looking into the distance before turning to back to Isaac and saying, "I've been camping across … Did you do the Duke of Edinburgh course when you were younger?"

Isaac shook his head.

Dylan looked at his own drink, eyes focused. "I ended up getting the silver," he said. "Got kicked off the gold one. Some bullshit about … Was rubbish, really; those teachers and a few people did not care for me that much."

"What for?" Isaac asked.

Dylan waved his hand as he spoke. "Could you get me one of the specials?"

"The specials?"

Dylan nodded. "I think they had some beers in today. Just today."

Isaac shook his head and muttered, "I think I saw that, yeah."

Dylan quickly resumed talking just as Isaac finished his answer. "What did they have up on the board?"

Isaac shrugged. He hesitated before saying, "As in, can I remember what they were?"

Dylan nodded slowly. "Yes, do you remember? I think this one is pretty strong, so I've forgotten."

Isaac sighed. "I don't remember."

Dylan turned his hand into a fist and wrapped the knuckle on the table. He looked away before looking back to Isaac. He tried again. "Rats. Can you get me … Actually, I don't know."

"All right, I'll get you whatever."

Just as Isaac was getting up and walking away, Dylan asked a question. "Can you text them to me, yeah?"

Isaac was a bit exasperated and turned around. "What? I'll just get—"

"Ask for pints this time," Dylan interrupted.

Isaac breathed out before responding, "They don't do … All right." He walked away. The bar was up a short set of stairs. There was a tall man walking down the stairs who moved suddenly to accommodate Isaac as he passed.

There was not much space at the bar. He walked to the left side of it and the back to the right of it without getting closer to it. A group of women stood looking around for a seat. Isaac looked back at the table that he and Dylan were on. There was space enough for three, maybe more. There had been other tables around them that were smaller, but Dylan had gone straight for the larger one.

Isaac looked back at the bar. Someone had just arrived and stood in front of him while he was looking around. He ordered two strangely worded drinks, in the largest size. The largest size was not a pint.

From his vantage point at the bar, he looked around. All the faces were pale and young-looking. The volume of conversation was enhanced by the low ceiling. The walls were lined with dark wood and dark green paint. People were sitting closer together, faces lit by candlelight. There were a few couples close to him. He took his drinks away from the bar.

Diane was sitting by herself at a table in the corner of the room.

Isaac snapped his head towards her. Her beer was half-empty and her face lit up by her phone, the white glow lighting up her blue eyes. She paid no attention to the world around her.

To get to her side of the room would mean forcing his way through the tables and chairs, the mass of people inside the pub. Across the lines of conversation and music, heavy jackets and people pushed together, she sat still. She did not look up from her phone, did not appear to be typing anything into it.

After a few moments, Isaac could pick out words from the conversations around him, different accents. People around him were talking about how cold it was, how tired they were, how the beer tasted, who they were seeing, what they'd been eating.

He kept looking at Diane.

He moved forward towards her, close to a pair of tables. There was room for him to manoeuvre through if he shifted to his side and forced his way past. He paused, body moving a little bit forward, a little bit backward. No one moved. He tutted and moved away, back round to Dylan.

Dylan was on his phone. He did not look up as Isaac placed the drink in front of him. He asked, "Did you get my text?"

Isaac shook his head as he sat down. "No, didn't want to hang around."

"You could have just come round and given me some options then," Dylan snapped at him.

Isaac spluttered out a response. "Didn't have any signal."

Dylan stared at Isaac before replying, "You could have asked."

"It's here now," Isaac muttered.

Dylan nodded, looking at the drink without touching it. He bit the inside of his lip, breathing out and not bothering to respond. Dylan sipped his drink slowly. His cheeks inflated a little, the drink rolling around in his mouth. He tilted his head back and swallowed slowly. He screwed up his face and moved the glass away from his face.

Isaac did not touch his drink. He looked back towards the bar, to where he had come from. He could only see part of it, a barman moving around and filling drinks up.

"I genuinely want it to happen, sort of. The zombie apocalypse," Dylan said, resuming their previous conversation. "It'd be a chance to start again. Life isn't as good as it was, you know? I always feel a bit held back by the rules just now, you know? Like I can't get what I want as much any more. People get too sensitive about things and they just … People are shit, people are really sensitive about dumb, dumb shit."

Isaac took a drink. A long drink.

Dylan kept going. "I've done nothing wrong. Really. I'm living my best life. I think it's a bit tied to jealousy, just a bit. I wasn't always this good with people. I used to be a speccy little – wore glasses a lot, but I'm not that person anymore. I'm great now. I've been doing yoga and it's a great place to meet people …"

Isaac held his glass in his hand. Dylan did not stop.

"… but it'd be a chance to start again. No rules, no limitations. I could actually be my best self. I'm great at yoga, I can shoot a bit, I'm good at camping – it'd be so much better."

"Are you still planning to move properly up north?" Isaac asked.

"Just for a bit. You've seen my pictures online? They're pretty spectacular! I climbed Ben A'an – it's one of the highest mountains in the UK, a proper Munro. Pictures were amazing, absolutely epic climb."

Isaac did not answer.

Dylan shook his head. "You've not really seen a lot of the country, have you?"

Isaac looked away. "No."

Dylan smiled. "Yeah, that's not a good thing."

"Didn't say it was," Isaac muttered into his drink.

Dylan stared into his drink, his lips pursed. He looked back to Isaac and said, "Thought you'd want to see more of everything. Why don't you try to? You really should have done that stuff in your late teens. Bit old for it now."

Isaac's hand was gripping onto the glass again. He did not talk for a few seconds, his knuckles turning white. He breathed out. Dylan stared at him in silence. When Isaac spoke again, he was staring at Dylan's drink. "Did not realise there was a time limit on travelling."

Dylan shook his head as he drank, staring into the glass, screwing up his face as he put it onto the table. He talked again. "I mean, I'm up north a lot on my conservation work. Why don't you come and visit me? Get everyone else up?"

Isaac stared at his hand. He had let it lie flat against the table, wet against spilt drink and sticky against the unwashed top of it. "Yes. I should try to do that."

Dylan wasn't looking at him any more; he was looking at his phone again.

To the left of them was a louder table, a group of seven squeezed into a small round table for four people. The men in the group were quite tall, five other women around them. They alternated talking to each other. Isaac looked over at them, at the back of one of the tall men in a long brown leather jacket patched at the elbows. The woman sitting next to him had black hair and a fringe. She wore a thin top with long black sleeves; there was a sliver of a tattoo at her wrist. She placed her hand on the man's arm.

Dylan kept staring at his phone, but he said, "I do wonder about you sometimes, Isaac."

Isaac turned back, staring at the ground midway over.

Dylan continued talking. "You should move up north. It's fresh up there."

"I've got my parents place to look after while they're away. I've got my job."

Dylan shook his head. Still looking at this phone, he said, "You still don't hear from them that much?"

"No. They're doing fine."

Dylan looked up from his phone. "Travelling still? Isn't that annoying? You've not tried to go out to see them at all? It's a bit weird that they don't want to talk to you."

Isaac shrugged. "That's not a problem really. We're adults now, we should be—"

"Aren't they worried about how you're doing, what you've been up to?" Dylan interrupted immediately.

"I tell them I'm fine all the time. What else are you meant to tell them?" Isaac muttered into his drink, whimpering a little. "They told me to work hard and all that, and I did. I did."

Dylan stayed still. Isaac glanced over at the table where the women outnumbered the men. Dylan followed Isaac's eyeline. Isaac finished his drink. Dylan's was still half-full. He leaned over again. He growled at Isaac, "Do you want another drink? Think I'd rather pick out my own after that last debacle. Honestly, that drink you got me the last time was shit. What were you thinking?"

Isaac breathed out before saying, "We got the same ones. I can get the next one."

Dylan was already getting up.

"I'm fine, I'll get them right this time," Isaac said.

"Did not get the right ones, did you?" Dylan snapped.

Isaac's hand was still wrapped around the empty glass. "I thought I was doing the right thing. It's not my fault!" he snarled back.

Dylan was shaking his head. "Nothing ever is. Don't worry, I'll get them this time. Why are you so keen to go up the bar again?"

Isaac looked towards the bar. "Nothing," he muttered.

Dylan followed his eyeline for a second but turned back to him. He talked slowly. "Nothing what?"

Isaac turned back to stare at his empty glass.

Dylan stared at Isaac for a few seconds. He said, "Well? Say something then. Why aren't you saying something? Do you realise how stupid you look?"

Isaac didn't look up at him.

Dylan shook his head and walked away.

Isaac didn't watch him leave. He breathed out. "Fuck sake."

He stared at the screen of his phone, tapping it with his fingernail. He checked through his messages. He did not look at the group next to him again, at the woman holding the man's arm. He glanced over to see her move it up towards his shoulder, then down again, towards his hand. As it lowered towards his hand, his moved, his palm opening to take hers.

Isaac waited. There wasn't anything around him to look at and no one else to talk to. He turned his head towards the bar a few times. He could not see Dylan, could not see him in the large mirror on the back of the wall, could not see bar staff moving over to him, could not see anyone moving or anyone taking any drinks.

The woman and her man next to him were still holding hands.

Isaac looked away. He stared at his empty glass. There was a little left in it. He took a drink from it, the little that remained draining slowly, slowly down the glass until it hit his lips, taking a second for the dregs to roll into his teeth, lathering his bottom gums with little impact. His glass was tilted at an angle and it took ten seconds for it to empty.

He was still doing this when Dylan came back. The drink he gave Isaac was darker in complexion. Isaac sipped – it tasted like something close to dark chocolate. Dylan sipped his without reacting and Isaac kept his facial expression placid. Dylan watched Isaac for a few seconds looking at his drink. He shook his head. He turned to face the group next to them for a few seconds, staring at the women in turn. Isaac did not say anything.

"How are Lyle and Will doing?" asked Dylan.

Isaac looked back at Dylan as he answered. "Fine, I think. My shifts have changed a bit. I mean, I don't see them that much. I'm paying the rent on time, which is all that really matters. They're all just working. We're all working just now. Pretty normal stuff."

Dylan had looked over to the women at the other table before looking back to Isaac. "It's normal to never see the people you're living with?" he asked, talking louder than before.

Isaac breathed out a response. "No. I mean, we're just doing our own stuff now. What's wrong with that? We're doing our stuff, our own stuff, I mean."

Dylan took a drink from his glass. He pointed at Isaac as he spoke. "They're going to kick you out. Just like me."

Isaac shook his head.

Dylan leant towards Isaac, his hands moving, his eyes moving between the glass, the table and Isaac. "They kicked me out after what happened. I mean, it was – fuck, you get weird at one party and it's suddenly the final straw, you know? I'll apologise for nothing. Isn't it weird that people just give you the silent treatment one day? Like, they were waiting for an excuse to have me out of the group, like there's something wrong with who I am or something stupid, something fucking stupid like that. It's a bit ridiculous."

"And no one wants to see you then. There you go," Isaac muttered into his drink.

Dylan shook his head. "No one likes you that much anyway. You know I always stood up for you, all right? When you were following me around and clinging to my coat-tails, they all thought you were crap."

Isaac had gone pale. His drink was back on the table. "No, that's—"

"You know it's true." Dylan wagged his finger. "It's always been true. No one liked you that much."

"I remember … You were awful, horrible to her—"

Dylan flashed a grin and shook his head as he interrupted Isaac, still wagging his finger. "Her side of the story is bullshit. At some point she needs to get over it – it's weird that she keeps banging on about it. Besides, it's not as bad as what you've been up to with your ex. Let's talk about something else."

"You brought it up," Isaac snapped back.

Dylan looked back at Isaac. "They'll kick you out too," he said, very slowly.

"They won't," Isaac spat. "I pay my rent on time, I tidy up after myself, I don't bother anyone. I don't do anything wrong. Why would they? I've had some issues with them, but it'll work itself out, it's fine. You stick to taking pictures of hills in the middle of fucking nowhere."

Dylan frowned and raised his voice as he snapped back, “I’m great at what I do.”

“Munros are shit, no one cares about you going for a shit walk somewhere.”

Dylan looked away and waved his hand. He muttered under his breath, “Let’s talk about something else. I’m bored of this.”

Isaac sipped his drink for a few seconds before putting it down quickly. “This drink is awful. It’s not even a pint and it’s too expensive.”

Dylan waited until he had finished a long drink of his own and wiped his mouth. He smiled as he said, “You aren’t paying for it.”

“You were flat-out horrible to her,” Isaac muttered, more to himself than Dylan. “It’s weird that you thought you could get away with it.”

Dylan put his drink down quickly and made to leave, not looking at Isaac as he said, “I’ll let you get on with your night. I’ve got a woman to see anyway.”

Isaac screwed up his face as he snapped, “You’ve got a woman to see?”

Dylan smiled triumphantly. “I always do. Weird how I can be this big ratbag of a guy when I’ve always got someone on the go when I’m back down here. Not quite sure how that works – can you tell me, Isaac, how that works? You’ve always wanted this life of mine, I know you have. You know the other guys have been ignoring me for the last few weeks, but you’ve kept talking to me. They’ve all avoided me like I’m some sort of creep. I’m not a creep. No way. I’m great with women and I think Will and Lyle are bothered by it.”

Isaac shook his head.

Dylan continued, leaning in and snarling at Isaac. “You’ve been holding onto my coat-tails for so long. All those women I set you up with – your ex, who you dumped.

I've heard all about that. Did you think we were going to go out like the old days, that I was going set you up with someone again?"

Isaac said nothing.

Dylan kept going. "Fuck, you are the worst. That's what you wanted, wasn't it? You think I'm a shithead, good for one thing?"

Isaac stared into his drink.

"Goodbye, Isaac." Dylan got his jacket.

Isaac waited until he was getting up before snapping at him, "Fuck off then."

Dylan shook his head. "No. You shut up," he snapped back. He left.

Isaac tutted. The group next to him had gone quiet, but after a few seconds they began their conversation again. Some of the women across from Isaac moved their heads to look at him. Isaac did not look back. Isaac took another drink from the glass. A longer drink. His hands were shaking.

The man in the brown leather jacket had leant his head to the left; the woman whispered into his ear. Isaac glanced over. Between her mouth and his ear, one of the other women was staring at Isaac. He looked away.

He kicked the chair that Dylan had been sitting on and it fell backwards onto the ground. He swore under his breath. "Fuck."

People had gone quiet now, the noise of the chair hitting the floor spiking across the bar. One of the bar staff was looking over.

Isaac stood up slowly, and people went back to chatting again. He went back towards the bar, carrying his jacket, glancing over at the group of women looking at him one last time. He ordered another drink.

Diane was still there, reading a book now. He breathed a sigh of relief. He looked at the table closest to him, at the space between the tables, people leaning forward over the small round tables. Long jackets littered the ground.

She had not looked up. Her drink looked the same as it had before.

He moved forward, beer and jacket in hand, reaching out with his leg and attempting to extend it through a tight space between two chairs. He managed to put his foot down. This put him immediately in front of another table, three women sitting down and talking to each other, the three of them looking at him as he made his first step. He moved his body through the gap, his jacket hitting against the back of a chair.

Diane was a few more tables over.

Isaac was stuck now. One of the women was watching him and she shifted her body away from him. Isaac was looking at his feet. He muttered in the woman's general direction. "I'm trying to get past."

She looked up from her conversation and slurred out, "Why?"

She moved her seat forward as much as she could manage it. He tutted as he moved his body through, his left leg scraping against the chairs. He did not look back at the women as he made his way past. They did not say anything until he was further away.

He moved between another set of tables. One person had seen him come over and, without saying, had moved. There were four people around the table, all watching Isaac as he moved past them. Isaac did not say a word to them.

Diane did not look up from her book.

A few people were watching Isaac now. He had managed to get himself stuck again – he could move left between two tables, but he'd be moving further away. If he moved to the right, he'd get stuck near the wall.

A tall man with an English accent rose from his seat, just

to Isaac's left. He roared out at Isaac, "Are you all right, pal? Where are you trying to go?"

Isaac moved to the right, away from the man, without looking at him. He moved towards the wall. Isaac dragged against it, moving past the last table, pushing into it, causing it to wobble a little. He was in front of Diane.

Isaac spoke quietly, under the music and the sound of conversation. "I've met you before."

She took a second to look up. She looked confused at first, nodding after a second. She did not say anything.

He tried talking again, louder this time. "Yeah, from that crazy party."

She raised her eyebrows and smiled, saying, "Oh, sorry – yeah – what are you doing?"

Isaac looked back at the room around him then back to her. "I mean, you seemed lonely," he said.

"I'm alone, sure, not really that lonely though. People can be by themselves sometimes."

Isaac looked at the back wall for a few seconds then back to her. He spoke again. "I mean, trapped. You looked trapped."

She looked confused. "Trapped?"

Isaac nodded as he said, "I mean, it's difficult squeezing past this many tables and people and stuff."

Diane looked around her, past the place where Isaac was standing, at the rows of faces and bodies and noise. She hesitated, her hand curled around her drink. She looked back at Isaac, speaking slowly. "I guess I am trapped. And yet you came."

Isaac managed to smile for the first time in weeks. "And yet here I am."

She looked at him apologetically. She spoke a bit faster. "I don't have anything to give you as a reward, unfortunately."

Isaac shrugged. He spoke at the same speed, in time with her. “How about a seat?” He looked around. She was sitting by herself and there was no other chair. Everyone around him in the small space he had to stand in was firmly sat down. There was a small section of the window that Isaac leaned on and he shifted the table to make room for his legs.

After Isaac had finished settling himself, Diane said, “You really came all this way to say hi?”

Isaac nodded, looking across the room as he replied, “My f … My friend is off, real shame. Were you waiting for anyone?”

Diane nodded, looking past Isaac, out the window, as she talked. “I’m waiting for some people. I mean … Also, my flat is cold and I had a book to read, so …”

Isaac screwed up his face and asked, “You came here to read a book again?”

She nodded.

“You were doing the same at the party. Which I get, I do, but pubs are pretty social places. You’d be better chatting to people, getting yourself out there. Not like … You know what I mean.”

Diane looked confused again.

Isaac drank, his face red, looking across the room before looking back to her, spluttering out some words. “But you know what I mean. It’s nice to get out. Especially in Edinburgh. You can find all sorts of things now. You can even pay seven pounds for a half pint!”

Diane laughed.

Isaac held up his glass against the light. “This one tastes of chocolate,” he said.

“Why would you want chocolate in a drink?” Diane asked. “You’d be better just buying chocolate and drinking normal drinks.”

Isaac let go of his drink when it was back on the

windowsill. He had his back to the window. There was a slight draught creeping in. His hand was flat on the windowsill, relaxed against it. He breathed out. He turned back to her and asked, "So, what do you do?"

She kept her hand around her drink. She asked, "What do I do?"

"For work, I mean."

She breathed in before she answered, looking away to the rest of the room. "Oh, I work at the galleries. Administrative work. I like it. Well, I like it well enough. Not sure I can do anything else just now, with the job market the way it is, so I'm doing this. What about you? What do—"

"Is that something you've always wanted to do?" Isaac interrupted.

Diane closed her mouth and looked through the sliver of window not obscured by Isaac. She could only see as far as the bus stop outside through the glass, people standing still as they waited. "I'd love to be a writer," she said. "I'd love that. I like the idea of it, in any case. I'd imagine it's a lot harder to actually do."

"What would you write?"

Diane looked back at her book for a second. "Novels? I've always read a lot. I grew up near a library. My mum used to take me there when I was younger, before she became too ill."

Isaac nodded and smiled. "Romance books and that …"

Diane looked back at him for a second, spluttering out, "And … what, sorry?"

Isaac pointed his finger at the book on the table. "Like, fiction and that? I can't – no, I don't – I mean, I'm not much of a reader."

Diane smiled at him. "Oh, that's all right."

Isaac looked across the room, the mass of people talking to each other. "Never really needed to. I'm good at engineering, that kind of thing. I'm doing … I was doing IT at uni. I dropped out but I still work." He took his drink in his hand again, drinking half of it in one go.

"Oh, I'm sorry to hear. University's a difficult thing."

Isaac stared at the walls, the shadows on the walls. He carried on. "I don't think I need it for what I do anyway. If there's one thing I've learnt from the job … I've learnt a lot on the job, not from the boss – he's not really that helpful, tell the truth, he kind of just sets out on his own and does his own thing – it's that you have to keep going. Fuck 'em all. You must keep going. Everyone does – they all moan about you, and you don't really need them for anything because you can just get your little bit, then save, then just keep working, and it's – ack …" He stopped. His hand was still clinging onto the glass, his knuckles white with the pressure he was putting on it. He started again. "You know? There's not a lesson to any of it. I just have to keep going. I've lost interest in what everyone says to me now. Thing is, I'm close to moving back with – back with my folks, by the looks of it – but it's fine. I've got my flatmates, as rotten as they are." He took a breath.

Diane did not say anything. She watched him without expressing anything, resting her head on her hands.

Then he carried on. "It's not really my fault that this has happened. Like, some other pals of mine made some weird choices and I'm kind of caught in the middle now, which isn't my fault. There's a lack of something. I'm doing my own thing now. But I'm lost a bit. I don't know where I am sometimes."

Diane nodded when he finished. "No – I get what you mean, I feel a little lost as well," she said.

Isaac took another quick drink, carrying on after he pulled the glass away from his mouth. "I don't know … what I do, to be honest with you. Is that bad? I'm not normally this good at … I'm a pretty … I've had a lot to deal with recently. It's tricky in my line of work because it's quite intense …" His voice drained away.

Diane spoke up. "What do you want, Isaac?"

There was a little bit left in in his drink. He was shaking. "We're talking a little too quickly," he muttered. "I don't talk about this stuff."

Diane kept looking at him. "What do you mean? It's all right to talk about it sometimes when you're drunk. Are you all right?"

Isaac looked away. He muttered quickly, "I said I don't need to talk about this stuff. I know who I am. I'm not that drunk."

Diane did not react.

Isaac kept going on. "It's weird that you feel the need to question me. I'm great. I'm working on my own now. I don't need other people around me to tell me how good I am, I don't need … that level of stuff. I need real things – none of this."

He looked at her for a second and then she said, "You're fine, Isaac – you're fine. You've just had a lot to drink, that's all. You're just feeling a lot right now, you're beating yourself up a bit too much. You should focus more on what you can do all right now, instead of trying to blame everything on the past and the people around you. I get that you feel lost just now, but it's fine, it's just a feeling."

"I would like your number, please," Isaac said suddenly.

Diane paused. She glanced at his faint reflection in the glass, darker and less pronounced. Someone across the room was laughing; a few people joined in with them. Isaac was not looking at her, only somewhere in the distance, something beyond her, past her. She took out her phone and showed him her number. He typed it into his phone.

"I mean, I'm not really looking for anything." she said

quietly. "But you're interesting, Isaac. More interesting than you think."

He got up to send her a message, looking at her name in his phone. He breathed out, mouthing the name slowly. "Look, I'm going to … I need to head off. Maybe I'll feel better later."

Diane nodded. "Have a safe journey home. I think if you keep to the wall, you'll get out easier." She pointed to a thin gap where the chairs and the wall were, leading out to the bar, and then out to the entrance. Isaac left, nodding at her as he went away, not looking back again. He walked past the window, the steamed-up window, slowly walking, not looking back in. As he passed the pub he walked faster, at his normal pace. "It's happening," he said.

Someone across the street looked at him. Isaac did not look over. He whispered to himself, "You're going to get it. You're going to get it all." He turned the corner, heading towards Princes Street Gardens. He turned to check no one was following him. There were cars on the roads but no foot traffic. He spoke out loud again. "I've done it. I've done it. I'm going to have it all."

He walked towards the Meadows, the quickest way home. It was lit up by pale modern lamps casting long shadows against leafless trees. The path was cast in white and shadow. Although they were always busy in the summer, the best time to be in the Meadows was on a night like this, cool and calm. The lights were powerful enough to see for some distance, far stronger than the ones on the road. The Meadows cut between the town and the suburbs, a low skyline of modern flats and Victorian flats, the lights of the city on one side, the south of Edinburgh on the other.

But at the same time, it is a dangerous place for people at night, young women especially. Which is a shame. It should not be dangerous at all. In a perfect world, there would be no need for lights. In the dark silence, the grass fields beyond the path and trees, a gap emerged in the sky, a pocket of night above the Meadows. On a cloudless night, like the one Isaac was under, you would be able to see a clear black sky above. If there weren't any lights around, you'd be able to see the stars.

CHAPTER TWELVE

When Lyle was telling Isaac what was going to happen with the flat next year, Will hung back from them. He took the answer sheet away from Isaac and started to draw on it, the blue pen from the quizmaster in hand. They had been in the pub for a few hours. It was midway through the quiz, and they'd lost all interest.

Will drew a sketch of a nude man on the edge of his bed, from the perspective of his back. The individual joints of his spine were prominent, his shoulders slumped. His neck was bent, face hidden, his hands by his side on the bed. Will shaded in some details as best he could.

Isaac was reaching for his jacket. Lyle waited, looking over at Will, letting him finish. Will shaded in more small details here and there, then put the piece of paper in his pocket on the way out. Isaac was already standing outside by himself.

Isaac did not try to keep up with them. They were walking along George Street – a place other Scots imagine when they think of Edinburgh, all high-end shops that are as expensive as they are empty, strange financial businesses and expensive bars. George Street is all edges and corners, framing the night sky in perfect gridlines. Though the buildings are not taller than anywhere else, it's more imposing than any castle or dark alleyway. Not something fear-inducing, not something dreadful, just a human reminder that there's a whole other way of living, a better way, built out of clean brick and fine shopfronts. All criticisms of it are met with nothing. Nothing is left when you walk through it, save a lingering sense of disappointment for something that was never yours.

They walked onward, quickly, past everyone else heading towards the attractions. The dark maroon clouds above were littered with other lights, scattering glimpses of the Christmas markets, chatter and laughter.

A tall woman in a thin brown overcoat nearly bumped into Isaac when he attempted to walk in front of Will and Lyle. Isaac shifted back to his original position and never attempted to move forward again. They kept walking, two in front, Isaac behind. The two talked, but not too much.

The road curved downward, downhill all the way, the streets wide, thick gardens to the edges, large buildings, all blocks, still ahead. They crossed junctions without looking, heading further north. They had walked half a mile away from the city centre but there was no traffic, just thick rows of parked cars on cobbled streets.

The yellow lights were replaced with cold white ones. The paving stones looked flat, almost like one solid whole. The lights coming from the windows along the street were all brighter on the inside. They were walking past a cricket pitch. There was a pub connected to it with a seating area at the front, electric heaters hanging from canopies. A few people sat outside.

They walked past a house which was removed from everything, elevated on a hill, high enough to look over the cricket field, just over the wall. It lay in a row of detached houses, all separate, all apart. One had sounds coming from it, even from some distance away, some level of bass, some measure of melody. The garden across from it was clean, mounds of earth around the edges of the lawn evened out, prepared for the New Year.

They walked up to the house. There were two tall windows on either side of the door. They protruded outwards, so it was easy to see inside. A man stood at the window. There was a light on inside. A solitary bulb, uncovered by any shade, lit up the empty room, the light almost amber in colour. The man in the window became animated, starting to wave. As they got closer, Isaac could recognise the person.

It was Cullen.

He turned on his heel, moving away from the window and out of the room. He opened the door with a grin, accepting a hug from Will. His face looked fuller, and he was slightly wider than when Isaac had last seen him. His hair had grown out more.

Lyle gestured back towards Isaac without looking at him, talking towards Cullen. "Isaac, this is Cullen. Isaac, we met Cullen at a gallery thing – I know – he's a big investor, knows my new boss a bit. He was actually at uni around the same time as us – crazy. This is Isaac; he's our flatmate."

Will and Lyle disappeared inside, and Cullen greeted Isaac with a handshake. Isaac looked at him without looking at him directly in the eye.

The hallway had a large mirror immediately on the right side as Isaac walked in, framed in a sprayed golden colour. It ran a good few metres down the thin corridor. There were several rooms on either side, the door open at the end of the corridor.

Isaac stood close to Cullen. He muttered, "Bit empty."

Cullen looked back at Isaac. "What is it?" he asked.

Isaac did not look at him. He muttered again, not

changing the volume of his voice, “Your new house is a bit empty.”

Cullen was smiling, walking behind Isaac as they walked down the corridor. He kept talking loudly, not dropping to Isaac’s volume. “Is it? It’s not empty.”

The corridor led towards the back of the house, to a large open-plan kitchen which led immediately into a large conservatory that cut into the large garden. There was a smattering of people in the kitchen.

There were sofas in the conservatory, wide leather ones, and Will was already lying back on one, beer in hand.

Cullen caught up to Isaac in the kitchen. He said, “See, it’s all grand.”

Isaac was silent, looking at the faces ahead of him. They did not look back at him.

Cullen had already moved away to the conservatory. Lyle had gone to the fridge and taken out some beer. Will had ventured off by himself, looking around for someone.

In the conservatory, Lyle handed over the cans to Isaac and Cullen. He spoke to Cullen, Isaac’s gaze fixated on a point between the two. “So, this is all bought then?”

Cullen took a drink before saying, “All from work I did abroad. I did some tutoring for some big guy in China who really took to me, see? They liked having me around enough that they got me some contacts in Vietnam, which led to a ton of work.”

Lyle smiled. He replied, “Nice!”

Isaac opened his mouth to speak but Cullen cut in. “It was grand, like. It’s bit different over there, everyone’s more … well, it’s strange coming back here. Like, you know how if you’ve ever been in a queue for something, like, you’re at a supermarket or … It’s just that but hundreds of folk, so many–”

“Really, so *many* people,” Isaac interrupted.

"Yeah, but imagine being in a city with more folk than in Scotland, you know what I'm saying?" Cullen said.

Lyle looked at Cullen for a second before looking back to his drink. They all stood in silence before Lyle spoke again. "Do you have any plans for this place, Cullen?"

Isaac turned away from them, looking back down the corridor.

Cullen kept talking. "Think the walls need painted in parts, but the kitchen's nearly brand new. Was an old family who lived here and they've looked after it well enough. I think my dad wants to come over and see it – he'll be all over it with things, he's always buying—"

Someone called out Lyle's name and he excused himself, leaving Cullen and Isaac by themselves. Lyle sat down with the other people. He was happy and contented, in his element, a person all to himself, the person that he was all along. He looked back at Isaac one last time before moving on with his life.

Isaac muttered to Cullen, "Bit mental having a whole big house to yourself. Actually, I think I met your dad once."

Cullen waved at someone in the conservatory. He muttered back, "Did you?"

Isaac looked over the faces in the conservatory, a group of women talking to each other. No one looked at him. "Yeah, when we moved in first year," he continued. "Short guy. Big glasses. Quiet. Not that imposing. It's been a few years, must be getting on a bit. Is his limp any better?"

Cullen took a drink. He did not look at Isaac when he replied, "Yeah, good guy."

Isaac nodded. "Yeah, seemed quiet. A bit mute. Not much of a person, if I'm honest. I can see why you act out so much. It's a great place you have here, Cullen."

Cullen took another drink. He muttered again, talking slower, "It's for the best, Isaac. We've known for a while."

Isaac cut him off by walking away, leaving him alone.

Will had found the person he was looking for in the conservatory. She was a woman with blonde hair, shorter than him. She stood close to Will.

Lyle was talking. "It's all kicking off – I might have to move to London or something. It's crazy how quickly it's happening …"

No one was looking at Isaac, who stayed away from everyone. With the noise and the echo from the conservatory, he could not make out everything that was being said. He looked around again. He took out his phone, pressing buttons. He had no notifications, but he pressed buttons anyway.

He went back into the corridor, looking at the other rooms. One had piles of books, twenty, thirty piled high, differing sizes, all collected in a corner, a pair of sofas already in, the walls a deep green.

He looked up the thin staircase which went upstairs. There were marks on the walls, etched in it – the marked heights of children, scratched into the wall, the name 'Ethan' etched three times, one by Isaac's knee, then further and further up.

He took a few steps up. There was a murmur in the conservatory, the hum of noise now muted. Isaac took a few more steps.

Cullen appeared at the foot of the stairs. "You don't want to go up there," he said firmly.

Isaac turned back around at Cullen. "Why can't I go up there?"

"Why do you ask questions like that?" Cullen sighed. "You sound like everyone's speaking down to you all the time."

"Why are you afraid of being questioned?" Isaac stepped back downstairs. Standing on the second step, he was head height with Cullen. "Why don't you like being questioned?"

Cullen was shaking his head. He spoke slowly when he responded. "Isaac, you know that's not true."

"You don't like being questioned," Isaac snarled.

"Calm down."

Isaac raised his finger to Cullen's face. "It's a fact!" he spat out.

Cullen smacked down Isaac's hand with the flat of his palm, and said firmly but quietly, "Isaac, I don't like it when you ask questions without thinking, like they're a way of being defensive. You're not even putting any thought behind your questions, they're … just there to put me off guard. You're dancing around. Have you ever realised how that makes you sound?"

Isaac did not look away from Cullen. "I don't care," he spat.

"You don't care?"

"No."

"You don't care at all?"

"No," Isaac hissed again.

Cullen sighed and shook his head. "Right then."

Isaac pointed back towards the kitchen. "Can you actually fuck off?"

Cullen smiled and shook his head again. "You're in my house, you can't say that."

"It's strange that you're just trying to be in my life suddenly," Isaac spat at him. "You couldn't make one yourself so just lied to everyone about what you've been doing. Just acting along. Have you ever realised how that makes *you* look?"

Cullen had screwed up his face. "Isaac, you've … *Oh come on*, you've been doing the same thing for ye—"

"I'm glad you gave up drinking. You always were a lightweight," Isaac interrupted, and then said, "Bet you can't stop thinking about—"

"You know exactly why that is!" Cullen snapped, raising his voice. He glanced away when he spoke to check they were out of earshot. "I'm more surprised that you're the one who's acting strange – your flatmates have talked a lot about you."

"I don't care what people think. I've not hurt any—"

"Because of you, I had to hit someone, leave them in the mud. People are hurt because of what you've said, what you've done." Cullen took a breath to calm down.

"Talking absolute shit," Isaac huffed.

"You keep saying you don't care what people think about you," Cullen snapped back, "but everything is a slight against you, every answer has to be something that you like. You want the honest truth? I did bump into your friends at a gallery thing, and I did not know who they were. I mean, so what? You've got some good people in your life, Isaac."

"What's that got to do with anything? I still don't get it."

Cullen drank before he answered, speaking at a slower speed again. "I mean, why haven't you spent time with them before? I don't know them all that well, but they're a decent crowd. Think your other friend was getting back into art, he was saying the other day—"

"His drawings?" Isaac laughed. "They're shit, he's always been shit. What other day?"

Cullen shrugged and looked away. "I mean, we were out for drinks. You weren't there, and–"

"Wasn't invited, why should I give a fuck?"

Cullen pointed back to the room, still staring at Isaac, continuing on. "Mate, your friends are doing stuff with their lives. Why is that such a strange thing to wrap your head around? Lyle's doing well in that new job of his – it's a proper job, he's not on his feet anymore. Will showed me a link to a site he's selling art on, he's doing all ri—"

"And? They're doing what they want. What's so good

about that? They've been awful to me. Always putting me down. They're always making snide wee comments."

"What do you want to do, Isaac?"

"I'm fine. Don't need anyone else."

Cullen sighed. "You know the really sad thing? I genuinely didn't know, didn't chase them up or anything – got chatting to Will about his stuff and then he mentioned his flatmate being weird and he just *went off.* Then Lyle came over and joined in. But then … it's not like they're angry, Isaac – they sounded bored, Isaac, *bored*, that's all it is. I mean, they said you've been at home a lot. What have you been doing with your money?"

Isaac was biting the inside of his mouth, looking away. The noise of the party was growing louder. Someone was laughing. He whimpered out a response. "I didn't really have a plan. I'm fine. I'll be better. I'll move in with new people, or by myself. I'll do fine without everyone else."

Cullen was calm again now. "But what about work, Isaac? That IT thing, it has to stop."

Isaac did not look at Cullen. "I'll be fine. I don't need to tell you everything. I'll be fine."

Cullen shook his head. "You got what you wanted," he said. "You wanted a clean break, a way to start again, and you did."

Isaac whimpered again. "You're taking my friends away."

"Isaac, I only know them in passing. And besides, your friends don't like you because you treat them like shit. It's not all about you, Isaac. Are you really surprised that something like this would happen, that the friends in your life would move on from you?"

"You've been setting me up to fail."

"You've got money because of me," Cullen said. "Why do you act like you do, Isaac? Why do your parents stay away from you, Isaac? Did something happen when you bullied that kid?"

"You're jealous," Isaac hissed. "You've always been jealous, and you've screwed me over. You know fine well that I'm fine. All right? I'm actually a pretty fucking good guy, and a lot of the scummy shit you've been up to is awful. Awful. Awful. You know what this is? It's cognitive dissonance, that's what it is. You don't know what that is, do you? It's when you hold two contrasting opinions, and you hold them …"

Cullen was looking away, mumbling, "Oh my God" under his breath.

Isaac continued, " … and they don't work with each other, all right? You're acting like you're this big friend to everyone, but you … So, you come back and it's all engines go? Just because no one else has the balls to talk to me about what they aren't happy about, like it's all my fault they can't measure up."

Cullen took a step away for a second. There was a growing noise at the other end of the corridor. "No one talks like you," he said seriously. "When was the last time you had an actual conversation with someone? When was the last time you left your room? Did you just read about that online?"

"You're pushing me out of my own life."

Cullen pushed Isaac back, pushing him onto the stairs, further into the darkness. There was a darker tone to his voice. "You didn't give a shit about the people in your life and *then* you're shocked no one wants to hang out with you? You wanted to be the best thing in your life at the expense of everyone else. You've got everything you ever wanted. You can't even be arsed to be in your *own* life."

Someone down the hall started laughing and more people joined in. Isaac turned his head away and wiped his nose, muttering, "Why don't you tell me then, why? Why did you do all those things? Why did you pick me in the first place?"

"I knew the risks. I knew what I was doing. We took small amounts, took our time. I spent so long being careful, checking if we were being watched. We never were. Not once. Not even once. That's why I picked you. You were always going to be the person for this. Remember I gave you all that cash? Then what, Isaac? Did you go to the police? Did you tell anyone else? Surely that would have been the rational thing to do, Isaac? You've never had it in you. But you've got something else inside you. Something worse."

Isaac said nothing.

Cullen continued. "I've seen some heinous shit in my time away, Isaac, but that look you gave me up north was something else – then not calling anyone. I called on a burner when I got home. I have no idea what happened to him. You would have left that man to die. I stole from people, but I never killed, not once. That look you gave me made me realise that I needed to stop before it got too much. I swung for that guy's ribs to take him out, not kill him – but you would have killed him, you would have seen him dead and emptied that house of everything."

"So, it's my fault you're like this?" Isaac snapped.

Cullen nodded. He kept talking quietly. "Yes. I idolised you back then, that first week, Isaac, but you threw me under the bus to make yourself look better. I wanted so much to be better than everyone and I think coming back here made me realise it. It wasn't the travelling at all that changed me, it's the coming back again that did it."

Isaac shook his head. "What a load of shit. All that for one week? You couldn't get your shit together?"

Cullen sighed. "Did you ever wonder why I just didn't tell you everything, Isaac? Because it wouldn't make a difference. I could tell you over and over to be a better person, to try harder, work on yourself, do more, be excellent to the people around you, all those things. You wouldn't do it. You wouldn't learn anything. I could tell you how to be good and you wouldn't do it. I don't think you want to be wrong. Sorry, Isaac. I've fucked this all up, and this is what it is. Living in a house somewhere, getting a job, pretending this is all okay. Do you honestly think this is okay?"

Isaac did not react for a few seconds. Then he shrugged. His voice lost the whimper and found itself again. "I've got my money; I'm going to live my life. I don't need you. You were just some guy in first year I didn't really like." He walked away to the kitchen without saying another word.

Cullen waited until Isaac was gone. He sat in silence for a few minutes, the sound of the party beyond him, out of sight. He headed upstairs. No one could see him. He began to sob, going towards the rooms he couldn't show anyone else, *wouldn't* show to anyone else. The light upstairs was left on. His tears were falling down his face, his face in his hands.

Will had stepped away from the others with the woman he'd been looking for. She whispered to him, "I'd like to get a dog. I mean, I like the idea of getting one, but I think the reality is a bit different."

Will whispered back, "I'll love it. It'll be fine."

They waited for nothing to be said. Her hand moved down and took his. The sound of the party next door was framed through the open doorway, so much so that it felt far away. The dark window outside was still. They looked at each other for a while without doing anything. Will nodded. He squeezed her fingers.

Isaac came in, looking for a drink. He started talking aloud in Will's direction. "Weird guy, that Cullen, don't think that much of him. Like, he just turns up one day and we're all supposed to be friends with him, or something. Weird guy. Should be moving away from strange folk like that."

Will was not really paying attention.

Isaac kept talking. "It's more than all right. It's a big deal."

Will watched the woman's eyes move, the way they scanned his face and found something he could not see.

Isaac watched Will for a few seconds. Isaac muttered under his breath, "I mean, all right then." Then he walked away.

Will turned to watch him go, the outline of him moving down the long corridor, out towards the front door. He felt for the drawing inside his jacket pocket. He let go of it, relaxing his shoulders. His other hand squeezed the woman's fingers.

CHAPTER THIRTEEN

A few months passed.

It was February. Isaac's parents had come home for Christmas and Hogmanay. Around this time Isaac moved back in with them. The winter came and went and the days that were dark became lighter and brighter, bit by bit.

For the first time since last year, Isaac was back in Edinburgh.

Isaac muttered under his breath, "It's all worked out fine." He smoothed his hair down, but the back kept flicking up. His hands were shaking as he did this, his fingers flicking out lines of dandruff.

There weren't any clouds in the sky. It was a dry afternoon which would look like a summer's day if it weren't for the lifeless trees and limited pedestrians. These days are more precious to Edinburgh than any long, warm summer day. These calm afternoons can come out of nowhere, a respite from the drudgery of cold rain and hard wind, a chance to take stock through the winter months. A soft reminder, if you ever needed one, that our troubles are temporary, that things will turn out the way they're supposed to.

Isaac had gone back to the flat to drop off the keys. It was empty. They had moved out already. He did not touch anything, did not look back into his room. He dropped off the keys and left for the last time.

He did not stop walking. He was meeting Diane that afternoon. He had been sending her texts without receiving much in the way of replies, but she had answered yesterday to say that she would like to meet him.

He was walking quickly, Arthur's Seat looming in the skyline beyond him. An older couple walked hand in hand in the middle of the pathway. Isaac was moving at a faster pace than them, so much so that he moved to their side, into the way of an oncoming runner, a woman a head taller than Isaac.

He came to the crossroads at the Meadows, the path splitting up towards the university and further into the park, heading towards Nicolson Street. He stopped to let a cyclist who was heading towards him go past. He hesitated as he stopped, unsure of where he was going. The cyclist sped past him.

He turned around again to face the two women, to look back at them, but they were far away, far away amongst the trees. He could not see their faces. He nearly walked into a pram pushing past him. There were odd crowds ahead of him, groups of twos and threes. Amongst them, some women were on their own. He looked at the women on their own as he passed, ignoring any in groups. He walked ahead, walking past people walking slowly, stepping onto the grass to pass people on the other side.

He left the park, making his way to Nicolson Street, closer to the wine bar where he was meeting Diane. It was further down the road on the opposite side from where Isaac was. Isaac moved to his right to cross the road, walking in front of an older man who was walking towards him

Isaac shifted his body to let the older man past him.

The man had turned and was looking at him, his hands by

his side. His face was red from the cold. His mouth hung a little open. His hands looked large.

Isaac turned away. When he walked further down the road, he looked back again. He walked a little faster. Isaac did not look back again except to cross the road when the traffic thinned out.

Diane was waiting outside the wine bar. She was looking the other way, hands in the pockets of her coat.

Isaac held up his hand. He opened his mouth and shut it. He lowered his hand. He kept his mouth open for a few seconds before words came out of it. "Hey, Aria—"

She did not look around.

Isaac tried again, speaking louder this time. "Hey!"

She turned her head after a few seconds. He went to hug her, her arms rising a little slowly. She moved backwards. Her voice was quieter. "Hey."

Isaac paused his movements, lowering his arms. "You awake?" he asked.

Diana wasn't smiling when she talked. "I've got a ton of paperwork to do. The new job is great but it's full on."

Isaac shrugged before he said, "Well, you could spend some time with me, like we agreed?"

Her hands were in her pockets again. She waited a few seconds, looking around, before she answered, "I mean, I'm technically ill, just getting some reading done before I come back in. Technically."

Isaac pointed to the front door, stepping towards it, motioning her to follow. He spoke quickly. "Yeah, but you're here now, so let's go inside."

Diane kept her placid expression as she replied, "Seems kind of … Are you sure you want to go in here?"

Isaac nodded slowly. "That's what we agreed, though?" There was a hint of confusion in his voice.

"I thought we were just meeting here," Diane replied

slowly, drawing the words out. She stood still as Isaac slowed his movements.

Isaac came to a stop, close to the door. "Yeah, but we can go in now."

She looked through the large windows at the single empty tables, a waiter in smart clothes standing by himself at the bar. She did not look over to Isaac as she talked. "I think we can just go for a coffee. There's a place just next to it."

Isaac did not follow her eyeline when he replied, "But it's right there … It's right there."

Diane looked to her left, her shoulders tensed. She turned her head away from him, and Isaac stopped to watch her go into the coffee shop next door before following her in. There was an old couple leaving at the same time, and Isaac got in the way of them. It was warm inside. Diane took her hands out of her coat to open it. Isaac kept his on.

There was a queue which looped round to the counter. There were not a lot of seats available. Isaac muttered behind her. "Looks pretty busy. Are you sure you want to go here?"

Diane nodded. She spoke without looking back. "Yeah, here's good."

"Do you want to get these drinks to go?" Isaac asked.

"No. We'll get a table," she replied.

Isaac stepped forward, standing next to her. He muttered again without turning his head, "Do you see any free?"

She turned her head, moving her head so she could try to look around him. "No."

"Then we should get these to go."

She waited a second before replying. She did not mutter. She spoke clearly. "People might … People *will* leave."

"I don't think that'll happen," Isaac muttered.

They moved forward. There was an older couple at the end moving towards a table in the far corner, away from everyone else. Isaac tutted when they sat down. Diane's eyes shot towards him but went back to looking towards the front.

"One of us should look for a table. Can you do that?" she asked.

Isaac kept looking at the old couple as they took their jackets off. "I thought you said there were none free?" he said with a snarl in his voice.

"I did, but you wanted to sit down in that other place. You could look for a table."

"Why are you being like this?" Isaac said, still muttering.

There was a group of people in front of them who had quietened down as Isaac had been talking. The queue rumbled forward.

"I'm sorry," Diane said.

"That's better," Isaac muttered, a triumphant tone in his voice.

Diane did not respond. She touched her hair a little, putting her hand back in her pocket. She said to herself, "Everything is fine."

"Yes, of course it is," Isaac said. Then he spoke loudly. "Been months since I've been in one of these places."

Diane did not respond. He continued, "I'm not really a corporate sell-out kind of guy."

Again, Diane, did not respond.

He added, "Much more of a local business kind of guy."

They moved further forward again, able to hear people making orders, able to make eye contact with the people behind the till.

Diane turned to him. She examined his face as she asked him a question. "Do you go to wee coffee shops a lot? What's your favourite one?"

Isaac scratched his nose. He muttered, "Well, yeah. Much better to support local businesses, you know? It's better for the local economy. I've always been a big supporter of that – in general, anyway."

The queue moved forward again. Isaac had his hands around his coat. He tried to say something, opening his mouth, but he was distracted by a group of women to his right, younger than him. Their accents were foreign.

He turned forward again.

The group was laughing. He stared back at them. They sat with winter coats on and were louder than everyone else. He kept turning forward and then back at them, looking at them in turn. They did not look at him. One of them stopped joining in and began looking away from the group.

Isaac muttered to himself, "This place is a bit touristy."

Diane sighed out a response, looking at the wall next to her. "Well, yeah. It's Edinburgh," she said.

"It's all students and tourists. It's not really your own place, is it?"

"It's got a university and a castle in the middle of it – there's going be students and tourists everywhere," Diane said, looking back at him. "It's hardly unusual."

But Isaac kept talking as if she hadn't spoken. "It's not like a local city, you know what I mean? It's not really for people who live here."

"Do you hang out with local people?" Diane asked. "You said you hadn't seen your friends for a while?"

He looked back at the group of women and muttered again, "Yeah." Isaac stroked his chin. There were some errant strands of hair that he had missed when shaving. He stroked it again, slower this time.

Diane turned her head a little. Her hand had left her pocket for a few seconds. Isaac watched her hand. It was still, completely still. She breathed out.

They walked forward again. They were almost at the front.

"You're quiet. Are you okay?" Isaac asked.

Diane thought about this for a second before replying, "Yeah, I'm just keen to get going. There's still no one moving anyway."

"We can just get these to go then. It's not a problem."

Diane spoke again, purposefully. "I wanted to sit down and chat for a bit anyway. I've been working away. It's just tiring around this time of year. Good for comfy pints in pubs with a big fire, that sort of thing."

Isaac turned to her, speaking with a tone of disappointment in his voice. "I did … did suggest that, didn't I?"

She did not say anything.

He tried again. "That's what you said."

"I'm speaking hypothetically," Diane replied.

Isaac looked away, back at the old couple sitting happily by themselves. He muttered, "Hypothetically."

"It's that time of year. I'm always pretty unproductive about this time of year. Are you working on anything just now? How are your parents?"

Isaac did not respond.

They moved closer to the till and they made their order.

Isaac tried again. "Let's get these to go."

Diane shook her head as she took her payment card back. "No, we can find somewhere to sit."

Isaac was turning around, looking around. He sounded a little stressed. "I said there wasn't anywhere to sit. I can't see anywhere to sit."

Diane did not look at him. She muttered, "Don't stress about it."

"I'm not stressed about it," Isaac snapped back. "I'm not stressed about it at all. I'm not stressed about anything, but there are no seats anywhere. It's a fact."

Diane sighed. "It's not … You're getting worked up."

The person behind the till was taking their time with the receipt.

Isaac muttered, "It … Should we be standing around …"

Diane looked over at the other side of the room, her face lighting up. "There's some space by the window."

Isaac shook his head. He did not look round. "No, there isn't."

Diane pointed towards it. "There is. Look. There were two people who had their jackets on when we came in. They were sitting but getting ready to go."

Isaac shrugged. He did not look over at her as he said, "I didn't see them."

Diane muttered under her breath, "You saw them but you weren't paying attention."

Isaac muttered back, "I was paying attention."

"It's not that bad," Diane insisted. "It's cold because we've been outside, but it'll be better in here. Can you take one of these coffees?"

She had one coffee glass in her hand. He made a move to reach for it, her hand sliding back a little. He picked up the one on the counter. The server waited for a few moments before they left. The person behind stared at them as they moved to the corner.

Isaac curled his fingers around the glass. It was scalding hot, his hands heating up, his wrist twitching. The Spanish women did not look at him at he passed and did not change their conversational tone.

Isaac sat down, moving towards the seat closest to Diane. She pulled the seat out herself, putting her bag on the floor, away from the window. They were side-on to it. She kept her jacket on, fiddling with something in the pocket. Isaac sat across from her. They were right by the window.

Diane looked to her left, a table next to hers. There were two women sitting down near them, a mother speaking to her daughter, who looked to be in her mid-twenties. They were both similar in height. They had similar hairstyles, the older mother with neat silver streaks through her hair, the younger one more blonde. Isaac was left facing the younger daughter.

Isaac leaned over to Diane. He spoke with a darker tone in his voice. "What's wrong with you? You seem argumentative. We've been texting for ages and you've not – we've just been chatting about things, that's all. I've done nothing wrong."

Diane did not answer. She glanced over at the older woman, who was listening to her daughter.

Isaac looked back at the younger daughter. Her vision did not stray from her mother's gaze. He stared at the space between them; he could not make out their conversation.

Diane eyed her coffee glass with suspicion. The leaf pattern on the latte foam was a little messed up from the journey over, the leaves stretched out and distorted.

Isaac turned his head, following her gaze to the glass. "Did you ask for the right thing? You don't look that happy with it. I think that wine bar had tons of choices, like, tasty things."

"I can't get a read on you." She spoke with a slight strain in her voice.

"What?"

"You send a lot of pictures when you're chatting to me, then whenever I reply to you, you don't text back for a while. Is it because I'm not sending pictures to you?"

Isaac shrugged. The mother was nodding at her daughter as she spoke. Isaac spluttered out a response. "I don't know what you mean by that."

Diane kept looking at him, talking steadily, slowly. "I don't owe you my time. I have other stuff on. You think you're the only person I speak to? I don't understand why you get annoyed by me not responding if you take ages to talk back."

Isaac shook his head, mumbling, "That's … That's not it …"He took a swig of his coffee. He went to nod but his hand was still hot, the glass still at a high temperature. His hand was shaking. When he put his hand back down, it slipped and the latte glass hit the table. Isaac flinched at the noise.

Diane was still looking at him. "I don't know. Do you remember back at the house – you were talking about being let down by your friends—"

Isaac raised his finger to interrupt her, wagging it slightly. He said, "You're being really argumentative. It's rude."

"I don't need to be nice to you."

Isaac responded immediately. "So, you're just being rude now, is that it? Can't even go to the right place, gets all *sensitive* about text chats. Far too emotional. Is something wrong?"

Diane looked out of the window. The conversation between the two women next to them continued. The condensation in the room had fogged up the windows, making it hard to see outside, vague shapes of people passing by. She kept looking outside anyway. Through the fogged-up windows, she watched a passer-by, an older person walking by themself. They were carrying a heavy bag. The old person kept going, people moving around them.

Isaac watched Diane doing this but did not follow her eyeline. His hand was down by his glass again. He nodded. "Uh-huh, nothing to say, typ—"

"Yes, actually. I've had a lot on my mind. How has your day been?" she cut in, not raising her voice, calmly placing word after word, one after the other. Then she took a drink of her coffee.

"Took you long enough," Isaac said. "I've had a bit of a mental morning. I got up early to study that coursework I'm doing – you know, the online course for coding – sat through a morning lecture, took tons of notes. I've been battering through stuff since I last saw you."

Diane waited for him to keep talking. But Isaac said nothing, taking a drink, putting it back down. Diane watched him. He still said nothing. She breathed out her nose before she said anything. "That's great. Well done."

Isaac continued as if he had not stopped talking. "I'm learning a lot from it. It's good to go over all my old notes again; I feel like it's making more sense now. I mean, I was good back then. I really was. Glory days and all that. I used to go out every second night and that, bit more difficult now because I think everyone's going to get better now, right? I'm going to look for my own place, get away from my flatmates – awful. Awful, both of them, really untidy people to live with, bit anti-social – I'm past them. I don't need them. I'm … It's coming around, it's all coming around. Like I've got all the pieces in place. I know, all right! I'm just … I'm just really excited to see you."

Diane took another drink of her coffee. The older person outside had made it down the street. She wiped the window to look at them. They had made it to the pedestrian crossing. She took another drink. She muttered to herself, "It's great. It really is."

The mother sitting next to them was sipping her coffee. The younger daughter was on her phone, the phone down on the table.

Diane turned back to Isaac. She spoke calmly. "I know about your ex-girlfriend."

Isaac was mid-drink. He turned away from the younger woman on her phone. His glass hit the table. He looked out the window immediately. "What were you looking at outside?"

Diane stared right at him. "I met her a few days ago."

Isaac turned back to the door, scanning the queue, then turned around again towards the rest of the room.

Diane continued to talk. Never altering her pace. "I met her through a friend of a friend. I was talking about you with a friend, and your name rang a bell, so—"

Isaac turned round again, interrupting with a snarl. "So, you stalked me online then? Bit creepy. So, an old ex of mine just started bitching about me and—"

"No!" Diane interjected, raising her voice.

Isaac stopped talking.

Diane continued. "She said you were great. You were attentive, but then you'd just retreat into yourself, like you weren't interested. Then you'd be fine again, but you became moody – she thought it was her." She took another drink of her coffee.

Isaac smirked. "So, you found out nothing then. So, you got paranoid over nothing. I did not deserve that."

Diane finished her drink. She started again. "Why were you texting her after you broke up with her?"

Isaac looked at the women next to him. They didn't look over at Isaac.

Diane kept going. "You were texting her after the break-up. Lots of things. Middle of the night. Horrible things, Isaac. She stopped replying, but you kept going. They weren't drunk messages—"

"This has got nothing to do with you," Isaac snapped back, raising his voice, his eyes scanning the room, the door, the women next to him. "She was mental. Really mental. She was horrible to me. You're trying to set me up. That's what this is. You just want me to feel bad. I don't. I feel bad about nothing. Nothing at all. I'm entirely innocent. Factually speaking, I don't need you, I don't need her. The facts don't lie."

Diane stared at him, never looking away. She reached into

her pocket and pulled out her phone. She left it on the table. The younger woman on the opposite table turned her head a little, the mother barely turning hers at all. Diane did not raise her voice. "I've got the messages on my phone, Isaac."

He looked around at the women sitting next to him. Her younger daughter turned her head back a little.

Diane started again. "Do you want me to read them out to you?"

Isaac looked away. He moved his chair hard enough that it made a sound. He dropped his voice. "Why did not you want to go to that wine bar? Are you setting me up?"

"Because you're trying to set *me* up," Diane replied calmly. "Telling me how to feel and where to go. I needed to go right at you, that's why I'm here. I'm not lost any more, Isaac."

Isaac was shaking his head.

Diane kept going. "I've seen the texts, Isaac. You've been texting her for months. You've been messaging her online. She switched numbers a week ago."

Isaac kept shaking his head. His lip was trembling.

Diane took a breath and continued. "I don't know what to think. I think you want to get better – I think you did a stupid thing and got scared, but you never let up. And now you're wanting a fresh start. Is it always going to be this, Isaac? You can't admit for one second that you've done wrong. I didn't see it before. You're lost, Isaac. You think that it's about admitting defeat, but it's not – you make mistakes along the way and move on."

Isaac looked at her. His lip stopped trembling. Then he smiled. "No. I'm done with you," he said calmly. "Honestly. You did this to be dramatic and show off how clever you are. I bet you feel really good just now. Is this just some big victory lap for you now? I bet you feel so proud of yourself."

Diane looked out the window for a second. The old

person was long gone. She turned back to Isaac and said, "Honestly? I'm glad I met you. It's like … you're a bright light, leading the way. A raging fire, about to burn out. I don't need to follow you, go near you. I know the way out now. I can go as far away from you as possible."

Isaac rested his hand on his chin. He looked away from her, turning his head to look outside. Isaac did not turn back until she was gone.

He stood up. The younger daughter turned her head away and began talking to her mother again. He walked past the Spanish women, who looked past him as he went.

He went into the bathroom to wash his hands. He covered them in soap, lathered them. He turned the tap off, his fingers slipping as he turned it off. He looked at his hands, the soap clinging to his fingers.

He looked up again. There was a painting on the back wall. A small fishing boat was crashing against the crest of a wave, the horizon a foul, rolling tempest, heavy rain and high raking waves, portents of something terrible. The light in the cabin was on, the captain at the helm, both hands on the wheel. He was alone. The sea was the colour of a furious, rushing nightmare, the kind you try to wake up from. The sky was darkness and lightning, the boat in the foreground, sucked into the chaos around it. There was no sight of land, bar a sliver of blue in the distance, barely noticeable. But, through it all, it was there. The boat was heading toward it, wrapped in water and weather, towards some sort of end.

ACKNOWLEDGMENTS

Thank you for taking a chance on a self-published debut novel. The success of this novel is reliant on word of mouth, so please leave a review on whichever site you bought this from. Please recommend this novel to a friend if you can.

Special thanks to RTJ, M, M, J & J.

A massive thank you for Craig Hillsley for his help editing this work.

Thank you to Leona Skene for her proof reading skills.

Thanks also to the following Fiverr users:

<u>Beta Readings</u>

missfrancis
Allthingsm4tt
Morgan_maia
Hannah_flood
Maddy216
Jessicabrown99
Mh6108

<u>Cover Design</u>

Dkmrgn

Editing

Katieevelynm

Formatting

Mrtwriter

Printed in Great Britain
by Amazon

23572927R00158